"Who are you, Creed?" Gina asked.

"Maybe you shouldn't know." His voice came from right behind her, sending her thoughts scattering. She turned toward him.

"You are with the American government." The memory came

"Mor~~e~~ care you a

"I thi

"Don't let it." He took a step toward her. "I'd never hurt you."

A few more steps, and he was right there. In front of her. He terrified her and excited her, all at the same time.

Author Note

In the troubled days after September 11, 2001, a wave of patriotism soared through the hearts and minds of American citizens. We developed a gut-wrenchingly new appreciation for freedom, as well as a deeper realization of why the United States military had to fight and die to give us the privileges we enjoyed every hour of our lives.

I certainly was no different. Because of that patriotism, my first book with Harlequin® Historical, *The Mercenary's Kiss*, was born. In it, Jeb Carson was a soldier of his own making for the U.S. Army, a man who possessed a fierce love for his country. He had a friend whose love for America ran just as deep. Another mercenary by the name of Creed Sherman.

Her Lone Protector is Creed's story, of course, and the battle he fought to help America survive and prosper.

I've attempted to depict the troubles and triumphs of that era as accurately as possible. The turn of the century was a time of immense industrial growth, with enemies at every turn. Yet immigrants like Gina Briganti surged onto our shores. Driven by their hopes and dreams, they worked hard—and succeeded—and enabled us to become the great nation we are today.

Thank you for reading Creed and Gina's story.

PAM CROOKS

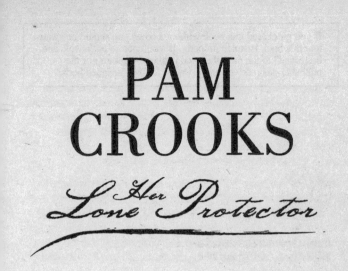

Her Lone Protector

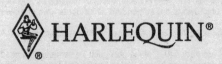

HARLEQUIN®

TORONTO • NEW YORK • LONDON
AMSTERDAM • PARIS • SYDNEY • HAMBURG
STOCKHOLM • ATHENS • TOKYO • MILAN • MADRID
PRAGUE • WARSAW • BUDAPEST • AUCKLAND

ISBN-13: 978-0-373-29429-9
ISBN-10: 0-373-29429-8

HER LONE PROTECTOR

Copyright © 2006 by Pam Crooks

First North American Publication 2006

This edition published by arrangement with Harlequin Books S.A.

www.eHarlequin.com

Printed in U.S.A.

Chapter One

Los Angeles, 1898

Creed Sherman could take care of himself in most any situation he found himself in.

Six years of protecting his country on foreign soil had forced him to adapt and survive. Before that, West Point Military Academy taught him discipline and strategy. He was a soldier. He thrived on risk and danger. Put him in a steaming, mosquito-thick jungle, he'd find his way out by sheer guts and determination. Put him at the front of enemy lines, he'd fight savagely to the death. Put a lethal weapon in his hand, and he'd know how to use it.

Put him in a women's dress shop, and he was seriously out of his element.

Panicky, even.

Hell.

He stood just inside the doorway of Collette's Fine Ladies Wear and frowned at the profusion of dresses in colors too numerous to comprehend. Hats in all shapes and sizes perched on glass counter tops. And he didn't even attempt to look inside the cases at the female fripper-ies *they* contained.

His head spun. He'd never been in a woman's establish-ment like this in his entire life. He was just off the train from San Antonio and headed home to his father's ranch not far outside the city limits. He wanted to buy his child-hood sweetheart, Mary Catherine, a gift to celebrate his homecoming.

He was going to marry her, if she'd still have him.

He had to have just the right gift for her—something ex-travagant and feminine. He ventured beyond the door. A mannequin draped in a gown of deep blue velvet snagged his attention. A pretty blue, he conceded. Might match Mary Catherine's eyes.

Or were her eyes green?

He frowned again.

It'd been a while since he'd seen her. Not since his West Point days when she'd headed east with his father to visit him, but damned if Creed knew what color her eyes were even then.

She had fair skin. That much he remembered. With hair like glistening gold. She wasn't very big, either. Barely reached his shoulder.

Might be she'd grown some, though.

Sometimes, it was hard to remember just what she looked like. Six years was a long time. Last he saw her, she'd been young and naive but sweet as sugar with lips full and soft and quick to smile.

She was a woman now. Mature. She'd have curves in all the female places. Probably lost her shyness, too. Wear her hair and clothes different.

A sudden eagerness to see her again swelled through him. He could hardly form a picture of her in his mind, but the letter in his pocket proved she was real and that she was in love with him. She told him so, over and over again, in words more eloquent than he could ever write to her in return.

One hell of a letter-writer, his Mary Catherine. A devoted one, too. Made a man feel good from all the nice things she always said about him.

Creed groped inside his shirt pocket and withdrew the last letter he'd received. Seeing her neat penmanship brought her alive, vanquished the years they'd been apart. He'd be with her soon. Within hours.

"My, but you look lost in here," a soft voice said, amused.

Fabric rustled behind him, and Creed turned. A dress the likes he'd never seen before drew closer, the woman inside it tall and confident. And beautiful. His glance lingered. Years in war-torn countries kept him from seeing the ways a woman could pamper herself like this one did.

A corner of his mouth lifted. "Is it that obvious?"

"It is." A puff of perfume reached him. "I'm Collette. Is there something I can help you with?"

"I need a gift for my fiancée." Might be he was stretching the truth calling Mary Catherine that. He hadn't yet asked her to marry him, but he was confident enough she would that he took the liberty.

"Fiancée?" Delicately painted lips curved downward. Collette's long-lashed gaze drifted over him, slow and leisurely, clear to his boots and back up again. Creed regretted not stopping for a haircut and shave after getting off the train, but if the female appreciation in her expression was any indication, it didn't matter that he hadn't. "Lucky lady," she murmured.

He grinned. "Guess I'll find out if she is soon enough."

She sighed dramatically, and he caught the twinkle in her eye. Collette was a charmer, for sure.

"So, what are you looking for, cowboy? Anything in particular?"

Cowboy?

Creed's grin faded. The word stung. He'd buried that part of his life a long time ago.

"Not sure yet," he said, shrugging off the dark turn of his mood. "Something nice, though."

"Something nice. H-m-m." Collette strolled over to a dress of shimmering yellow. Reminded him of the daffodils in Ma's spring gardens. "This just arrived from Paris last week. It's the latest rage."

Creed stared at the sleeves on the thing. Snug from the wrists to the elbows, they ballooned out from there to the shoulders and looked like puffed out, overblown wings. Mary Catherine would be wider than he was in it.

"It's a promenade costume," Collette said. "Does your lady like to walk in the park? She'd be the envy of everyone there."

Mary Catherine lived on the spread next to his father's. She'd work as hard as any of the other ranch women in the area. Who'd have time to drive to town for a walk in the park?

"What else can you suggest?" he hedged.

"You don't like it? Perhaps something more useful would be better." Collette seemed to know the way of his thinking and held up a short bouncy cape thing. "It's the perfect wrap for spring." She draped it around the yellow dress with a flourish. "Isn't that beautiful?"

He nodded politely but couldn't see how the cape could keep anyone the least bit warm. It barely reached a woman's elbows, and it was so damn frilly, Mary Catherine would be lost in it. Her taste tended to run to the…plain.

At least, it used to.

He began to feel overwhelmed with indecision. How the hell was he supposed to know what she'd like?

"You don't know this woman very well?" Collette asked gently.

He took courage from her perception. She was an astute businesswoman, and he was desperate for her help and expertise. "I've known her near all my life."

A perfect eyebrow arched. "And you don't know her tastes?"

He shrugged. "I just haven't seen her for a while, that's all."

"I see." She regarded him knowingly. "How long?"

Creed glanced down at the date on the letter still in his hand. Three years since she'd written him. Damn, where had the time gone? But then, he'd been out of the country. The rest of her letters just hadn't caught up with him yet. He stuffed the paper back in his pocket.

"Too long," he said.

"I see," she said again. "Well." She glided to a shelf, her skirts swishing. "We'll look at apparel more—shall we say—practical?" She lifted up a limp blob of lace and ribbons with an expectant smile.

Creed tried not to look stupid. "What is it?"

She blinked at him. "Why, it's a breakfast cap. See?"

She held it over the top of her head to demonstrate.

He frowned. "Women need to wear a hat to eat breakfast?"

Collette sighed and returned it to the shelf. "Some do."

Mary Catherine wore braids most every day, he recalled. He didn't figure she'd need a ridiculous-looking hat to cover *them*.

Collette moved to a glass counter. Creed had to admire her patience. His own was wearing mighty thin.

"How about handkerchiefs, then? We have some lovely ones," she said.

Handkerchiefs. A woman couldn't have too many of those, could she? Relief swarmed through him. His decision was made. "I'll take one of every style you have."

Collette looked relieved, too. "I'll wrap them in pretty paper for you."

"Thanks."

"You could bring her back later, you know," Collette said, working efficiently to tally his bill. "Let her pick something out herself. Then you'll know she'll like what you buy her."

"I will, as soon as I can."

"Are you new to town?"

"Could say that."

He didn't tell her of the foreign lands he'd been to or the men he'd killed, all in the name of his country. What would she know of war? Of patriotism? He figured her biggest worry of the day was deciding what color dress to wear in the morning.

Well, it was men like him that gave women like her the privilege.

"Welcome to California, then," Collette said graciously and slid the invoice across the counter for his signature. Creed obliged her, then paid his bill, and she handed him his purchase, covered in rose-colored paper. "Enjoy your stay here, Mr.—" she glanced downward "—Sherman."

"I will."

Behind him, the tiny bell on the door tinkled, signaling the arrival of another customer. Creed touched a finger to his Stetson, turned to leave and had to sidestep a tall, dark-haired man entering the dress shop, his arms full of boxes. Barely able to see over them, he flashed Creed a look of surprise and mumbled an apology. Creed strode to the door.

"Not one of your regulars, is he, Collette?" the man

muttered, grunting under his load. "He looks rougher than most."

"No, this is Mr. Sherman's first time here. He—"

Creed pulled the door shut behind him, tucked his pathetically small package under his arm, and headed for his horse hitched right outside.

In the next moment, the door flung open again.

"Mr. Sherman? Mr. *Creed* Sherman?"

Creed paused, one eye narrowed beneath the Stetson's brim. Lean and muscular, but average-looking in his dark suit and shiny shoes, the man hurried toward him. Creed had never seen him before.

"You're looking at him," he said.

"I can't believe it. I've been expecting you, sir. Just not this soon."

He pumped Creed's hand, but Creed's attention snapped at his words. "You've been expecting me?"

"Yes, sir. I received word only this morning that you'd arrived in California."

He tensed. "From whom?"

"General William Carson, sir. His wire ordered me to contact you."

"Ordered you. To contact me."

"Yes, sir. There's a serious matter I'd like to discuss with you. Let me correct that. A matter I *must* discuss with you."

Gut instinct told Creed he wasn't going to like what the man had to say. If the general was involved, then the matter was serious. Damn serious.

Creed didn't want to hear it. He was going home. To Mary Catherine.

"The name's Graham Dooling, Mr. Sherman. I'm with the United States Treasury Department. More specifically, the Secret Service."

Creed breathed an oath and braced himself for what would come next.

"President McKinley is due to arrive in Los Angeles next week for a private holiday with his wife. He's requested that his visit be kept secret for the time being. I'm part of a detail of agents sent here to prepare for them." Dooling took a discreet step closer. "However, we've received some disturbing intelligence that his life is in danger."

Suspicion coiled through Creed. "If you're with the Secret Service, what the hell are you doing making deliveries to a dress shop?"

Dooling grimaced. "Collette is my sister. She's been expecting a shipment of gowns from New York for an important customer of hers. I merely picked them up from the courier as a favor. It was my great fortune that you happened to be in her shop at the same time."

Could be a trap. Creed tensed. He'd been drawn in by the enemy with a clever ruse before. Damn near lost his life over it, too.

But feigning an assassination attempt on the president of the United States was unusually shrewd.

"How do I know you're who you claim to be?" he demanded.

Dooling nodded, as if he expected Creed's suspicion and understood it. "I'll share some information with you, sir. General Carson is the father of your best friend. You and Jeb Carson have been inseparable from your West Point days. You've fought brilliantly on foreign soil, soldiers in the truest sense. Patriots, both of you. You've acquired a reputation that most soldiers could only dream of."

"And what reputation is that, Dooling?" Creed taunted softly.

"A mercenary, sir."

"A mercenary." His mouth quirked. The term amused him. But Dooling was dead serious.

"A soldier-for-hire who will risk his life behind enemy lines. Your success has been awe-inspiring, to say the least."

The information, while not well-known amongst the ordinary citizenry, might easily be gleaned from someone in the military. If Dooling was acquainted with someone of the general's rank, he'd have access to the Army's gristmill.

Creed leaned a hip against the hitching post, crossed his arms over his chest, Mary Catherine's gift crushed against him.

"Go on," he said.

"Not long ago, you participated in a skirmish in Mexico against fierce revolutionaries there. Victorious, of course. You've recently parted company with Jeb and a certain young woman."

Creed's gaze didn't waver. "Her name."

"Elena, sir. Jeb's new bride. General Carson's daughter-in-law."

Elena. Graham Dooling would never have known of her if General Carson hadn't told him. Elena was the clue the general knew Creed would need to convince him to take the job of protecting the president of the United States.

Damn.

Creed didn't want this. He didn't *need* it.

"I'm not interested," Creed said, straightening and heading toward his horse, a palomino newly acquired from the nearest livery. He stuffed the package of handkerchiefs into his saddlebag.

"But Mr. Sherman!" Looking crestfallen, Dooling watched him climb into the saddle and take the reins firmly in his hands.

"Find someone else," he ordered grimly. "Plenty of soldiers in this country who could help you as easily as I can."

"You're wrong, sir! There's no other with your—"

But Creed wasn't listening. He tugged on the reins and kicked his horse into a run away from Graham Dooling and Collette's Fine Ladies Wear.

He was going home, damn it. Mary Catherine was waiting for him. Ma and Pa, too. His brother, Markie, and the rest of his father's outfit.

And not even the president of the United States was going to stop him.

Chapter Two

The Sherman ranch sprawled out before Creed as far as he could see. Acres and acres of prime rangeland, dotted with cattle, grazing horses and fields of swaying wheat. But as his lingering glance took it all in, it was the house standing tall and regal that stirred Creed the most.

He hadn't been back since the day he headed east all those years ago, a young man of seventeen, steeling himself against his mother's tears and his father's disappointment. Gus Sherman didn't want him to be a soldier, not at West Point or anywhere else. Creed was his oldest son. Together, they had a ranch to run. Over and over again, the Old Man ranted that it was Creed's duty to follow in his footsteps and spend the rest of his life wrangling cows and wild horses and ornery weather. The ranch was his heritage. His responsibility.

But Creed hadn't listened.

He wanted to be a soldier. Nothing—and no one— would stop him from being one.

They'd parted ways in anger, but time had a way of healing wounds. The Old Man even made a trip out to

West Point to visit Creed his first year as a cadet. Ma had been feeling poorly and wasn't up to traveling. Mary Catherine had gone in her place.

Just thinking of her warmed Creed clear through, and he spurred his horse closer to the house, to home, the anticipation of seeing his family again building within him. He'd stop in to see them, clean up some, then head out to Mary Catherine's place.

A couple of dogs loped toward him, mutts he didn't recognize. Ma would've taken them in, he knew. She had a soft spot for strays.

Their barking announced his approach, and one of the cowhands appeared from around the side of the house. Seeing Creed, he paused in midstride, a bag of feed balanced on his shoulder.

Creed leaned forward on the saddle horn and grinned wide. He'd know that face anywhere.

"Hey, Markie," he called. "Look who's home."

His younger brother blinked. The bag of feed dropped to the ground with a dull thud. "Creed?"

His name came out on a hoarse croak, and Creed's grin broadened. He swung out of the saddle, met Markie coming at him, and they fell into a long-armed hug.

"Last I saw you, you were somewhere between hay and grass. Not anymore. You've grown up, kid," he said. Pulling back, he poked Marcus on his bicep. "Put some meat on those scrawny bones, too, didn't you?"

"I'm not twelve anymore." He shook his head, as if he still found it hard to believe Creed had come home. "And you're not seventeen."

"Hell, no." He didn't want to live those years again. The Old Man had given him enough grief by then to last a lifetime. "Let me get a good look at you."

Creed took in the calluses on his brother's hands, the skin browned from long hours in the sun. He'd been born frail, sickly like Ma, his stature slighter than Creed's. But now Markie's shoulders were firm from muscle. Hard work had given him the strength he once lacked.

He'd become a man Pa could be proud of.

Had the Old Man even noticed?

"Still love this place so much?" Creed asked.

"More than you, I reckon."

Creed shrugged. He didn't bother to deny it. "You always did. Guess Pa depends on you now."

"You didn't leave him a choice."

The barb caught Creed by surprise, but he ignored it. Today was his homecoming. He refused to ruin it with a pointless argument. He glanced at the front door. "Is he in the house?"

"You never wrote, did you, Creed? Never kept in touch with us while you were off fighting your wars."

Creed braced himself against the accusation. And maybe the guilt from it, too. "I'm hoping Ma has some of her rhubarb pie waiting for me."

"You should've written, Creed. Come home now and again, damn it!"

Creed's patience snapped. "Well, I didn't, did I?" he shot back. "War is hell, Markie. I was too busy saving my own ass and fighting for yours that I didn't take the time!"

Markie's nostrils flared.

Creed exhaled a loud breath.

Why was he engaging in a yelling match when he'd only been home all of two minutes? He lifted his Stetson and raked a hand through his hair.

"I'm going in," he said and spun toward the porch.

"Wait." Unexpectedly, Markie grabbed Creed's arm,

halting him. "Let's have a drink first. I've got a brand-new bottle of Old Taylor whiskey stashed down at the bunkhouse. Seal's never been broken. We'll drink and…talk. Get caught up, you know?"

Creed acknowledged his brother's attempt at reconciliation with a terse nod. "Later. I promise. There are some things I have to do first."

"They can wait."

"No, they can't." Creed's gaze dropped to the fingers clamped around his forearm. Instinct told him something wasn't right in his parents' house.

Something Markie didn't want him to see.

He jerked his arm free. Wild horses wouldn't keep him from going in now. He strode to the porch, to the door.

"Damn it, Creed. Don't go in there yet!"

Creed gripped the knob and pushed. The door swung inward. His glance clawed the front room, the furniture he'd never seen before. One of those newfangled talking machines sat on a table, orchestra music playing from its oversize horn.

It wasn't like Ma to have such luxuries.

The scent of fresh-baked bread hovered in the air, and Creed headed toward the kitchen. She'd be fixing the noon meal for the Old Man, and he'd go there first after a morning of hard work. Might be he was already with her, and Creed could—

He saw his father first, dancing in slow time to the music swaying into the room, his tall, lean body angled just enough to shield the woman he held in his arms. But a glimpse of the pale hair piled on top of her head—and that vivid memory he'd held inside his heart for more than seven years—told Creed it wasn't his wife Gus Sherman danced with.

Instead, Mary Catherine.

Maybe he swore. Maybe the shock of seeing them hurtled across the room like a bullet and barked his presence. Maybe Mary Catherine's own intuition of the arrival of the first man she'd ever loved warned that he'd finally returned.

She pushed away from his father with a gasp, her eyes wide as moons. "Creed! Oh, my God, Creed."

The Old Man took a step toward him, but a snarl from Creed stopped him cold.

"You should've sent word," the Old Man said. "Let us know you were coming."

Creed emitted a mirthless laugh. "And spoil this pretty surprise you have for me? Not a chance, Pa. I wouldn't give you the pleasure."

"Creed, please," Mary Catherine said. "Let us explain."

"Nothing to explain, darlin'," he drawled. "What I'm looking at says it all."

"There's more to the story, and you know it," Pa growled. "I've always known you to be fair. Give us a chance to tell you what—"

"What I'd really like to know is what happened to my mother." How could Pa betray her like this? How could he destroy what Creed believed had always been a happy marriage? His glance flicked over Mary Catherine, a full-grown woman, and his lip curled in disgust. He leveled his father with a searing gaze. "What'd you do? Divorce her? Wasn't she good enough anymore? Did you find a young girl more satisfying in your bed—"

"Creed! That's enough!" Pa roared.

He clenched his teeth. Raw fury coursed through him.

"I'm so sorry you have to find out like this," Mary Catherine said, her voice shaking. "She died two and a half years ago."

His world rocked. *"What?"*

"The tuberculosis got her. She'd been living on one lung for a long time," Pa added. "She went fast and quiet in her sleep."

"Why didn't you tell me?" Creed demanded hoarsely. The shock of her death rolled through him. "Send me a wire. I would've come home, damn it."

"And leave whatever battle you happened to be fighting at the time?" Pa fired back.

The insult struck low. *"Yes!"*

"We notified the War Department," Mary Catherine said, looking hurt. "How could you think we wouldn't?"

"I didn't get the message." His brain tore backward through time. Two and a half years ago. He would've been in the Sahara Desert then. Out in the middle of nowhere. For weeks.

The damn wire never found him.

"There was nothing you could do, anyway," Mary Catherine said, calmer now. "We made her as comfortable as we could."

"We?" he snapped.

"Mary Catherine nursed her to the end," Markie said. He entered the kitchen and stood next to Pa. The three of them, together, staring at Creed.

The outsider. The absent son who'd chosen his country over his family and now paid the price for the years he'd never get back.

Had it been worth the cost?

The music ended, and Creed's head pounded from the oppressive silence blanketing the room.

"I courted Mary Catherine proper," Pa said, his voice a low rumble. "I want you to know that."

"She's young enough to be your daughter."

"I married her with the same vows I spoke to your mother. In a church and before the eyes of God."

"Is that supposed to make me feel better?"

"She'd been saving herself for you. But, damn it to hell, Creed, how long did you expect her to wait?"

"She told me she would!"

"You never wrote me," Mary Catherine said. Her lower lip quivered. "I thought you didn't love me anymore. I never knew where you were or if you were dead or alive. My feelings for you just—" she shrugged helplessly "—withered and died."

His lip curled, the repugnance churning inside him, obliterating her honesty. "So now you're my mother."

"Creed," his father began, the word a low warning.

Mary Catherine's head lifted with a defiant toss. "Yes. I am. You may as well know, too, I'm expecting a child. Gus's child. In the spring, you'll have a new brother or sister."

His gaze shot to her belly. For the first time, he noticed the roundness there, barely hidden beneath the apron tied to her thickening waist.

"Well, isn't that just too rich," he purred. "Guess it proves the Old Man still has what it takes in bed, doesn't it?"

His father lunged at him with a bellow of rage that shook the rafters. Creed reacted, taking his weight with a defensive shove that hurtled his sire backward until he staggered and toppled to the kitchen floor. Mary Catherine cried out in alarm and rushed to his side. But when Creed moved to help him up again, Markie stood in front of him, blocking his path.

"Why don't you just go, Creed," he hissed. "You've stirred up enough trouble for today."

The accusation finished off what had been one hell of a lousy homecoming.

"You know, Markie, that's the best damn thing I've heard since I got here."

He spun and stormed out of the house. The door slammed shut behind him with a finality that left him cold and bitter.

Alone.

He rode hard toward Los Angeles and didn't look back.

"Hurry, Mama. The elevator's run already. We cannot be late." Gina Briganti hooked her arm through her mother's and urged her faster along the crowded sidewalk toward the shirtwaist factory where they both worked. Only then did she realize Mama was limping. "What? A pebble again?"

"*Sì*. Again." Sounding tired even though the morning hadn't yet reached the eight o'clock hour, her mother halted, balanced herself on one foot and leaned over to untie her shoe. Gina kept a firm grip on her elbow and tried not to think of the precious seconds the stupid pebble cost them.

But then, it was no wonder Mama was always troubled with the pesky things. Her leather soles were worn through to her stockings.

Louisa Briganti shook the stone out, then tied her shoe back on, and they resumed walking, arm in arm. Gina endured a twinge of guilt for her impatience. It was just like her mother not to complain about her discomfort.

"Maybe we should begin to take the horse car," Gina said, thinking of the comfort, the luxury, of riding on a streetcar, pulled by a horse over rails. She thought, too, of the time they'd save by not having to walk to their jobs at the factory every morning. Or home again at night. "Our shoes, they will last longer."

"It costs a nickel to ride the horse car, Gina," her mama

said with a reproving cluck of her tongue. "Four nickels for us, both ways every day. That is a dollar and twenty cents a week. Too expensive!"

Gina sighed. Always, everything was expensive.

They lived like paupers, saving what little money they made at the factory working six days a week, sometimes seven during the busy season. And yet, it never seemed to be enough.

"Then you should take some money we save and buy yourself good walking shoes, Mama. Think of them as an investment."

"My shoes are fine. They have much use in them yet."

Gina snorted. "We should have tossed them into the gutter long ago."

"They are *fine*."

Gina rolled her eyes, but she couldn't stop a reluctant smile. "You know I am right, Mama. You are too stubborn to admit it."

Mama smiled, too, and patted Gina's hand lovingly. "It is more important you have your dream. That is why I do not buy new shoes."

For a moment, Gina didn't say anything as they hurried past a boy of about twelve in an oversize cap hawking newspapers on the corner. The mouthwatering smells from an Italian delicatessen hovered in the air. The Premier Shirtwaist Company factory was two blocks over. "Sometimes I think the dream, it will never happen."

"You must not give up." Her mother peered past a horse and buggy parked in the street before determining it safe enough to cross. "Next year, maybe. The one after that, for sure, eh?"

Gina didn't think she could wait that long. Patience had never been one of her virtues, and her dream of one day opening her own dressmaker shop often seemed impossibly frivolous.

And other times, she wanted it so much she could scarcely breathe from it.

Like now, the beginning of another long workday. The prospect of toiling for hours in the tedious monotony of shirtwaist-making with several hundred women was much too depressing. The only good thing she could look forward to was that it was Saturday, because Saturday meant shortened hours and payday.

Payday, most of all.

If only Mama wasn't so determined to send a portion of their meager wages to her family in Italy. If only they could keep every dime they made for themselves, Gina's savings would build faster and she could open her little shop sooner. If only they…

Gina couldn't think of "if onlys."

It was the right thing to do, sending Aunt Rosa money every month, Gina told herself firmly to alleviate the guilt from her selfishness. Many people did. Immigrants like herself and her mother who were compelled to help their struggling families back in their native countries.

Families who depended on the riches that could be made in America.

Except the sooner Gina could open her shop, the more money she could make, and the more money Mama could send her sister, and the sooner Aunt Rosa could come over for a visit.

Mama would love that more than anything. To see her sister again.

Unfortunately, Mama didn't agree with Gina's logic of keeping their money for themselves, no matter how hard Gina tried to convince her.

Even more worrisome, Mama wasn't so strong any-more. She'd lost weight since they left their beloved Sicily three years ago after Papa died. Each season, she lost a little more. Some days, Gina worried a brisk wind would lift her right up and carry her away if Gina wasn't there to hang on to her.

Her arm tightened protectively against her mother's. It was just the two of them in this big, powerful country. The Great Land of Opportunity. Mama needed her to take care of her. There was no one else.

Resolving to get through the day as she always did, Gina joined the throng of women streaming toward the freight elevator that would take them up to the ninth floor of the Premier Shirtwaist Company.

By late this afternoon, with the money she made, she'd be a little closer to fulfilling her dream.

Chapter Three

The shirtwaist was a fashion phenomenon.

Its very design rebelled against tight-fitting corsets and bulky bustles and softened the demand for an hourglass figure. Women had fallen in love with the concept of wearing a blouse and skirt, no matter the season or their class in society. They found the shirtwaist liberating. Incredibly versatile. Simple and comfortable.

Gina despised them.

Perhaps despise was the wrong word, she mused as she carefully hung a pattern piece onto the wire strung across the sewing table. Just weary of sewing thousands of them. Shirtwaists were available plain or chic, tucked or lacy, in gauzy fabric or durable cotton. But a blouse was just a blouse no matter which way it was designed.

Ah, but to create a beautiful, full-length gown. Now *that* was exciting! She loved the challenge, the creativity, and poured her ideas into a sheaf full of sketches she kept stashed under her bed. She fantasized about fine silks, brilliant wools and stunning velvets. One day, she would stop making boring shirtwaists and create gowns that would steal a woman's breath away.

"Here you are, Gina." Julia, the Premier Shirtwaist Company bookkeeper, handed her an envelope that contained her wages for the week. She thrust a battered clipboard toward her. "Initial next to your name, please."

Gina abandoned her frivolous thoughts and quickly checked the amount before she signed for the money. Today, one of the sample makers at Premier had taken sick. Gina spent the day in her place, tracing patterns of the new shirtwaists the salesmen would sell to department store buyers. It was an honor to be chosen for the job. Only the most talented of seamstresses were allowed to work on them—everyone knew the importance of having a fresh design for the company's product line. Even better, she was paid a higher wage because of it.

Luckily, the money was all there. Gina didn't trust her boss, Abraham Silverstein. He often cheated his employees, and it'd be just like him to pretend he didn't notice what Gina had done all day.

"Here's your mother's, too," Julia said, riffling through her stack of envelopes. She looked rushed; the end of the workday was only minutes away, and she had many employees to pay yet. "You'll give it to her, won't you?"

"Yes, of course." Gina jotted her initials next to both their names, and the bookkeeper hurried away.

The extra bonus in her wages lifted Gina's spirits. Maybe she would treat Mama to some of the *gelati* served by the Italian delicatessen across the street. It was early yet; they'd have time to indulge before their walk home.

She searched the massive workroom for her mother's table, her gaze skimming over several hundred women's faces before she found Mama sitting next to Serafina, her best friend in the factory. Serafina was from Sicily, too, and would love to join them for a refreshing dish of the *gelati*.

"We're short two dozen cuffs, Gina." Abraham Silverstein approached her, his stocky legs moving quickly past the long tables crowded with dozens of machines each, his belly stretching the buttons on his expensive silk shirt. He looked angry, as if the oversight was her fault. "The order must go out tonight. See that they're cut and sewn. I'll have the foreman bring the unfinished waists to your table."

Her spirits plummeted. "But it is almost time to go home. Less than twenty minutes."

"You'll work fast then, won't you?"

He was off again, barking orders in his gruff voice and leaving Gina no choice but to obey. She didn't dare argue with the factory owner, not when he could easily fire her for it. Worse, she'd already been paid for the day. Her time spent on the cuffs would be lost.

Her mood soured, and she hurried to her mother's table. Mama smiled, moved her foot off the Singer's pedal and tiredly pushed a curl off her forehead. "It will not be long now, eh, *bambina?* Our day will be finished."

"I must sew two dozen cuffs first," Gina said irritably, handing her mother the pay envelopes. "I cannot leave yet."

"What?" Mama stared, aghast. "Who says this?"

"Mr. Silverstein." Gina glared at him over her shoulder. "The big ox."

He was scolding another of his employees, a long-haired young man who had only begun work this week, an unskilled worker who started his training at Premier as a thread cutter, snipping stray threads from massive piles of waists. Gina didn't know his name, but it seemed his work for the day hadn't been satisfactory.

"We will help you, then," Mama said, tucking their pay envelopes securely into her purse.

"*Sì, sì,*" Serafina said. "Go, Gina. Have Sebastian cut the cuffs. With the three of us, it will not take so long."

"*Grazie,* Serafina." In her haste, Gina slipped into her native tongue. Sebastian was her friend. He'd see that she had the cuffs quickly.

He worked on the floor below them. As a cutter, he was highly respected and paid far more than the rest of the factory workers. It was his job to cut thousands of pieces of fabric in the most efficient manner possible. His skill with the razor-sharp blades never failed to amaze Gina.

Grateful now for that skill, she rushed down the narrow stairwell leading to the eighth floor. She didn't want to wait for the elevator. Every minute counted. She found him standing with the rest of the cutters and their assistants, their work done for the day as they waited out the clock to go home.

Seeing her, his expression registered surprise. Handsome with the dark skin of his Italian heritage, his hair thick and black as jet, he was only a few years older and loyal as a puppy. Mama was quite taken with him. She'd told Gina many times what a fine husband he'd make.

"*Bella Gina.* What are you doing down here?"

She ignored his flirting and reached for the pattern pieces she'd need. Like they were upstairs, the patterns— thin paper edged in steel—hung on lines over the cutting tables. "Quickly, Sebastian. I need two dozen cuffs. Will you help me?"

"Yes, sure, but two dozen? Now?"

She huffed a breath, exasperated all over again at the timing of Mr. Silverstein's order. "Yes. Can you believe it? It is so late!"

Sebastian was already laying the patterns onto the yards of fine cotton stretched out before him, his big hands handling the delicate paper with ease. "Someone cannot count, eh?"

"I think not," Gina said, not bothering to hide her annoyance. "Oh, *thank* you for doing this, Sebastian."

He winked. "For you, *mi amore,* anything."

"Now, I make you late tonight, too." Feeling guilty for it, she glanced at the other cutters. Most of them weren't married. It was Saturday night. They would all go out and drink too much beer together.

"Relax, Gina. You do me a favor." Sebastian had lowered his voice so it wouldn't carry. "Nikolai wants me to go to a meeting tonight after we leave the factory. Now I have a good reason not to go."

"Who is he?"

"Nikolai Sokolov. One of my assistants. The big one with the moustache."

She eyed the man covertly. Yes, she had seen him many times. An arrogant-looking Russian with broad shoulders and harsh features. He always stared at her whenever she walked by.

"What kind of meeting?" she asked, her attention more on the cutting blades than Sebastian's conversation.

"An anarchist meeting."

Gina cared little about the ravings of the men who despised the values that made America such a powerful country. The cuffs were more important. "How much longer?"

"What? You want me to make a mistake and waste the precious fabric?" Sebastian chided gently. His blade glided through the cotton. He tossed leftover pieces into a bin heaped with scraps and tissue paper and repositioned the knife for one last cut. "Then it takes me twice as long, and Mr. Silverstein is not happy. Trust me, *mi amore.* You will have your cuffs, and they will be perfect."

"I know, Sebastian." She tried to smile away her impatience. "That is why I come to you for help."

She clasped her hands tightly, drew in a long breath, stared up at the high ceiling. Sebastian was right. She couldn't rush him. A few minutes wouldn't make much difference. Not really. The delicatessen would still have their sweets, no matter what time she left the factory tonight.

"Later, I go for *gelati* with Mama and Serafina," she said. "Would you like to come, too? My treat. This I can do for you since—"

But Sebastian wasn't listening. His attention had shifted to his fellow workers and their assistants. They listened raptly to a sullen, angry-looking youth Gina recognized as the new thread cutter Mr. Silverstein had been scolding earlier. How the young man managed to slip downstairs before the final bell, she didn't know.

"What is it, Nikolai?" Sebastian demanded, straightening from the cutting table.

"My brother, Alex," the Russian said. "Silverstein has just fired him."

"That so?"

"He has also cheated Alex of the wages he earned this week. He says my brother's workmanship is poor and that he is not entitled to be fully paid for his time."

Sebastian's mouth tightened. "Too bad."

The Russian grunted. He reached inside his coat pocket and withdrew his cigarettes and match, his hard gaze on his sibling. "Yes. Too bad."

He lit the tobacco, one cigarette for himself, one for his brother. They began speaking in the guttural language of their country. Alex paced back and forth, his agitation obvious. Barred from the language they couldn't understand, the other cutters lost interest and meandered to the coat rack.

Gina watched the brothers in disapproval. It was strictly

forbidden to smoke in the factory. Signs were posted everywhere. How could they be so careless?

But then, Sebastian didn't seem to mind, his concentration once more on cutting the cuffs. She suspected he, too, had stolen a few puffs off his cigarette when Mr. Silverstein wasn't looking.

The factory's closing bell rang, and the shrill sound startled Gina from her thoughts. The electric motor which powered scores of sewing machines shut off. Wooden chairs scraped against the floor as workers left their tables and headed for the coat racks. Nikolai and Alex Sokolov took one long drag off their cigarettes and tossed the butts into the scrap bins.

Sebastian smiled and handed Gina the cuffs, all two dozen of them. Before she could thank him, flames erupted from the bin behind her with a sudden, explosive *whoosh*.

Chapter Four

Creed threw back another swallow of whiskey. He cursed himself for being all kinds of a fool.

How could he think Mary Catherine would wait for him? How could he be so blind? So stupid?

And the Old Man. Stole her right out from under his pathetic nose. Never in a hundred years, a *million,* would Creed have thought it possible.

Pa and Mary Catherine. Husband and wife.

He slouched lower in his chair and closed his eyes. The self-pity rolled through him in bitter waves.

But of all that had gone wrong the entire day, learning Ma had died was the worst. If only he could've told her goodbye…

He opened his eyes again and focused on the bottle of Old Taylor whiskey sitting in front of him. The words on the label blurred into Mary Catherine's penmanship. The notes she'd written, the promises she'd made, the love she'd professed.

Creed removed her last letter from his shirt pocket. Three years he'd carried the thing with him, day in and day out, close to his heart.

Not anymore.

He lit a match and touched the flame to a tattered corner. Within seconds, his memories, his hopes and dreams, disintegrated into a sorry-looking pile of ashes.

He finished off the whiskey in his glass, but didn't pour himself another. He had to think. Make some decisions. Get his life back in order.

Going back to the ranch was out of the question. He could find a job somewhere, he supposed. California was a big state. He could learn a trade. Make a decent living.

But, hell, he was a soldier. He'd never been anything else. Never wanted to be, either.

You've fought brilliantly on foreign soil...a mercenary...a reputation most soldiers only dream of...your success has been awe-inspiring....

Graham Dooling's words dropped into Creed's memory, and his mind cleared. There was nothing for him here in America. Not anymore. His place was in fighting for his country in lands beyond the continent.

It was what he did best.

Creed stood up, tossed a few coins on the table and pushed his hat onto his head. Anticipation hummed through him. His good friend, Jeb Carson, was working at the War Department now. Creed would wire him and request the most dangerous assignment the government could give him.

Now that he thought about it, he was itching for a good fight. The thrill that came from laying his life on the line. Making his own rules. Pitting his guts and brains against a ruthless enemy—and winning against them all.

What did he have to lose?

The bartender gave him directions to the nearest Western Union Telegraph office. He strode outside, paused on the boardwalk, and scanned the busy Los Angeles business district, vastly different from the impoverished countries he'd lived in the past six years. He'd been in one hell of a hurry to come home. Now, he couldn't wait to leave again.

Collette's Fine Ladies Wear was across the street. Had it been just this morning he'd been in the store, eager for a gift for Mary Catherine?

He frowned and shoved aside the memory, his thoughts distracted by the scent of smoke in the air. Might be the Italian delicatessen on the corner burned something in their kitchen. But a crowd was gathering in front of a tall building on the opposite corner, a factory of some sort, and it was then he saw the flames shooting from an upper story window.

The door to Collette's dress shop opened, and Graham Dooling ran out, his sister right behind him. Clearly, they'd just spied the fire, too, and rushed to the street to help.

"Graham!" Creed barked. "Do you know if anyone is inside?"

Any surprise Dooling might have felt at seeing Creed again was lost in the seriousness of the situation.

"I suspect the Premier Shirtwaist employees, sir. They work every Saturday."

"Sometimes Sundays, too," Collette added worriedly. "It's their busy season. The hours they keep are horrendous."

"How many?"

Collette stared at the flames. "Oh, God. Hundreds."

"Hundreds?" Creed gaped at her, his alarm increasing tenfold. "Of *people?*"

She trembled. "Yes."

Creed broke into a sprint toward the factory. None of those employees had come out yet.

Why?

"You got a fire department around here?" he snapped over his shoulder. "Call 'em, damn it!"

"Yes, yes. Of course." She hurried to the nearest alarm box and pulled it.

Graham ran beside him, his attention riveted on the flames high above them. "I'm glad you're here, sir. If anyone can help these people, you can."

Creed counted nine rows of windows. The fire was burning on the eighth floor. Only a matter of time before the ninth began burning, too.

Ladders would never reach.

A sick feeling washed over him. How could he get all those Premier Shirtwaist Company employees out in time?

How could anyone?

Gina stared in horror at the fast-spreading flames. It'd taken only seconds for the scraps of airy cotton and tissue paper in the bin to explode into a firebomb. Didn't Nikolai and Alex realize how careless they'd been? How stupid? She whirled toward the group of cutters, but the brothers were gone.

"Get the fire pails!" Sebastian yelled, running toward the ledge where the bright red containers were kept, always full of water. "Hurry!"

Gina dropped the cuffs and joined the men splashing at the flames, but their efforts were no match for the hungry fire. Already, it leapt from cutting table to cutting table. Beside each one, a bin heaped with hundreds of pounds of scraps like Sebastian's fed the bomb until it raged out of control.

"We need more water!" Gina cried.

"Coming! Coming!" Leon, who operated the freight elevator every morning and night, bolted into an alcove to fill pails from the water trough kept there. In his haste, he left the elevator's doors open. Air blew up from the shaft, and the fire raged higher.

Flames licked at one of the pattern pieces strung over Sebastian's table, then another and another, until the whole line of them dropped. Gina's arm came up, protecting her face and hair from flying embers. Piles of shirtwaists in various stages of construction burst into fiery balls. Bolts of cloth and rolls of tissue paper, too—everything!—burst into flame.

Smoke billowed and swirled in a raging cloud, and Gina coughed, her eyes stinging.

"We must get out of here!" Sebastian yelled and grabbed her hand. "Hurry! The elevator!"

Suddenly, one of the windows shattered. Two. Three more. The flames roared through the openings—demonic, angry flames that rocketed from the eighth floor up toward the ninth in a rampage—

The ninth floor! Holy Madonna. *Mama!*

Gina yanked her hand from Sebastian's. "I cannot leave yet! My mother!"

"No, Gina! You cannot go up there. We have to get out. Now!"

Mama wouldn't know how terrible the fire was, or how fast it was spreading, until it was too late. Sebastian reached for Gina again, but she bolted toward the stairwell, finding her way by sheer instinct. She couldn't see him anymore, or hear him. The smoke was too thick, too blinding. But the stairs were next to the elevator. She had only to get to them to find her mother.

Screams from terrified workers met her in the narrow stairwell, barely the breadth of a strong man's shoulders, yet the workers stumbled down two and three abreast. Gina flattened herself against the wall and forced her way up against the downward rush, her body pummeled, pushed, kicked. She prayed she wouldn't lose her footing and be knocked down in the exodus.

At last, she made it to the ninth floor. The windows here, too, had been shattered, and the openings sucked flames in from the outside. The monstrous fire ignited stacks of packing crates and bales of finished waists. Burning pieces of tissue blew and floated along the floor, in the air, up to the ceiling. Panicked seamstresses jumped from tabletop to tabletop, over rows of sewing machines and piles of cotton, looking for a way to escape.

The inferno raged. And raged.

"Mama!" Gina screamed, her gaze searching countless panicked faces. Her mother had to be here. She wouldn't have left without Gina. *"Mama!"*

Suddenly, miraculously, there she was, sobbing, reaching. Gina, sobbing, too, fell into her arms.

"Thank God I found you." Gina shuddered in violent relief and forced herself to think. She took firm hold of Mama's hand, pulled her toward a door only Mr. Silverstein ever used, the one leading to his office and another set of elevators.

"The door is already locked for the weekend." Mama gasped and tugged her to a stop. "We cannot get out that way. Many people have already tried. All that is left is the freight elevator and stairs, and they are both too crowded. Oh, Gina, so many people. We will never get out of here."

"We will, Mama. We have to."

She abandoned Mr. Silverstein's exit and headed for the freight elevator instead. Distraught employees pounded on the closed doors, but Gina knew Leon wasn't this high. She had just seen him on the floor below, and he would've filled his car with workers from *there* and taken them to the ground level.

Please. Let him come back for us.

"The roof!" someone cried, and part of the crowd shifted to this new avenue of escape, but Gina wavered with indecision. What if the fire burned through the ceiling, clear through to the roof? What would they do then?

And then, before her very eyes, the elevator came up, the doors opened, and there was Leon, his car blessedly empty. The crowd surged forward, nearly lifting Gina from her feet and carrying her with them.

"*Oh, mio Dio!* Our pay envelopes, Gina! They are in my purse!" Mama yanked at the death grip Gina held on her hand. "We cannot leave them behind!"

"No! Forget the money!"

She fought to keep Mama's hand clutched in her own, but her mother pulled free. Gina was helpless to go after her, not when the other women held her fast, pressing her into the elevator with them. Their bodies crushed her against the back of the car. She couldn't move, couldn't breathe.

The doors began to close. Her panic rising, Gina strained to see into the hellish shroud of smoke and flames between them.

But Mama was gone.

Creed and Graham ran into the factory entrance nearest the fire. The vestibule was deserted, but from somewhere, a stairwell, maybe, Creed detected the faint, chilling sound of people screaming.

"Run to the building next to this one," he ordered, noting the close proximity between the two structures. "Enlist some help to get the workers to safety by way of the roofs."

"Yes, sir."

Graham took off again, yelling at several policemen hustling toward him. Creed sprinted to a stairway, his blood turning cold as he thought of the horrors that awaited him on the top floors.

A low hum behind him announced the arrival of an elevator. He swung toward it. The car slid to a stop, the doors opened, and a couple dozen crying women tumbled out. How the small cubicle managed to hold so many, Creed would never know. The cable should've snapped from their weight.

The elevator emptied except for one.

"Go with them, Gina," the operator pleaded, pointing to the workers scattering out of the vestibule and into the street. "Save yourself while you can."

"I must find my mother, Leon. Please, pull the car up to the ninth floor again. Hurry!"

Even in her anguish, she was beautiful. Black eyes. Olive skin. Hair, thick and gleaming, the color of rich sable.

But it was her anguish which clawed at Creed most. How it contorted her thinking, defied her logic. She had to know the severity of the fire, the dangers of going back up. That she might not make it down again—alive.

And he'd have none of it. He strode toward her.

"You're getting out," he ordered.

Her gaze jumped to him. "I will not."

"It's real bad up there, mister," Leon said. "Not sure I can make a trip back. The heat. It's too much. Could bend the rails." He swiped at the sweat on his cheek. "But I got to try. Those girls aren't going to make it down if I don't. And Gina here needs to find her mother real bad."

"Please go, Leon!" she said, grasping his arm in desperation. "Hurry!"

"Then I'm going up with you." Creed stepped into the car. Where was that damn fire department? "We'll do what we can until help gets here."

Leon levered the door closed, lifted his arm and tugged on the cable. Nothing happened. He tugged again, to no avail. He swung his head back, as if he could see nine floors up.

"The fire's in the shaft," he choked. "It's burned the cable. We're not going anywhere."

The woman, Gina, made a sound of dismay and flung herself at the lever that kept the doors together. She yanked them open and bolted into the vestibule.

Creed swore and bolted out, too. He caught up with her, halfway to the second floor. Grabbing her elbow, he pulled her against the wall of the narrow stairwell.

"You crazy fool. What the hell do you think you're doing?" he demanded.

"Let me go!" She pushed against his chest, but he didn't budge. "I must get to the ninth floor!"

"You can't! You *know* you can't!"

"I must find my mother. She is there! I have to help her. Let *go* of me!" She planted both hands on his chest again. Her strength caught him by surprise, and he took a fast step back to keep his balance.

She raced up the stairs once more, toward the third floor, Creed right behind her. He snaked his arm around her waist and hauled her back against him, lifting her clear off her feet and keeping her there.

"Listen to me, Gina. That's your name isn't it? Gina?"

"Yes. Gina Briganti," she said, an automatic response, he suspected, considering how much she was squirming against him. "Put me down!"

"Five seconds." He hissed the words in her ear, his chin and cheek pressed against that silky mass of hair of hers. "That's all I'm asking. Five lousy seconds to hear what I have to say."

She didn't respond, just kept squirming, kicking, clawing.

"I'm stronger than you are," he grated. "I can hold you a long time. The more you fight me, the longer it'll take before we start looking for your mother."

Instantly, she stopped. Her bosom heaved. Creed put her down, and she whirled toward him, black eyes flashing.

"Talk!" she snapped.

"My name's Creed Sherman." He didn't know if she cared who he was or not, but telling her his name was a start in getting her to trust him. "I'll do all I can to help you, but we're going to do it my way, you hear?"

Her eyes narrowed in suspicion. "What way?"

"The safe way." He pointed up the stairs. "I'll go ahead of you to find the best way to get to the ninth floor if there is one. If not, we head back down. Understand?"

Footsteps sounded above them. The stairwell was narrow. Wouldn't be room for the both of them if a herd of people came clamoring down.

Gina cried out something in Italian and clutched his shirt front, pulling him flat against her.

Hysterical women, coughing, crying, their hair and clothes singed from fire, stumbled down the steps. Each one bumped into him, as if they couldn't see he was there. Or didn't care if they did. Just when Creed thought they were all past, one more appeared.

"Serafina!" Gina gasped, staring at her over his shoulder. "Oh, Serafina! Have you seen Mama?"

Creed stepped back, and the woman blinked, her eyes red and dazed. "Gina?"

Gina pushed him aside, and the two women collapsed into each other's arms.

Serafina cried loudly. "You do not find Louisa?" She pulled back, grief-stricken, her cheeks streaked with smoke and tears. "Mother in Heaven, she is lost to us. The fire—it is so terrible. No one can survive it."

"Lost to us?" Gina pressed her fingers to her mouth in horror, and Creed's gut tightened.

"We'll keep looking," he said fiercely.

"Do not go up there." Serafina trembled and made the Sign of the Cross. "The fire is everywhere. No one can escape. Not anymore."

"But you made it, Serafina. Maybe Mama is coming still."

"No. We come from the sixth floor fire escape before it breaks. It is not strong enough to hold so many. We saved ourselves by climbing in a window. And those that could not—" she clutched a handkerchief and sobbed into it, her plump shoulders shaking "—Louisa was not with us. Oh, Mother in Heaven, she is lost." Sobbing all over again, she hurried away.

Wide-eyed, Gina stared after her. She dragged her stare back to Creed and sucked in a whimpering breath. Suddenly, she pivoted, lifted her skirt hem, and rushed up the stairs again.

"Maybe your mother made it to the roof," he said, acutely aware he was doing the following once more.

"And maybe she still waits for the elevator. She will not know the cable is burned. No one will."

They were on the fourth floor now, and the smell of smoke was getting stronger. Up to the fifth, they climbed. The sixth. The seventh. The smoke stung the back of his throat. Gina coughed and dragged in air.

The eighth floor was next. The one where the fire had started. Creed reached out, grasped her arm, forced her to halt. From here on out, things weren't going to be pretty.

"Is there any other way of getting to the ninth floor? Another set of stairs? Elevators?"

"No," she said, winded. "Except Mr. Silverstein's entrance, and his door, always it is locked from the rest of us."

"Where is it?"

"On the other side of the building. We cannot get there from here. Mama would not have been able to use that door. Too many people tried."

"So these stairs would be her only way to get to the ground level."

"She did not come this way. She would not have had time."

Creed peered at the stairwell, illuminated only by a dirty skylight. He could hear the fire, snarling and snapping, a horrific monster just beyond their reach. The air was thick. Heavy with heat. They couldn't go much farther.

But he had to find a way to get up those stairs. He needed to get to the ninth floor. He'd noticed fire hoses mounted on the walls on each level they passed. He could use them to fight his way through the flames with more guts than brains to help Gina find her mother.

There would be a tank of water on the roof; turning the iron valve would release the water into the hoses. But before Creed could remove the hose from its bracket, before he could turn the valve for the rush of water, glass shattered.

An explosive fireball roared into the stairwell, a roiling mass of flame that threw him back against Gina and sent them both toppling down the stairs.

Chapter Five

Pain shot like a rocket through his head, and incredible heat seared every inch of his skin. Smoke filled his lungs, choking back the air he needed to breathe.

But it was sheer instinct that propelled Creed from the depths of unconsciousness to the horrifying reality that if he didn't get the hell out of the stairwell, he would die. And so would Gina. The snarling, snapping flames were too close, too demonic, too determined to burn them alive if they didn't.

The blast had thrown them down like rag dolls, and he lay sprawled on top of her, his body a shield against the worst of the heat. With Herculean effort, he heaved himself up; his glance clawed over her. She didn't move, didn't make a sound, didn't make any reaction at all, and a raw fear gripped him that she was dead.

He swore. There was no time to determine if she was. He had to get her out, get them both out, and in spite of the narrow breadth of their surroundings, he managed to heft her over his shoulder, like the feed bags he used to carry when he was a kid. Holding her tight with one arm while using the other to brace himself against the wall, he descended the debris-strewn stairs they'd only just climbed, his teeth gritted against the disorienting smoke, forced to trust his feet to find the way when his eyes couldn't. Past the seventh floor, the sixth, he traveled with as much speed as he dared, meeting no one coming up, no one going down.

By the time he reached the third level, the air showed signs of thinning. By the time he stumbled to the second, the roar of the fires above had lessened, but frantic voices below grew clearer with every step. Barked commands, he realized, from firemen and policemen desperate to gain control of a tragedy gone wild.

They were too late. Terrible damage had already been done.

His lungs burned from exertion, from the poisons he'd inhaled from the factory's hellish top floors, and staggering into the vestibule at last, a storm of humbling relief swept through him.

The place was eerily deserted. The elevator stood open, abandoned, Leon long gone to save himself after the car was rendered useless. Creed headed straight for the building's exit doors.

Suddenly, two grim-faced firemen burst through, dragging a heavy canvas hose behind them. Creed did a quick sidestep to evade them. They were too intent on hustling up the stairs to notice him or the woman he carried.

Creed watched them go. In the coming minutes, as the men climbed closer, deeper into the inferno, Creed and Gina would be far from their minds, the least of their troubles.

Another time, he would've followed them up in a brazen attempt to do what he could to help. Now, he had Gina to think of. He had to get her out of this godforsaken place. And hope she was still alive.

In several long strides, he was outside. His lungs filled with crisp, clean air, and he breathed in deep, as long and as much as he could.

Never would he take fresh air for granted again.

A heavy cloud of smoke hung over the factory, but beyond it, the sky still shone blue and hinted at the coming dusk. Seagulls soared in graceful abandon as they meandered their way to and from the ocean. Beyond the perimeter of the Premier Shirtwaist factory, to the thousands of people unaware, it was just the beginning of another Saturday night.

But to those closest, their lives would never be the same again.

Including Gina's.

She hung limp and heavy over his shoulder, and he shifted her body to cradle her more comfortably in his arms. Her dark head lolled against his shoulder, and a small moan slipped from her throat. It moved him, that moan. Creed never considered himself to be a religious man, but he breathed a prayer of thanks to the Almighty that she wasn't dead as he'd earlier feared.

She'd been knocked cold from the fiery blast, and he didn't know how bad she was hurt. No blood that he could see, or broken bones, but she needed a doctor to know for sure, and he raked a glance around him to find Graham Dooling. Of anyone, the man would do what he could to help Creed locate one.

But the crowd gathered behind the police lines surrounding the factory made searching for Dooling all but impossible. Word of the blaze had spread fast, aided by the giant plume of blackened smoke billowing into the sky. Grief-stricken relatives of the garment workers screamed for information about their loved ones. Horse-drawn fire wagons raced to help fight the blaze, their sirens wailing, their efforts hampered by the hordes of curiosity-seekers streaming into the streets.

Creed turned away from it all and headed toward a well-groomed park on the city block adjacent to the Premier. The place offered a small piece of serenity amongst the chaos. He could take Gina there for a little while. Get her medical help and maybe learn some news about her mother.

Scores of young women were already there, clearly of the same mind. From the smoke smeared on their faces, he discerned they were mostly factory workers, the lucky ones who'd managed to escape just as the fire broke out. A small number were being consoled by family members fortunate enough to have found them. Others sat alone, crying, dazed and devastated by all that had happened.

He found a quiet spot away from them, dropped down to one knee, and eased Gina onto the thick grass. She didn't move or make a sound. He knew what it was like to be knocked unconscious, understood she needed a little time to bring herself out of it.

But he lingered over her, worrying, his gaze caught on the finely-sculpted angles of her face and the dark coloring of her heritage.

A beautiful woman, this Gina Briganti.

Might be she had family looking for her, too. A sister or a cousin. A husband. Or her mother—he could only hope, for both their sakes.

She hadn't mentioned anyone, though, and the thought of her being alone, fighting the nightmare of the fire and all its repercussions…

At some point, it'd become important to stay with her. She didn't know it yet, but she needed him.

And hell, maybe he needed to be needed right now.

Didn't take a brilliant man to figure he was still hurting from Pa and Mary Catherine's betrayal. Would probably always hurt from it, at least some. But he refused to think of them and how they were living out there, a couple of lovebirds on the Sherman ranch, a world away from the turmoil here in the city.

He grimaced and drew back. Hell of a day so far, and it wasn't even over yet.

Exhaustion hit him fast and hard, and he sank onto the ground next to Gina. His body had been pummeled by chunks of plaster and wood from the explosion in the stairwell, and he felt the bruises to prove it. His throat burned from the smoke. And every muscle ached....

His eyes shut. He needed to close his mind to the holocaust he'd just witnessed. To rest a minute or two. Then he'd have to find Dooling—and soon. Between the two of them, they'd scour the far corners of Los Angeles to track down Gina's mother.

"Gina! *Mio Dio!* Gina!"

Creed's eyes flew open at the anguished cry. A black-haired man, a few years older than she was, dropped to his knees beside her, grasped her shoulders and gave her a good shake.

Creed sat bolt upright. Abrupt protectiveness shot through him, and he grabbed the man's wrist to keep him from shaking her again.

"Easy," he growled. "You might hurt her."

The other man turned grieving eyes toward him. "Is she—is she dead?"

"No." Understanding why he'd think so, Creed released him. "We were in a stairwell by the eighth floor, and a ball of flame came at us. She was knocked out."

The man made the Sign of the Cross.

"She's alive," Creed said, for both of their benefits. "Best thank God for that."

"*Sì.* I do." The handsome face crumpled, and he grasped her shoulders again, more gently this time. He bent low and pressed a kiss to her forehead. "*Mi amore.* I must know that you are all right. Can you hear me, Gina?"

Amazingly, she stirred, as if his plea—or maybe it was the familiarity of his voice—reached into the deep abyss that held her captive. She made a slight grimace, then fell victim to a spasm of deep, wracking coughs that curled her onto her side and left her gasping for air.

Alarm filtered through Creed. Inhaling that smoke had made her sick. Maybe she needed some water. Why hadn't he thought of it sooner? He dragged a glance around the park, but saw no one who might have some to share.

Yet he was reluctant to leave her to make a more thorough search. He didn't know who this man was, and until Creed knew she'd be all right, he had no intention of leaving her with anyone.

The coughing ended, and she lay back, spent from the effort. Her gaze touched on him before flitting to the man bent over her. Recognition widened her dark eyes; she raised herself up and flung her arms around his neck.

"Sebastian!" The smoke had given her voice a raspy sound. "Oh, Sebastian! I cannot find Mama! Have you seen her?"

He made a sound of despair. "No, Gina. You did not see her on the ninth floor?"

"*Sì,* but only for a little while before she remembers our pay envelopes and runs back for them. I could not keep her with me, Sebastian! I could not leave the elevator, and Leon, he could not go up for her again. The cable burns, and Mama is still up there, and—"

He appeared horrified. "*Mio Dio,* Gina. She is lost, then."

"No!" Stricken, she pushed away from him. "She is not lost. I will find her. She looks for me, too. I know she does."

"Gina." Sebastian touched her cheek. "*Bella Gina,* the fire is terrible. So many will be lost today."

Her breath quickened. "Not Mama."

"You must understand—"

She made a quick, negating shake of her head. "I will find her, Sebastian."

He drew in an unsteady breath. "I hope that you will." He hesitated. "What of Serafina?"

"I see her by the third floor." Gina paused, as if to gather her composure. "But she does not know where Mama is."

Sebastian nodded, slowly, gravely, and said nothing more.

Creed didn't know how Sebastian fitted into Gina's life. Might be he was her husband. Or betrothed. Could be either one, since he obviously had great affection for her. But it rankled that the man offered no hope about her mother. Until they had solid evidence to the contrary, Creed intended to help her keep looking.

"I will take you home to my family," Sebastian said. He made a move to rise, his hand on her elbow. "We will wait there for word about Louisa."

She jerked from his grasp. "No."

"It is better you come with me," he said. He reached for her again.

"I cannot leave, Sebastian. I will not!"

"*Mi amore,* please. Many terrible things are happening because of the fire. It is not good you are here to see them."

Creed's patience snapped. Hadn't the man been listening to anything she said?

"The lady stays," he growled.

In unison, they turned toward him.

Sebastian locked an imperious gaze on him. Creed had a pretty good idea how he must look—eyes reddened from smoke, his shirt and Levi's covered in dust and soot, and he'd long since lost his Stetson. Sebastian would know Creed had no affiliation with the Premier Shirtwaist Company's factory, might even think he looked out of place in a city as sophisticated as Los Angeles.

But Creed had never backed down from a fight. And right now, Gina needed someone on her side.

"Who is this, Gina?" Sebastian demanded.

She hesitated, her gaze still on him, the faintest furrow forming between her dark brows. Creed knew her mind was scrambling.

And why did that annoy him?

"I am sorry," she said finally. "I do not remember your name."

She'd been distraught in the stairwell when he'd introduced himself. Consumed with getting to the ninth floor. Understandable that the words didn't sink in.

But he knew with certainty he'd always remember everything about her, from her name, to the way she said it, to the way she looked when she did. Her beauty before the fire, and after, and all her anguish in between.

"Creed Sherman," he said.

"Yes," she murmured with a slight nod. "Yes, that is it."

"You do not know him?" Sebastian asked. "Yet he speaks for you?"

She snapped her attention back to him. "He does not!"

"Then it should not matter if he wants you to stay. It is more important I think you should go." A third time, he took Gina's arm. "Let me take you home, *mi amore*." His voice lowered to a gentle, coaxing tone. "Just for a little while, eh? Until the nightmare is over."

She didn't move. "The nightmare does not end if I do not find Mama, Sebastian. You *know* it will not."

"I'll see that she's taken care of," Creed said roughly.

Again, she turned to him. Her dark gaze seemed to search into his soul to judge for herself whether he could be trusted. She couldn't know the man he was, or what he'd done, or all he was capable of, and he found himself holding his breath.

"Yes," she said. She seemed to draw strength from her decision. She gave Sebastian a quick nod. "I am safe with him. He risks his life in the fire to help me."

Sebastian released her and drew back. His shoulders squared. "I will help you, too, then. But it will not be easy. Tell me what I can do."

She swept an arm outward, showing him the crowd which filled the park, the streets. Factory workers, civil servants, the curious—and the morbid.

"So many people. And it is dark soon. I cannot ask them all if they see Mama." She appealed to him. "Surely, someone does!"

"*Sì, sì.* I will ask everyone I know. I will do my best for you and for Louisa."

Tears welled in her black eyes. "*Grazie.*"

He smoothed the hair at her forehead. "You must be strong, Gina. I am afraid the news will not be good."

She drew in a quavering breath. "I must hope that it is."

He kissed her cheek, one side before the other, and hastened to his feet. Gina followed him up, her gaze clinging to him as he disappeared into the crowd.

Creed rose, too. Her relationship with Sebastian was none of his business. Wasn't like Creed to pry, but with this woman, he had a need to know.

"Do you belong to him?" he asked.

"Sebastian?" She appeared taken aback. "No."

Creed kept his expression blank. "Easy to tell you mean a lot to him."

"Yes." She appeared distracted, her gaze caught on someone in the crowd. "I think it is Julia over there. Maybe she sees my mother."

Creed caught her arm before she could leave. "Not so fast."

Her dark gaze darted up at him in surprise. He kept a firm grip on her, saw how her chin barely reached his shoulder, that she was full-breasted and thin-hipped and slender enough to make him wonder if she got enough to eat every day. Again, a peculiar feeling of protectiveness swirled through him.

"Hell of a blast back there in the stairwell," he said quietly. "You hurt anywhere?"

"No."

"It's best to find a doctor to know for sure."

"I do not need one to tell me I am fine. Only *I* know if I am fine."

She had a stubborn streak in her, for sure. "I'll bet your throat is sore from breathing in smoke."

Her fingers touched her neck. "A little, yes."

"Some water will help it feel better."

"I do not want any water."

"There's a delicatessen across the street. I'll get you a glass there."

"Creed." Impatience threaded the word. "I do not need a doctor or a glass of water. I only need—"

"—to find your mother. I know." He gave in. She was beside herself with worry. Nothing he could say or do would convince her to do anything else. "All right. We'll work together on it. Where's this Julia you mentioned?"

He scanned the maze of faces in the direction she indicated and snagged on one he recognized. Graham Dooling's. The Secret Service agent looked rushed, intense, clearly on the hunt for someone as he wove his way through the people scattered around the park.

"Gina, wait," Creed said, not letting Graham out of his sight.

"Why?"

"I have a friend over there. He might know something."

"Who?"

"Graham Dooling. He works for the government. Could be he'll have an idea what to do." Creed slid a sharp whistle between his teeth. The sound caught Graham's attention; seeing Creed, he immediately sprinted toward them.

"I've been trying to find you, sir," he said. "I heard the blast from the upper floor of the factory. I knew you were headed that way. I thought the worst."

"We made it, but barely." The grimness in Creed's tone revealed all he didn't say. "The explosion kept us from getting to the ninth floor."

"'Us', sir?"

"My name is Gina Briganti." She stepped forward, and the desperate hope in her expression was enough to give Creed's heart a stiff yank. "We try to find my mother, Louisa Briganti. Do you hear about her?"

Graham's regret was genuine. "I'm sorry, ma'am. I haven't. There are so many—"

He halted. Easy to see even he was affected by her anguish and disappointment. Creed guessed that because of it, Graham refrained from explaining how difficult it would be to track down so many this soon after the fire broke out.

"The police are doing all they can, Miss Briganti. Right now, getting the blaze under control is their main concern.

After that, they'll have to find some way to get a listing of the workers on duty today. When they do, they can cross off the names of—of everyone found."

"Could take a day or two," Creed said, just so she'd know it'd be hard to do.

A tiny gasp escaped her. She whirled toward the crowd. "Julia might have a list."

"Julia?" Creed and Graham repeated in unison.

"Premier's bookkeeper. It is payday today, and she has a list with her when the fire breaks out so we can sign for our envelopes. She is here. I see her not long ago."

Creed exchanged a hopeful glance with Dooling. It'd be a stroke of luck if the woman had some sort of roster with her, which could be a valuable tool in the quest to account for every factory employee.

And he fervently hoped there was someone on that list who had seen Gina's mother.

Chapter Six

No one had.

Gina was devastated no one knew where Mama was. Were they so frantic to save themselves they paid no attention? Many of the seamstresses knew Louisa Briganti and liked her. They would have helped if she needed it.

At least, Gina hoped they would.

She knew as well as anyone the fire, the smoke, were horrifying. So hard to see, to breathe. But what had happened when Mama went back for her purse?

Gina couldn't bear to think of all that might have gone wrong. She *refused* to think of it.

In the end, it had taken the fire department only thirty minutes to get the blaze under control. Those who survived were raced by ambulances to the Los Angeles Infirmary, located nearby. Those that didn't were lowered from the factory's top floors by block and tackle, placed in pine boxes and brought to a makeshift morgue set up near the waterfront.

Gina hadn't found her mother at either place.

Oh, the relief.

The worry.

Where was she?

Every name on Julia's list had been accounted for. Except Louisa Briganti's. It'd been a stroke of luck the young bookkeeper thought to rescue her clipboard from the fire, along with the company's ledger, to keep important financial records from being destroyed. It was a big help, Julia's list. Because of it, the police made two more.

One for the living. One for the dead.

Louisa Briganti wasn't on either one.

But somewhere, she waited for Gina to come. Gina clung to the hope that Mama was looking for her, too, at this very moment.

Safe. Somewhere. Waiting. Looking.

Deep in her heart, Gina believed she was alive. Perhaps it was the bond they shared, a daughter with her mother, that made her believe, some mystical sense of *feeling* that continued to give her hope.

And if Gina didn't believe, she'd go crazy. How would she live without Mama? Alone?

Now, hours later, they'd come full circle. Back to the factory. Though it was well past midnight, Gina had insisted they go back. She had foolishly hoped Mama would be there after all, sitting on the curb, wrapped in her thin coat, waiting for Gina to come for her.

But Mama wasn't there.

The acrid scent of smoke still lingered in the air. Gina barely noticed. She stared up at the building, once a fire-breathing monster, now shackled and tamed. Black soot stained the brick on the upper levels. Lamps had been brought in by the fire department, and their dim light shone eerily through the vacant openings which once held the glass from the windows, their sashes gone, a gruesome reminder of the horrors of the afternoon. Outside, a scattering of policemen guarded the building; inside, firemen watched the banked flames so they wouldn't erupt again.

The crowds were gone. The streets were silent. And the Premier Shirtwaist factory would never be the same again.

"Gina. It's three in the morning," Creed said quietly. "I'll take you home."

She dragged her thoughts to the man beside her. What would she have done without him? He'd been tireless in their attempts to track down her mother, as determined as Gina, though he had never seen Louisa Briganti before in his life.

At Gina's insistence, his friend, Graham Dooling, had already left for home. She'd given him the name of her apartment and the street where she lived, in case he heard news before she did. He promised to contact her immediately if he did.

Creed Sherman and Graham Dooling. Both strong, honest Americans. They'd done what they could for her and her mother.

"There is nothing there for me now," she said.

"Could be she's found her way and is waiting for you."

It was something Gina hadn't thought of. Mama already being home. She wouldn't have gone there without Gina and yet...

It wasn't impossible. Mama hated doctors, hospitals. If she was found hurt, she may have been stubborn and refused the ambulance. She may have demanded to go directly home instead, preferring Gina's care over anyone else's.

The thought reinforced her hope. Perhaps it was what Creed Sherman intended. To keep feeling the hope.

She peered up at him. The firemen's lamps didn't reach this far, and the dark night shrouded his features. But she could feel him watching her. Not once had he strayed from her side since she saw him from Leon's elevator. He helped her think when her brain was thick from worry, her heart heavy from fear.

She felt safe with him, and so she wouldn't tell him he couldn't take her home. She didn't want to walk by herself in the dark anyway. Besides, she had nowhere else to go, and fatigue had settled deep into her bones.

She shivered in the chilly California air and pulled the wool blanket someone from the infirmary had given her closer about her shoulders. "It is a long walk."

"Walk?" She sensed his frown. "You mean you don't have a rig parked somewhere?"

"No."

Gina thought of Mama's shoe and how pebbles often found their way inside the worn-out sole. Only this morning, no, *yesterday* morning, Gina had fussed with her about it, and now she didn't know where Mama was. She swallowed down a hot rise of tears.

"I have a horse," he said. "Just across the street."

She could only nod, barely comprehending the luxury of riding when she had always, *always,* walked. He took her elbow, his grip loose but steady through the blanket. He kept his stride matched with hers as they crossed the brick-paved street, the rhythmic click of their heels against the clay the only sound to break the silence.

They halted next to a sleek palomino tied in front of a saloon, one of many in the business district, its name hidden in the shadows of the night. At their approach, the horse snuffled softly, as if relieved he hadn't been forgotten. Creed patted the pale hide in reassurance and unknotted the reins.

"You know how to ride?" he asked.

She hadn't ridden since she left Sicily, but it'd once been her passion. At least, before Papa died.

"Yes," she said quietly.

"Climb up, then."

He took her blanket, freeing her hands to grasp the saddle horn and mount. She remembered to take her foot out of the stirrup so he could use it next. He swung up easily; leather creaked as they both settled in. The palomino shifted and took their weight.

"Wrap this in front of you," Creed said, draping the blanket against her. "I'll keep you warm from behind." He reached around with one long arm and took the reins. His chest pressed against her back, giving her a hint of just how warm she would be. "How far do you live?"

Iron hooves clomped away from the saloon, and a barrage of sensations assailed her, delaying her response. The motion of a powerful horse under her when it'd been so long; the muscular thighs of a man she didn't know, who kept her warm with his arms and chest, and maybe she should be afraid of him but she wasn't. The chill in the air nipping her nose; the odd sensation of being alone, just the two of them, in the middle of the night...

But Gina chastised herself. She couldn't let herself be distracted by Creed Sherman. He was only being kind and wouldn't be here if not for her mother. After he took Gina home, he would know she no longer needed his help. His kindness would be complete. She would never see him again.

"A little more than a mile," she said. "Turn left, please."

The palomino changed direction, heading away from the business district. "You mean you walk over a mile to the factory every day? And back again?"

His low voice sounded husky in her ear. Almost intimate. But then, there was no need for him to talk in a loud voice. Not with him sitting this close, his chin sometimes brushing her hair.

"It is not so far," she lied proudly.

"Except when it rains. Or the wind blows cold. How about when you're dog-tired from working all day?"

Gina said nothing. What could she say? He had already guessed the truth.

He fell silent. She got the impression he didn't approve of her and Mama walking every day, but what business was it of his? He had a beautiful, strong horse. He wouldn't know what it was like not to have one.

The blocks passed swiftly. With them, her hope increased that she would find her mother at home. When they approached her street, she instructed Creed to turn, and as the black shape of their tenement apartment building loomed, her gaze shot to the row of third-floor windows.

All of them were dark.

Her hope crashed.

Mama would have left a light on.

The despair, the worry, hurtled back again, and Gina struggled to breathe from the onslaught. Creed dismounted first, then took her blanket and tossed it over his shoulder before assisting her down. With both feet on the ground again, she struggled hard for composure.

"She is not there," Gina said.

He dragged his gaze over the apartments. A moment passed. "No way to know for sure until you go inside."

Impatience cut through her. Why didn't he understand what Gina knew, deep in her heart? Mama wasn't here, but she was somewhere, all alone, and Los Angeles was a very big city, and Gina didn't know how to find her. Not anymore.

But she bit back the words. He spoke with a man's logic, not a daughter's worry. He was only being kind, encouraging her, and he had done far more than anyone would have expected.

"Thank you for bringing me home," she said. "Thank you for—for everything."

"I'm going in with you," he said.

"What? Into the apartments?" This she had not expected.

"To make sure you get in all right. Here's your blanket."

She took it. "There is no need for you to go in. I can find my way."

"The place is dark, and it's late. Not safe for a woman alone."

"I have done it many times."

Well, not so many without Mama, maybe, but he didn't need to know that.

"This is one time you're not." He tied the palomino to a hitching post. As if he didn't think they'd be safe either, he took his saddlebags and hooked them over an arm. With the other, he made a sweeping gesture toward the apartment's front door. "Lead the way, Gina."

She couldn't win over his bullheadedness, and she was too tired to keep trying. A wide sidewalk separated the dirt street from the steps. From the top one, she pushed the door open and went inside.

A long, narrow hall divided the front apartments from the rear ones. Mrs. Sortino, the landlady, kept only a single light burning near the wooden staircase which ran through the center of the building, more for her benefit than any of her boarders since her rooms were on this level. Gina took hold of the handrail as she always did—the higher they climbed, the darker the staircase would get.

It wasn't long before she heard Creed swear behind her.

"Hold up," he ordered. She recognized the sound of a match striking flint. Instantly, pale golden light fanned out around them. "Is it always this dark?"

She understood the annoyance in his tone. Many times,

she felt the annoyance, too. "Mrs. Sortino says it is expensive to have a light burn on all five floors."

"She does, does she?"

"So we must be careful at night. I know many who have fallen."

He muttered something unintelligible, but Gina ignored him and kept climbing. At the third floor, she veered into the hallway lining the front of her apartment.

But at the door, she halted. Only now did she remember she had left her purse at the factory. Everything in it would be gone. Burned. She didn't have a key.

Creed's glance bounced from her to the knob and back up again.

"Can't get in?" he asked.

She jiggled the knob.

"No." She drew in a miserable breath.

Creed extinguished the match, plunging them into darkness, then lit another, giving them light again. "Here. Hold this."

He handed her the matchstick, and she held it carefully between two fingers while he rummaged in his hip pocket. He removed a long, thin piece of metal, something like a nail, and inserted it into the keyhole. A few flicks of his wrist, and like magic, the door opened.

But Gina didn't go inside.

Alarm held her frozen, her heart pounding. This skill of his—he was a thief, and he intended to rob her of what little she had, maybe even kill her, because thieves *knew* how to break into people's homes. She had trusted him like a fool, and oh, holy Madonna, what *else* could go wrong tonight?

He went still, as if he could read the emotions tumbling through her like words on paper.

"Gina." He shook his head slowly. "I learned to pick locks a long time ago. In the army. It was part of my job to—it's not like you're thinking. You can trust me, I swear it. I'm not going to hurt you or steal anything." His mouth went hard. "Do you really think I would?"

Her throat worked. "Maybe. I do not know."

"I'm not."

From somewhere in the shadows, something skittered past them, and she whirled with a cry of fright. The match light shone on a pair of glittering eyes staring up at them.

Mrs. Sortino's cat, on the prowl again. Recognition left her wobbly, giddy, precariously on the verge of tears.

Creed opened the door wider. "Let's go in, Gina. We're going to wake your neighbors if we don't."

She collected her flailing composure. "You cannot."

"I can't what? Go in with you?"

The low-voiced challenge lingered in the air between them. Clearly, he thought nothing of the impropriety. Again, that odd sense of intimacy curled through her from being with him, carrying with it a growing awareness of this American, his power, his mystery, but mostly how vulnerable he made her feel.

"You are—are very nice to bring me up to my apartment, but now I am here, and you must leave," she said.

A muscle moved in his cheek. He returned the pick to his pocket. "Not yet."

She bit her lip at his persistence. The walls were paper-thin; her neighbors might come out any minute and find her here, standing in the hall at a scandalous hour, arguing with this handsome stranger.

If he had any intentions of hurting her, he would have done so by now, she knew. Yet she dreaded the prospect of finding the apartment cold and empty, and did she really want to be alone anyway? "Then you cannot stay with me for more than a few minutes."

He grunted. She went in. He followed, dropped his saddlebags to the floor and locked the door. Before his match went out, he lit a third and bent over Mama's kerosene lamp. Soon, light spilled bright around them.

Immediately, Gina's gaze searched the tiny front room, the bedroom and the bed still made from yesterday morning, the kitchen where coffee cups sat on the table, ready for filling.

Without taking a step away from the door, Gina accepted the truth, and her heart broke from it.

Hot tears burned her eyes. "She does not come here after the fire."

Creed dragged his glance to her.

"No," he said.

A sob welled into her throat. It was the last of her hope, another frightening disappointment on a night full of them. The wool blanket slipped from her grasp; her knees buckled from the faint that threatened to pull her under.

In an instant, Creed was beside her. He hooked his arm around her waist and half carried her into the nearest chair, a plain wooden one at the kitchen table.

"You're exhausted." He released her and headed for the cupboard. "You have anything strong to drink?"

He found a bottle of wine, a gift from Sebastian on her last birthday. Without waiting for her response, he uncorked it, sloshed some into one of the coffee cups and held the porcelain to her lips with a firm order to swallow.

She did, until every drop was gone. The warmth flowing down her throat and into her belly melted her weariness, gave her some strength. She wished she would've fainted after all to escape the terrible worry about Mama.

"Have some more." He refilled her cup and took the liberty of pouring himself one, too. He pulled out the remaining chair and sat across from her, then drained his wine in a few good gulps. He set the empty cup down. Silent, assessing, he watched her.

She drank the second round more slowly, aware of how the wine seeped into her blood, soothing her, leaving her numb. She dared to meet the intensity of his perusal, let herself not think about her mother for a little while but become intrigued by the deep amber color of his eyes, so different than the men of her country.

Besides Sebastian, no man had sat at her table before. Creed filled the tiny kitchen with a bewildering kind of aura no one at Premier possessed, not even the most respected of highly paid cutters, like Sebastian. Or her boss, Mr. Silverstein. Something in Creed's life had given him a hard edge. She suspected it made him fearless, too. And why should she find that fascinating?

"You save my life in the factory," she said quietly.

He nodded once, the vaguest of gestures. She might have missed it if she hadn't been concentrating on him so much.

"You carry me down the stairs?" She thought of the explosion, the fury of it, and shuddered.

"Couldn't leave you on them, could I?"

"All eight floors." Oh, she would have been heavy.

"Every one."

Her glance touched on the breadth of his shoulders, the bulge of his arms inside the sleeves of his shirt. She wouldn't be here if he hadn't been so strong. "Thank you."

He seemed unaffected by her gratitude or what he had done, the dangers of going with her to the top of the factory when the fire was so hot, so wild. Perhaps he had done this before? Saved innocent people when they didn't know how to save themselves?

He leaned forward. "What happened up there, Gina? Do you know?"

She blinked. Her thoughts on him jolted to a stop.

"How does the fire start?" she asked.

"Yes. All the victims—if the owner of the factory is at fault in any way, then he needs to be held accountable."

Her blood turned cold. She set the cup on the table with a thunk.

"No," she managed. "Not Mr. Silverstein."

"Your boss?"

"Yes." For all his faults, he would never have done anything so horrible.

"What then?" Creed's voice sounded rough, determined. "Faulty sewing machines? Cutting equipment? Wiring?"

"No."

She had not had time to think of it. She had been too frantic, too desperate to find her mother and save them both from the fire.

But now, the truth came. Vivid and ugly.

With it, the first stirrings of rage.

"Gina. Tell me what you know."

The rage bubbled inside her until it welled in her throat. Until she could barely breathe.

"The fire, it is set," she ground out. "On purpose."

He breathed a stunned oath.

"I see it happen. They smoke, even when they know they must not."

"Who was? You know their names?"

Her lip curled. Never would she forget.

"Yes. I know the names. Nikolai and Alex Sokolov.

They are angry at Mr. Silverstein. And so they start the fire in a bin of scraps."

Creed stared. "You're sure about this?"

Irrational tears stung the back of her eyes. "You think I will lie?"

"No." A muscle in his jaw moved. "No, but you can't be wrong, Gina."

She swiped at a stubborn tear. "I am not wrong."

"What can you tell me about them?"

"They are brothers. They work on the eighth floor. I am on the ninth, and so I do not know them as well as Sebastian would."

And now, because of what they had done, so many had died, so many were hurt. Mama was gone, and Gina could not find her, and oh, she *hated* them for what they had done.

Frustration and grief and worry all rolled into one choking sob, and she covered her face with her hands. She had to stay strong, because if she wasn't, she wouldn't be able to think on how to find her mother. Or how to go on if she didn't.

Gathering her will, she straightened from the table and stood. "You must go now."

An eye narrowed. "I think I'll stay."

"You cannot."

"I'm not leaving you alone."

"Mrs. Sortino will evict me. She does not approve of men staying with unmarried women."

"You going to tell her? I'm not." Creed rose, too. "You need someone with you. Under the circumstances."

His stubbornness, his hardheaded *kindness,* was her undoing, and the tears rushed back to stream freely down her cheeks.

The great, ravaging grief she hadn't allowed herself to feel.

Until now.

Creed reached a hand toward her. "Gina."

She didn't want him to see. To know how much she hurt. Always, she took pride in being strong, and now, she wasn't.

She turned from him, went to her bedroom and shut the door.

Chapter Seven

Creed swore at the closed door.

He had a need to barge through it to give her some comfort. Hell of an ordeal she was going through. Daughters tended to be close to their mothers. Real hard for Gina to be apart from hers, not knowing if she was dead or alive.

He raked a hand through his hair and grimaced. Most likely his own mother felt that way often enough over the years. She would've worried plenty—about where he was, who he was with, and yeah, if he was dead or alive.

He shifted under an onslaught of guilt. Now, she was gone. Forever. He'd never get the chance to tell her about the soldier he'd been and what he'd done for his country. How he'd learned to survive when the odds were against him. How he'd been victorious over the enemy—or managed to escape one by the skin of his sorry hide. Mostly, the thrill of it all, driven by a patriotism Ma would've been proud of.

She'd never know. Maybe that was why it'd become important to him to help Gina find her mother. Until they had proof Louisa Briganti was dead, Creed was going to go on believing she was alive.

It was understandable that Gina was scared. She didn't know him well enough to take the comfort he was willing to give. She just needed to have time and privacy to work through the grief on her own.

He slid a somber gaze around the apartment. The place was small. Barely enough space for one person to live, let alone two, though tenements were notorious for squeezing entire families into flats this size. The front room contained a single window, a small table and a pair of worn chairs. Behind it, the kitchen with a fireplace and coal-burning stove; off that, the only bedroom which, he presumed, Gina shared with her mother.

The apartment was clean, tidy, but sparsely furnished. Easy to tell the women had little money to spend on luxuries, and now with the factory burned, Gina would have no job. How would she pay the overpriced rent the landlady was sure to charge?

He released a troubled sigh, picked up the wool blanket Gina had dropped by the door and spread it over the threadbare carpet. Her world had been knocked upside down, for sure. She was going to need some help to get it right again.

He blew out the lamp and lowered himself onto the blanket. Using his saddlebags as a pillow, he laced his fingers behind his head and stared up at the dark ceiling.

His mind turned from her into a jumble of thoughts about Pa and Mary Catherine. Markie. The disturbing intelligence report he received about President McKinley.

The wire to the War Department, most of all.

Gina's situation had kept him from acting on it, but he'd send the message first chance he got. He was leaving America, no question about it. He just had a few matters to attend to before he did.

Might be Graham could help him dig up some information about the Sokolovs. Sebastian would, for sure, considering he worked with the men.

If the Sokolovs were guilty, they'd have to pay the price. Creed intended to see that they did. In full. He'd delay his plans to leave the continent if that's what it took to avenge the scores of innocent factory workers the brothers' actions had hurt.

But especially, he'd stay to avenge the beautiful Italian woman weeping softly in her room.

It'd been a short night. Seemed Creed had no sooner closed his eyes before sunshine poked through the thin curtains to wake him again.

At least he couldn't hear any more crying from Gina's room. Sometime before dawn, she must've fallen asleep from pure exhaustion. He frowned at the thought, but he knew the rest would help her feel better. A new day tended to improve one's outlook on life.

She'd need to eat, too. Same as he did. Neither of them had had supper last night, and the growl in Creed's belly told him breakfast was a need he couldn't ignore.

He rose, found some water in a pitcher, soap in his saddlebags, and gave himself a good wash. After donning a set of clean clothes, he headed straight to the kitchen to see what he could find to eat.

Which wasn't much.

A little coffee, a half loaf of bread, a few eggs. One large potato. But his interest caught on a pair of sausage links, wrapped in paper.

He set to work cooking it all up without feeling the least bit contrite for taking the liberty. It was plain to see Gina and her mother ate like birds. Maybe that was the only way they could afford to eat, but Creed intended to change that with a trip to the grocer to give their shelves a good restocking. He'd make sure to heap Gina's plate this morning, too, and see that she ate every bite.

He stood at the stove and turned the sausages frying in the skillet. Just as he was about to add the chopped potato, her bedroom door opened, and she stepped out.

She was wearing a different dress, navy blue with little pale flowers all over it. Nicer than the one she wore to work. No shoes, though, and her long, sable hair was undone. The way it gleamed and hung thick on her shoulders told him she'd just brushed it.

"You stay, I see," she said.

His gaze dragged from her hair. Her eyes were puffy, rimmed in red. From her glower, she felt less than friendly this morning.

"I said I would," he said carefully.

"You should not be here. All the apartments will talk about the man Gina Briganti kept last night."

"Let 'em."

She made a sound of exasperation, swept past him with a huff and soaked a washcloth from the water left in the pitcher. Barely an arm's length separated the stove from the table, and she bumped into him on the way back. Without bothering to excuse herself, she pulled out a chair at the table and dropped into it.

"That is easy for you to say. You do not know Mrs. Sortino." She propped her bare feet on the opposite chair, tilted her head back and laid the washcloth over her eyes with a weary moan.

Her moan stirred his sympathy. "Don't think I care to, either."

"Or my neighbors," Gina went on, as if he hadn't spoken. "If one of them see you, they are very quick to report me."

"Surrounded by busybodies, are you?"

She clucked her tongue. "They want my apartment."

His glance swept their cramped quarters. "Your apartment?"

"The window."

Creed struggled to follow her logic. "Not all of them have one?"

"No." She sighed, as if he were being obtuse. "Only the front do. The rear do not. Mama and I are fortunate to get this one."

He couldn't imagine being confined in a place like this without being able to see the outdoors. He'd always preferred wide open spaces and plenty of fresh air. Which came from being raised on a ranch, he supposed. One of the few things he and Pa ever agreed on when it came to the home place—the benefits of living there.

Her explanation made it easier to comprehend her concern about his staying with her. Vindictive neighbors would make anyone's life uncomfortable. Didn't change things, though. He had no intention of leaving until he was sure she was strong enough to be on her own.

He placed each sausage on a plate and made room in the skillet for the eggs. "I'm not going to apologize for being here."

"She will raise my rent."

"Greedy, too, is she?"

Gina groaned. "Very."

He knew ways to keep greedy people happy and cooperative, thanks to the army, and he dismissed the Sortino woman from his mind. He divided the potatoes between the plates, slid an egg onto each and brought both to the table.

"Let's eat," he said.

He added silverware, cups steaming with coffee, and

still she didn't move. He reached out and plucked the wash-cloth off her face.

"Gina."

Her eyes opened. "What?"

She looked so innocently annoyed, he had to work hard to hide his amusement.

"Were you napping under there?" he asked.

She frowned. "I am not awake all the way yet."

"Put the fork in your hand," he said.

"I want coffee." She brought her feet down to the floor and sat straighter in the chair. He slid the cup closer, and she went for it.

Silence fell between them. Her expression turned brooding, and she sipped the hot brew slowly as she stared out the sunny window, slight furrows between her dark brows. Creed let her do the thinking she needed to do.

He took advantage of it to watch her, his attention held by the exotic shape of her face in the morning light. The slight hook on the bridge of her nose, the delicate jut to her chin, the slender column of her neck, half hidden by the silken mass of sable hair hanging loose against her shoulders and back.

Hair meant to slide long and free through a man's fingers.

The blood flickered in his veins. She fascinated him in ways he didn't bother to comprehend, a woman hauntingly beautiful, passionate in love, in anguish. Proud and vibrant.

A woman he wasn't likely to forget for a good long while after he left American shores.

Finally, she set the cup down and picked up her fork.

"I had a *visione* in my sleep," she said.

She appeared preoccupied. He suspected she was still thinking about it.

"Want to tell me what it was?" he asked.

She fiddled with her fork, which, he noted, had yet to scoop up any breakfast.

"My *visione* shows Mama in a dark place, far away. I cannot reach her, but I try many times. She talks to me, very clear. She is afraid, not for herself, but for me. When I wake up, I feel the evil that makes her afraid. But I also feel she is alive."

Creed had never put much stock in the supernatural. As a soldier, he'd learned to trust the solid facts of reality along with skill and gut instinct. Anything less could result in death, his own or someone else's. Her vision didn't make much sense, anyway, since her mother was more of a victim of the arson than Gina, who had escaped it.

"I go to Mass this morning," she said suddenly.

He shifted thoughts with her. His glance drifted over her dress. Her best, he suspected. The reason she wore it.

"To pray to the Madonna," she added.

He nodded respectfully. Tried to remember the last time he stepped into a church.

"I ask her to help me find my mother." She finally speared a small piece of the sausage and slipped it neatly into her mouth. "I ask her how to find the Sokolov brothers, too."

The evil in her vision.

"Leave that to the police, Gina," he said sharply.

"I do not trust the police."

"They're a hell of a lot more qualified to track down men capable of arson than you are."

"I do not have the money to pay the police to do what I need them to do."

His mind worked to fathom her thinking. "You don't have to pay them to do anything. It's their *job* to protect citizens."

"I cannot trust them."

"If a crime has been committed, they have the ability to solve it. You don't."

"But they do nothing because I am only a poor immigrant from Sicily. Then I do not find Mama, eh? The Sokolovs go unpunished. I trust only myself to do these things."

He thought of all the countries he'd been to in the past six years. Fragile governments plagued by treason, assassinations, revolt. Governments desperate for reform who needed the United States military to help them because they couldn't depend on their own. They hired mercenaries—men like himself—for the tactics, the skills, they'd learned to infiltrate secret societies hell-bent on overthrowing them one way or another.

Oppressors of the innocent. Betrayers of the people. Unfortunately, they came in all levels of government, a fact of life from the first day of history.

Still, he chafed at her jaded outlook. "You think our police are corrupt?"

She hesitated. "Maybe not all. But some."

"In this country, it's an honorable thing to serve the citizens."

Her dark eyebrow arched. "What? You do not know about corrupt lawyers? Politicians?"

"I know about them."

"They want only power and riches. They do not care about honor. They care only about the money they can make."

"A few," he conceded.

"In my country, Sicily, it is everywhere." She scooped potatoes onto her fork and lifted them to her mouth.

"The Mafioso," he said.

"Yes." Her expression melded into sad bitterness. "They hurt many with their greed."

He regarded her. "Have they hurt you, Gina?"

"Yes."

"How?"

She took a breath, let it out again. "My father is once a shoemaker. Very talented. He repairs the shoes, but mostly he loves to make them. The quality of the leather, his workmanship, the styles, he makes them magnificent."

Creed waited, drawn in by the story she was ready to tell.

"People come from many miles to buy his shoes. Even the Mafioso. They see Papa's business grow, and they want some of his money, too."

"Yes," he murmured. They would.

"But Papa does not want to give them what he works hard to earn. He refuses to pay them. Then one day, he receives a letter." She swallowed, the fear in her still real. "From the Black Hand."

Creed knew about them, too. The secret group that demanded money by sending notes, unsigned but imprinted with an inked handprint of the sender. Those that didn't comply risked harassment and murder, not only to themselves but to loved ones.

"We cannot ask the police to help. They are too afraid, or maybe they are part of the Mafioso. The corruption, the bribery, it is everywhere. Even as high up as Premier Giolitti in Italy."

No wonder she mistrusted the police. Hell of a shame it was, too, when most of them in America were as honest as the day they were born.

"Papa does everything he can to protect Mama and me, but he cannot protect himself. The Mafioso—they hurt him so he cannot make shoes ever again. He loses his business. Soon, he gets sick. Four years ago, he dies."

"I'm sorry," Creed said and meant it.

She toyed with the last of the potatoes left on her plate.

"Mama and I are very sad, very unhappy. We love Sicily, but we must leave. We do not want to be afraid anymore. So we use the money we have left to come to America. For Papa, we want to succeed here."

Again, Creed's glance took in the tiny apartment, the over-worn furnishings. Working six days a week at the shirtwaist factory hadn't done much for her success that he could see.

She fell silent, but her throat moved, as if she fought a welling of despair. "And now maybe I fail."

The despair cut through him. "At what?"

Her dark eyes filled with moisture. "If I do not find Mama, if my *visione* is a—how you say?—a mistake, I cannot afford to live without her. I am very alone. I become very poor. I cannot pay my rent, and then where do I go? I lose everything." She swiped miserably at a recalcitrant tear. "I lose my dream, too."

His fist clenched to keep from taking her into his arms and soothing all that needed soothing in her. "What dream?"

"To own a dressmaker shop." She sniffled. "For three years, Mama and I save for it."

An ambitious undertaking, for sure, even for one with considerably more wealth. "You like to make dresses, then."

"Very much."

"Want to tell me about that, too?"

She hesitated, as if she debated whether she should. Then, she nodded.

"It is better that I show you." She stood and entered her bedroom. In moments, she returned with a sheaf of papers. He swept aside their plates to make room on the table. "These are my designs."

One after another, she pulled sketches from the pile. With each one, her worries seemed to fade, and she became more animated. Her slender finger pointed at sleeves, necklines, billowing skirts. Her descriptions were precise, her voice breathless, her vision of fabrics vivid. Real.

· And Creed was impressed. He'd never claim to be an expert on women's gowns, but Gina's designs were as good, if not better, than those he'd seen in Collette's shop only yesterday.

"Do you design the shirtwaists, too?" he asked. "Seems to me it'd be a place for you to start."

Her black eyes rolled. "There is nothing to the blouse. Even Mr. Silverstein does not design them. He adds a tuck here or a ribbon there, but he only copies the ones very popular in New York." She gathered the sketches, carefully layering them into a neat pile. "Then he brags to the salesmen how special his shirtwaists are."

Creed rubbed his chin. "Once they're sold, your factory makes them and ships them out to department stores."

"Yes," she said. "Thousands every season. The shirtwaists, I mean."

"Silverstein is a rich man, then?"

She sniffed. "He keeps most of the money for himself because he does not pay his seamstresses a decent wage." She glanced at the clock and gasped. "Oh, the time! Mass starts soon, and I am not ready!"

Creed stood. "I'll do the dishes. You finish getting dressed."

She snatched the sheaf of sketches and hurried to her bedroom.

He watched her go. He'd been fascinated by the glimpse she'd given him into her life and troubled by the fears that haunted her. She'd had a tough time of it, for sure. And now, with her mother unaccounted for...

He collected the plates and wondered how long it would be before she'd be happy again.

Chapter Eight

Gina finished pinning her hair into a topknot and used Mama's hand mirror for a quick inspection of the results, turning her head back and forth to make sure she didn't miss any strands. She hadn't, but her scrutiny lingered in the glass.

Her eyes weren't as red anymore. And there was a little color to her cheeks. She had Creed to thank for that, and the breakfast he'd made her eat. She felt stronger with a hot meal in her stomach. Less miserable. Better able to face the day and learn what she could about her mother.

She set the mirror aside. Still, it wasn't like her to talk so much about her past. Or her future. Never had she told the story about Papa to anyone, not even Sebastian. Except for her mother, she hadn't shared her dream or showed her sketches to anyone, either.

With Creed, it'd been easy. He'd been interested, concerned…incredibly strong when she felt weak and lost.

Her thoughts drifted backward to how his tawny eyes had been bold, intense, never leaving her face. When he looked at her like that, making her feel like she wasn't at all alone, well, she couldn't stop herself from talking so much.

But she couldn't spend any more time thinking about him, she reminded herself firmly. She must rush to church, and she put on her hat with more speed than style, then grabbed her coat from its hook.

She hurried into the kitchen. Creed had just finished drying the last of the dishes, and his shirtsleeves were rolled up to his elbows. Thick veins corded his forearms, which were darkened by the sun and roughened by a sprinkling of burnished gold hairs. Again, she thought of his power, how he overwhelmed her tiny apartment. A man of the world, this one. Unlike any she had known before.

He glanced up at her approach. His gaze drifted over her, slow and appraising, from the hair piled onto her head to the toe of her shoes. And back up again. For the life of her, she couldn't move. She didn't think of her need to get to Mass on time; instead, she wondered what rolled through his mind while he looked at her like this.

And how it would feel to be touched by him.

"Beautiful," he murmured.

She curled her fingers to keep from fussing with her pins again. She didn't know if he spoke of the way she twisted her hair or the dress she wore or something else. "Thank you. This dress, it is not new, and the hat is not, either, but—"

"Doesn't matter. You still look beautiful."

He left her flustered, unable to think of another thing to say. He strode toward her, lithe and masculine, and she was sure he intended to touch her, after all.

He merely took her coat and held it open. "Is your church far?"

She tried not to feel disappointed he didn't. "About six blocks or so."

She slipped her arms into the sleeves and turned back toward him, busying herself with the buttons.

"It'll be faster to take my horse."

Gina bit her lip at the prospect of sitting so close to him again. "Maybe."

He gathered his saddlebags and met her at the door. She'd remembered to bring the extra key hidden in her drawer and made sure it was safe in her coat pocket. Now, there'd be no need for him to pick her lock like a common thief.

Not that he'd be coming home with her again.

She quickly negated the thought that he would. He had a life of his own. She didn't need him in hers anymore, now that the worst of the fire was over. She must go on without him, and she intended to tell him as much. After they arrived at the church, anyway, since he made it clear he would take her there.

They left the apartment, and with Creed right behind her, she descended the steep, narrow stairs with as much haste as she dared. A baby squalled somewhere below them, and the sound grew louder the closer they approached the ground level; the musty air gave way to the smells of bacon frying and coffee boiling.

Once on the main level, eager to make her escape, Gina headed toward the front door. But the one to the apartment closest to that, the one she dreaded most, suddenly burst open.

Gina would swear on her father's grave that Mrs. Sortino could see right through a wood slab.

"Miss Briganti!"

Her heart dropped to her toes.

"I want to talk to you, missy."

She halted. Turned. Felt Creed move closer to her side.

"Good morning, Mrs. Sortino," she said.

The door opened wider, and the woman lumbered out. Gina heard she had once been married to a mouse of an

Italian. She took his name and his money and ran the tenement like a dictator, but no one ever knew what happened to the poor man. She was as big as a bear, gruff as one, too, and Gina admitted to being a little afraid of her.

"Heard about the fire," Mrs. Sortino said. Always, she smelled sour from stale garlic and yesterday's sweat. She wore her authority over her tenants like a thorny crown. "You made it out, I see."

"Yes."

Beneath bushy eyebrows flecked with gray, her sharp eyes shot to Creed, back to Gina. "Where's your mother?"

Gina's heart squeezed. "She—she is still missing."

"That so? Sorry to hear it."

Gina didn't know if the words of sympathy were genuine. She sounded as gruff as ever saying them. "It is terrible—not knowing."

"Now the factory's going to be closed a spell, ain't it?" Again, she gave Creed one of her shrewd, grizzly bear looks.

"Yes, but I do not know for how long. I am sorry, Mrs. Sortino. Mass starts in only a few minutes. We are in a hurry."

"You know the rent'll be due the first of the month, same as always. If you won't be able to meet your obligation without your mother to help you, I'll need to know it right now."

Gina refused to think of where she would go if she had no money for rent. "I understand."

"Another thing."

She braced herself…

"There will be no men spending the night if you ain't married. And I know you're not. It's grounds for your eviction if it happens again."

"Eviction? Now, now, Mrs. Sortino." Creed spoke in a lazy drawl Gina had not heard from him before. He draped his arm casually over her shoulders, mortifying her with his recklessness. "I was just spending a little time with my favorite girl, that's all."

"Rules is rules, and she knows it."

"Hell of a day she had yesterday."

"It don't matter."

As big as Mrs. Sortino was, Creed was bigger. The old bear had to look up at him to defy him. Gina wished she could disappear into a crack in the floor.

Creed sighed. "You're right. You have to forgive me." Magically, a folded bill appeared between two lean fingers. "Let's just forget this talk about eviction, shall we? In case I decide I want to stay with her again."

Mrs. Sortino snatched the bill into her grimy paw. "There could be worse things, I reckon. Just don't be tellin' all the other tenants. I ain't runnin' a brothel around here."

A brothel! Gina's eyes widened. But before she could manage to defend herself, Creed took her elbow and hustled her toward the door.

Before going through it, he turned back again.

"In case you decide to come looking for more of where that came from, you can be damn sure the city building inspector isn't going to like hearing how you refuse to put lighting in the stairwells. Isn't safe for the tenants, you know." His fingers lifted in a cocky salute. "Good day, Mrs. Sortino."

Leaving the woman sputtering after him, he whisked Gina outside into the bright, crisp morning air.

Gina frowned up at him in disapproval. "You should not pay her so much money. She does not deserve it."

"I've learned all lowlifes think the same," he said roughly.

"And now she thinks the worst of me."

"As long as she gets her money on the first of the month, she'll leave you alone."

In that, perhaps, the bribe would succeed, and some of Gina's disapproval faded. "Well, you are very brave with her. I cannot be so bold." He guided her toward his horse, still tethered at the curb. "But do not think you can stay with me again tonight. You cannot."

He glanced over at her. A corner of his mouth lifted. "What if I like the idea of being a kept man by you?"

Did he tease her with the words she'd used to chastise him just this morning? Or did he mean his own? Before she could decide, his attention shifted from her and caught on something else.

Graham Dooling waited in a shiny runabout carriage parked next to the palomino. Dressed in a dark suit and freshly-starched white shirt, he looked too important to be on this dusty street with its crowded tenements. A sharp mingling of hope and fear burst inside her that he brought news about Mama.

"'Morning, Graham," Creed said.

"Good morning, sir. I took a chance you might have accompanied Miss Briganti home last night. When I saw your horse, I figured you were still here."

"I'm taking her to church."

"I see." His compassionate gaze swung to Gina. "I've been most concerned about you. Any word about your mother?"

Her hopes fell. Clearly, he had none, either.

"No," she said quietly.

"My sympathies, ma'am."

"We'll make another trip to the infirmary and the police station in case she's been found," Creed said, untying the reins. "After church. We're late as it is."

The man took the hint. "Perhaps I can drive Miss Briganti in the buggy, sir. It'd be more comfortable for her, certainly."

Creed cast Gina an inquiring glance, and she nodded a bit uncertainly. When had she ridden in a carriage as nice as this?

"We go to St. Philomena Church, six blocks away," she said.

"We'll be there shortly. Do you mind if we talk along the way, Mr. Sherman?"

Creed and Gina exchanged a glance. Whatever the man needed to discuss must be important for him to seek Creed out. In their short acquaintance, she discovered Graham Dooling was not a frivolous man. He took everything he did with utmost seriousness and efficiency.

And his reason for being here must mean trouble.

Creed rode his horse on the driver's side of the runabout. "I'm listening, Graham."

"I'm sure you're aware, sir, that anarchism is sweeping the world. We live in an industrial age, and America is at the forefront. Our cities are changing like never before. Unfortunately, the anarchists are resisting the trend, and their numbers are increasing at an alarming rate. A secret group of them is active right here in Los Angeles."

"That is what the Sokolovs are," Gina said.

Creed and Graham swiveled toward her.

"What?" they demanded in unison.

"I remember. It is what Sebastian said. Anarchists."

"Who are the Sokolovs?" Graham asked.

"Two brothers," Creed said.

"Nikolai and Alex," Gina added.

"She saw them set the fire last night at the factory," Creed finished.

"What?" Graham's head whipped back and forth between them.

"It is true," she said, somber.

Creed doubted Graham swore often, but he did so now, with relish.

"The name is Russian?" Graham said, once he'd recovered enough to think the news through.

"Yes," she said. "Nikolai is very big, very arrogant. His brother, younger, not so big."

"How does Sebastian know they're anarchists?" Creed asked.

"They ask him to come to one of their meetings."

"When?"

"They want him last night. Before the fire, at least."

Suspicion coiled through him. "Is he one of them?"

"No." She appeared offended that Creed would ask. "Sebastian tells me he does not want to go."

The carriage pulled up in front of the church, and their conversation had to end. Her dark-eyed gaze took in the congestion of horses and buggies on the street, and her expression turned sad.

"Many of the seamstresses who work at Premier belong to St. Philomena," she said in a hushed voice. "Their families come to pray for them. For all of us." Both Creed and Graham moved to help her down, but in her hurry, she was out of the rig before they could. "Thank you, Mr. Dooling, for taking me."

"Of course," he said.

Her glance met Creed's.

"I'll wait," he said before she could tell him goodbye, or thanks, or anything else to send him on his way. She should know by now he wasn't going to leave her.

She nodded once, then pivoted toward the church.

"Gina," he called.

She turned back.

"Say a few for me, too, will you?"

Her expression softened. "The Madonna listens."

His gaze lingered over her until she slipped between the heavy doors and was gone. He'd committed his share of sins over the years and envied the faith that seemed to run deep in her. It was good she had an inside track to heaven. He hoped it would give her peace in the end. She'd need all the prayers she could offer up to get through the worry about her mother.

Creed sighed and delved into his shirt pocket for a rolled cigarette, but the memory of breathing in all that thick smoke in the factory dropped into his brain. Made him want to cough all over again. He grimaced and put the thing away.

He hooked a knee over his saddle horn instead and contemplated the man beside him. From the grim expression on Graham's face, something troubled him, and it went beyond his concern over the rising wave of anarchism.

"So, why are you really here, Graham?"

The Secret Service agent swept a discreet glance around him, as if to assure himself no one would overhear.

"It's in regard to the matter we discussed yesterday," he said. "Outside my sister's shop."

The intelligence the Secret Service had received about President McKinley, that his life might be in danger.

Unease kicked through Creed. "What about it?"

"His itinerary has been finalized. He'll be arriving in two days by train. Washington has notified us just this morning."

Creed stared.

Two days.

"I'm sure you understand, sir, the importance of making it absolutely, *positively,* safe for him to visit."

He knew, all right. In America, a man didn't come any more important than the president. And Creed had been proud to serve one for the past six years.

But, hell, two days.

Only yesterday, Creed had planned to be gone by then. Gone somewhere far away....

"There's more, sir. Washington has ordered the excursion be kept top secret. His wife is an invalid, and her health is of great concern to him. Her doctors felt that a quiet holiday in the California air would be beneficial."

"Almost impossible to keep news like this from reaching the public."

"My fears exactly, sir. The anarchists strongly oppose his authority in our government. They despise all this country stands for. Once they learn he's coming, his life will truly be in danger. As will his wife's."

Creed's grim glance slid down the street, to a row of glass-front offices. Sunlight touched on bold block lettering on one window in particular. He squinted, reading the words....

Western Union.

An easy ride away.

He could be there.

In minutes.

He thought of President McKinley. And patriotism. He thought of Nikolai and Alex, two men whose ideals clashed with everything Creed had ever believed in, stood for or fought about. He thought of the horrible fire in the Premier Shirtwaist Company factory, the pain and destruction and the lives who had been hurt, and the Sokolovs' heartless part in all of it.

But most of all, he thought of Gina.

He wasn't going to send that wire to his friend, Jeb Carson, in the War Department. Not for a good long while yet.

He had a hell of a fight on his hands, right here in America. The first stirrings of excitement, the ardent need for justice, took root inside him. Six years of fighting, learned in the halls at West Point, then perfected behind enemy lines in war-torn lands, had taught him the need for it. The importance. He'd sweated and bled, suffered and feared, for his country.

For freedom.

He was prepared to die for it.

He'd learned to survive because of it.

He could do nothing else but protect the president of the United States and avenge Gina's mother at the same time.

"General William Carson assured me you'd know what to do," Graham said, watching him.

"He did, did he?"

"He said you were one of the best soldiers he's ever known. His son, Jeb, too. Both of you, the *best*."

Creed grunted. Jeb would be safe from the fighting out there in Washington. Was probably home right now, in his kitchen, having breakfast with his new wife and son.

"You'll help then, sir?" Graham asked, hope obvious.

Living the good life. A life Creed had once hoped for with Mary Catherine.

Then, Gina Briganti burst into his world. And everything changed.

He straightened in the saddle, his mind dallying over the image of her in his mind—dark-eyed, olive-skinned, blood-warming, beautiful.

"The Sokolovs need arresting, don't they?" Creed asked. "The president needs protecting. Guess I'll do what I can to get both jobs done."

Graham blew out a breath. "Thank you, sir."

"Don't thank me yet. We're a long way from throwing the brothers and their kind behind bars."

"Any idea how we'll go about doing that?"

His mind sifted through what little he knew. And came up with Gina, his one link to the Sokolovs.

Once Mass was over, with her help, they'd find her friend Sebastian and ask him a few questions.

Chapter Nine

Gina shouldn't have tolerated Creed's stubborn insistence to wait for her until after the Mass ended, but in truth, she was glad he did. So much sadness from the families of the factory workers. Not enough hope. And, oh, the despair…

She left the church weepy and not as strong as she should have been. Seeing Creed outside, knowing he would be there, well, once again she didn't feel so alone.

The discussion he'd been having with Graham Dooling ended when she joined them. Maybe it was his concern for her, showing in the amber depths of his eyes. Or the way he kept watching her, as if to assure himself she would be all right. She understood his need to find the Sokolovs. But why Mr. Dooling needed Creed's help to find the secretive anarchists left her perplexed. Who was he that he had the skill? The courage?

Still, she'd been honored when Creed asked for her help to locate Sebastian. Her friend would do his best to answer the questions Creed needed to ask. She'd been only too happy to help in this small way.

But she asked that he take her to the Los Angeles Infirmary first, just in case someone had found Mama and brought her there. What if the good nursing nuns hadn't known to contact Gina to let her know?

Creed had been quick to agree, and she made the brief trip in Mr. Dooling's buggy. He departed from there, leaving Creed and Gina at the infirmary's entrance, with a promise that he would be in contact again soon.

Now that they were here, Gina was too nervous to go inside. She was afraid of what she would learn, that there was no news. Or bad news. What if her *visione* was wrong? That it'd been just a strange dream?

"Best to go in and get it over with," Creed said in his low voice.

She could not look at him. "Yes."

"Been hell for you not knowing."

"It has not been easy, no."

"I'll go with you. You know that."

Her head lifted then, and her gaze met his. His loyalty left her bemused and grateful. She'd known him only a short while, and yet…was he this honorable with all the troubled women he met?

"Gina! *Bella Gina!*"

She whirled at the sound of Sebastian's voice. He strode through the infirmary doors with his arms outstretched, and she went right into them.

"Oh, Sebastian! I do not expect to find you here!" she exclaimed against his coat.

He released her, lowered his head and kissed both her cheeks. "I have been worried about you. Louisa, too. Have you heard anything?"

She drew back. "No. That is why we come. I hope someone finds her and—"

She halted at his crestfallen expression.

"She is not here, Gina. I come to visit many people from Premier, the other cutters, my assistants... I want to visit Louisa, too. And when I ask if she is here, they tell me no. Everyone is identified. They do not have a Louisa Briganti anywhere."

Gina pressed her fingers to her lips. "Oh, Sebastian."

"The firemen, the police, they would have brought her here if they found her. It is the closest place."

Her eyes closed, the worry, the grief, unbearable. "Yes."

He gently touched her cheek. "The fire is out now. They are cleaning out everything that was burned. I have been told that Mr. Silverstein wants to reopen the factory as soon as possible." He hesitated. "If Louisa is there, they will find her."

Fierce denial shot through her at what he implied, and she jerked back. "She is not there, Sebastian! If she is, I know it here—" she thumped her fist against her chest "—deep in my heart. I have a *visione*. She is somewhere, and she is still alive! I *know* it!"

He made a pitying sound and shook his head slowly.

"Gina," he whispered, his black eyes sad.

And oh, she didn't want his pity or his sadness. In that moment, she *hated* him for it, and she blinked furiously to keep tears from falling.

"If there is anything I can do," he murmured, reaching for her again.

"There is," Creed said.

Sebastian froze, and his gaze shot toward Creed before jumping back to Gina. His expression darkened. "You are with him again, eh?"

"Yes," she said, refusing to justify herself.

"We're hoping you can help us with some information," Creed said.

Sebastian's eyes narrowed. "What kind of information?"

"We must find the Sokolovs," Gina said.

"Nikolai? Alex?"

Creed nodded. "They've got some explaining to do."

Sebastian's expression turned guarded. "I do not know what you are talking about."

Frustration snapped inside her.

"The fire!" she said. "Nikolai is responsible."

"I cannot say that for sure," he hedged.

"What?" It was all Gina could do to keep from throttling him. "You see him with his cigarettes. You see him smoke them. You know he is angry at Mr. Silverstein. He starts the fire, Sebastian. You know that he did!"

"He needs to be held accountable," Creed said in a hard voice.

From the time she'd met him, Sebastian had been her friend. Charming, flirtatious, fun. But always, he was cautious, avoiding trouble. Why couldn't he be a little more fearless?

"Think of what he does," she said, impatient that she must explain everything to him. "Do you forget you barely escaped the fire with your life, like the rest of us?"

His nostrils flared. "I do not forget."

"He's an anarchist, isn't he?" Creed demanded.

Sebastian's eyes darted to Gina. Her chin lifted. She didn't feel guilty for revealing the information or that Creed knew it was Sebastian who'd told her.

"Yes," he admitted finally.

"Where does he hold his meetings?"

"They are secret. Nikolai will be angry if I told you."

"He'll never find out from me that you did."

Still, Sebastian hesitated.

"You want him to hurt more people?" Creed demanded.

"No, no." He shifted uneasily. "The meeting was supposed to be held last night, but with the fire—he will have one tonight instead."

"Tonight." A muscle moved in Creed's jaw. "Where?"

"There is an abandoned warehouse outside of town. The old Swanson place on First Street. Nine o'clock."

Creed nodded. "Good."

"You know this because he asks you again to come to the meeting?" Gina asked.

"Yes."

"Do you decide to go?"

He appeared offended that she asked. "After what he has done, no. I have already told him I would not be there." He hesitated. "Stay away from him, Gina. He is a dangerous man."

"Yes." More than she ever suspected.

"I do not like the way he looks at you."

Many times she'd noticed him staring but until now, she hadn't given it much thought. She shivered. "I do not think he comes back to Premier."

"Not if I have anything to say about it," Creed muttered.

Sebastian centered a cold glare on him. "And what makes you think he will listen to anything you have to say?"

Creed matched the glare with a hard one of his own. "I've made it a habit to rid the world of vermin like them."

His dark eyebrow arched mockingly. "Oh, you have?"

"And I've got a strong appreciation for the freedoms in America. The Sokolovs are a threat to them that must be stopped."

Sebastian seemed to recognize the truth in Creed's words and could find no argument for them. He retreated and reached for Gina's arm.

"Come. I will take you home," he said.

"She's not ready to go back," Creed said.

Again, the glares came between them.

"She is in mourning for the loss of her mother. She should not be in public like this," Sebastian said.

"I do not mourn!" Gina grated. "Not yet."

His expression turned imploring. "You should go home and wait for word from the authorities. They will not be able to find you if you are out on the streets."

She understood he had her best interests in mind, yet the thought of returning to her empty apartment with nothing to do but worry was more than she could bear. She laid her palm against his cheek. "When it is time for me to go to the apartment, then I go."

His glance flickered toward Creed, and hurt shadowed his handsome face.

"He is a stranger," Sebastian said, as if Creed was not standing there, just a foot or two away. "You have only just met him."

"But I am safe with him." She couldn't explain the feeling of certainty, yet it was there, deep inside her, like it had been last night, after the fire. "You must not worry for me."

"How can I not?"

"We have a few errands to run first, that's all," Creed said quietly. "I'll make sure she gets home. You have my word on it."

Again, their gazes locked, but this time, there were no glares. Finally, Sebastian nodded in resignation, then pressed a kiss into her palm. "If you hear anything about Louisa, you must promise to send word. I will do the same."

"I promise," Gina said. "*Grazie*, Sebastian."

He took a step back, his glance flickering over Creed one last time before he turned and walked away.

Her heart squeezed. Sebastian had always made his attraction for her very obvious, very flattering, and she couldn't deny she enjoyed his attentions. But was she in love with him? Had she ever been? More confusing, had being with Creed ruined the relationship she and Sebastian once shared?

"Are you doing okay?" Creed asked, guiding her away from the infirmary and down the sidewalk toward his horse, hitched just across the street.

"I am not sure," she murmured, truthful.

Nikolai Sokolov was responsible for tearing her neatly arranged life apart. Because of him, her future had never been so bleak. She didn't know what would become of her treasured dream of one day having her own dress shop. Or her job, and oh, Mama—

"Watch out!" Creed barked.

Her thoughts scattered. He snatched her arm and jerked her back to the sidewalk when she would have stepped absently off the curb toward his tethered palomino.

The frantic clang of the bell on a flat-topped ambulance warned of its approach as it careened around the corner, narrowly missing them. The horses thundered past in a cloud of dust, their haste driven by the urgent needs of the patient they transported.

Gina pressed a hand to her breast in reaction. She would have to be more careful! If Creed hadn't been with her, she would've been trampled and in need of the infirmary herself.

More observant this time, she checked both sides of the street before leaving the sidewalk. Deeming it safe, Creed beckoned her forward in his low voice, his hand clamped firmly on her elbow. As they crossed, her gaze lifted to the tall Premier Shirtwaist Company factory building, several blocks down, the scorched roof towering over the others around it.

Deeply, she had prayed to the Madonna to help her seek revenge against the Sokolov brothers. Now, knowing they'd be at their anarchist meeting tonight, perhaps her prayers would be answered, and she would find a way to make them pay for all they had done.

Nikolai did not know the man she was with.

He did not wear the drab clothes of the common laborer at Premier. Nikolai might have recognized him if he had. This one was different. American, not of the city, and he carried the air of the world about him. Tall, proud. He walked with confidence, a man with money to spend, power to flaunt.

A man of authority.

Nikolai's lip curled in contempt.

The kind of man he had grown to despise.

It had been the ambulance speeding by that yanked his attention from the fragrant Kulich he'd just bought, the bread still warm from the bakery's ovens. Only after the vehicle raced by did he see them at the curb.

He moved backward, deeper into the doorway. He had not expected to see Gina Briganti this morning, and her beauty reached out to him, even with the street and half a block separating them. The olive skin, the black eyes, so different from the fair-skinned women of his native Russia. The memory of her voice, intriguing with its Italian accent, soft, filled with spirit, with passion.

Many times, he had lusted for her. Seeing her now, he lusted again.

But she knew too much about him, that it was his lit cigarette which started the fire in the scrap bin on the eighth floor of the factory. She would not understand why he had to do it. She would think it was wrong. She would be righteous, angry, and tell the police what she knew.

Maybe she already had.

They would find him and put him in their filthy jails. Forbid him from doing his work against the injustices of society. They would not understand the need which always burned inside him—to destroy the authority found in all levels of the American government and free the laborer from organized hypocrisies.

Nikolai had no regrets about what he had done, the lives he had cost. Abraham Silverstein fired Alex for the flimsy reason of poor workmanship. He did not care that Alex was young and did not yet have the skills Nikolai possessed. Silverstein thought only of the money he saved from not paying the wages Alex had rightfully earned. Nothing else.

Silverstein had to be punished. His greed and tyranny against all the employees at his factory had to be stopped. Burning his factory was only the first step of Nikolai's scheme for revolt in America.

The bakery door opened, and Alex stepped out, a small loaf of the Kulich in his slender hand. He was only fifteen, not yet a man. But he had Nikolai to take care of him. There was no one else.

They were raised in Russian poverty, deprived of affection throughout their lives. Nikolai had grown to crave the love Alex unabashedly gave him. The admiration.

The trust.

Alex had been born frail, their mother often too drunk, too depressed, to care for him, their father abusive and cold. Many years, Nikolai planned their escape. When the time was right, when he managed to scrape together enough money for their passage, he took Alex and left for America.

Alex almost died on the long, arduous journey. If not for Nikolai's devotion, he would have. But they were here now, in California. Together, they had survived.

And they would triumph.

"She works at Premier," Alex said, his blue gaze on the couple, like Nikolai's had been. "I remember her."

His thoughts returned to Gina, the man she was with. "Yes."

"She came down to the eighth floor to talk to your friend Sebastian."

Nikolai nodded in approval as the couple stopped next to a horse, a fine-blooded palomino. "It is good you remember so many details, Alex. You must always be aware of what is happening around you."

Gina said something, and the American lifted his broad shoulder in an easy shrug. He untied the reins, but neither of them climbed into the saddle.

"Do you think she knows?" Alex asked in a hushed voice.

She began walking with him, the horse trailing behind. They appeared in no hurry, as if they had the whole day to stroll together.

"Yes. She knows."

Alex said nothing, and Nikolai dragged his gaze toward him. Sunlight glinted on the blond hair hanging long and shaggy beneath his woolen cap; crumbs from the Kulich had gathered on one side of his mouth. Pale fuzz grew above his lip, the moustache he struggled to grow, a sign of the man he tried to be.

"What are we going to do, Nikolai?" he asked.

His worry moved Nikolai, as it never failed to do.

"I will take care of her."

"So she will not go to the police?"

He refrained from explaining she may have already done so. Possibly last night, after the fire, when the police were everywhere. Maybe she told the American, too.

"So many questions, Alex." He gave him a gentle nudge

on his shoulder, thin even through his coat. "Eat your bread, and you will be strong."

"Like you?" he asked with a grin, tearing off a chunk and stuffing it into his mouth.

"Like me." Nikolai thought of the bulk on his six-foot frame, how Alex would never match it, no matter how much bread he ate. "I am strong for both of us."

Alex made a sound of agreement around the food he chewed, his worry clearly gone, his trust in Nikolai absolute. His attention strayed from Gina to a pair of noisy starlings feeding on an apple core carelessly thrown into the gutter.

The sight struck Nikolai. So much like himself and Alex, the little birds. The lowest of laborers, they lived without respect, hungry and dirty, always the pests of society.

Bitterness roiled through him, and his gaze found Gina and the American again, now farther down the street. He took a bite of his Kulich, savored the taste of its nuts and raisins, the butter on the crust.

She knew of his guilt in setting the fire. She had no proof, no evidence, but with the American's help, she could destroy his dream of freeing the oppressed laborer, the work he had only just begun.

Nikolai knew it, deep in his gut.

The beautiful Gina Briganti must be stopped before she did.

Chapter Ten

"You should not buy me the horse," Gina said with a frown. "It is—how you say?—too extravagant."

She remained seated in the saddle beside him, though they'd finished with their errands for the day and had returned home to the tenements. The hitching posts were right in front of them.

A corner of Creed's mouth lifted. It was as if she was afraid the big bay would disappear if she got down and went inside.

"I only rented him for you," he reminded her for the dozenth time. "He's yours to use for as long as you need him. When you're done, we'll take him back to the livery. It's that simple."

"But he is expensive to rent."

"The liveryman gave me a good price."

"You should not spend your money on me."

"I wanted to." He guessed it'd been awhile since anyone had given her anything. A damn shame it was, too. He swung his leg over the cantle, dropped to the ground. "Now let's go inside."

She bit her lip and didn't move. Easy to tell it went against everything she stood for to keep the mount.

With a mix of amusement and exasperation, he set his hands on his hips. "Look. You can't walk everywhere. Los Angeles is too big a city. Until things settle down for you with regard to your mother and all, well, it's just easier to have a horse."

She sighed. "Yes. Maybe."

"No maybes about it."

After eyeing him dubiously, she finally dismounted and faced him, her gaze no higher than his shirt button. That pride of hers, making it hard to accept his gift.

"I am happy to have the horse. Thank you," she said.

"You're welcome," he responded drily, thinking of Graham's fancy runabout. What would she have done if he'd rented one of those instead?

A quick glance at the sky from beneath the brim of his new Stetson showed dusk would be settling in soon. He gauged the number of hours he had left before the Sokolovs' meeting started. He intended to be there. It would be the first step in setting up the brothers' arrest.

He had time to eat with her before he left, and the prospect appealed to him. He untied the smallest of the bags of groceries from his saddle and handed it to her.

She clutched the bag to her chest and lifted her chin. "There is no reason for you to stay."

He regarded her. "You shouldn't be alone yet."

"I have food. Now, a horse. I am fine."

His inspection caught the fatigue in her expression, the worry and grief in her eyes.

"Do I have to go through this with you all over again?" he demanded in a low voice.

"Maybe your family waits for you. Maybe your job. I think you do not have so much time to spend with me."

Family? Creed forced back a smirk. Pa and Markie didn't need him. Mary Catherine sure as hell didn't, either. No one needed him, except Graham, maybe, and he didn't count.

"I'm all yours, honey," he drawled. "For as long as it takes."

She seemed uncertain at what he might mean, and her mouth opened to protest. Then, as if she thought better of it, it closed again.

"Many times, you tell me this. You try hard to make me believe you." She sighed. "So I do, a little bit." She eyed the heavier bag of groceries he held in the crook of his arm. "We have a feast tonight, then, eh?" She settled hers on her hip and headed toward the front door of the tenement. "You cook breakfast this morning. I do the supper. You like orecchiette with sausage? Or I make the veal cutlets and roasted peppers."

He held the door open, and she went through. She knew how to make a man's belly gurgle in anticipation for sure. How long had it been since he'd had a full-course home-cooked meal?

"Doesn't matter to me. Just slide it hot under my nose, woman, and I'll eat it," he said. "You won't have to tell me twice."

Gina tossed him an amused smile over her shoulder. The rarity of it struck him, the way it showed the whiteness of her teeth and all but transformed her face. He wondered what it'd be like to hear her laugh out loud or to see her completely relaxed and happy.

Would he ever?

Thoughtful, he joined her in the center hall. The passageway was deserted, the apartments on the front side of the building quiet. Must be the time of day when folks were gone or getting ready to settle in for the night. Either way, he couldn't see himself living in a crowded place like this—ever. Didn't matter how desperate he got to have a roof over his head.

From inside one of the apartments, someone pushed their door closed, and the scrape of the latch reached them in the stairwell. Gina paused on the step.

"Mrs. Sortino," she whispered with an annoyed roll of her eyes. "Always, she watches."

"The old buzzard doesn't have anything better to do?" he whispered back.

"I do not think so. She knows everything about everyone."

How could Gina stand it? His jaw clenched with some pretty strong annoyance of his own.

On the third floor, Gina halted outside her rooms and fished the key out of her coat pocket. But before she inserted the metal in the lock, she froze.

The door stood ajar.

Creed swore under his breath.

Their glances met.

They both knew she'd locked it this morning, before they left for church.

Either the damn thing went faulty since then or someone had broken into her apartment. Who or why, he couldn't fathom. She didn't have much of value for anyone to steal, and could it be some sick bastard taking advantage of her grief and misfortune after yesterday's fire?

Creed put a finger to his lips, ordering her silence. He thrust his bag of groceries at her, nudged her aside and went for the knife he kept sheathed at his waist.

His muscles coiled. Carefully, he pushed the door open. The interior of the apartment was dark. Someone had closed the curtains, and he braced for whatever awaited him inside. One step, two, he ventured into the room.

Then three…

A force came at him with the power of a charging bull and sent him hurtling off his feet into the kitchen table. His body slammed hard. Wood splintered. He lost his hold on the knife, but his brain comprehended only the buffet of boot steps against the thin carpet.

Out the door. To Gina.

She screamed, and he heaved himself off the caved-in table in pursuit. Groceries littered the hall floor. A hulk of a man gripped her in his big arms and bolted toward the stairs. Bellowing a roar of rage, Creed flung himself at them.

"Put her down, you son of a bitch!"

He yanked savagely at the man's grip until it broke free. Gina stumbled back, precariously close to the steps, and she cried out, her arms flailing for balance as she tried to catch herself before she fell. Instinctively, Creed reached for her, his attention split between saving her from breaking her neck and the man who threatened that and more.

Her assailant took advantage of the distraction and drew his arm back with a snarl. Creed grabbed Gina's wrist at the same moment he swung away to avoid the blow, but the meaty fist was quicker and clipped Creed's jaw before he could. His head snapped to one side. Pain exploded, and he sprawled onto the floor, bringing Gina down with him.

Her head cracked against the wooden slats with a sickening thud. For a few heart-stopping seconds, she didn't move. Creed needed a few of his own to clear the stars.

Footsteps thundered down the stairs.

From somewhere close, a door whipped open.

"What the hell is going on out here?" a gravelly male voice demanded.

Creed untangled himself from Gina's skirts and clawed a look over her. "Gina, are you all right?"

She blinked, shaking off the daze. "I think so."

A shotgun cocked from the same direction where the voice came from. "Get away from him, Miss Briganti. I got him covered."

She scrambled to sit up, swayed a little when she did. "No, no, Mr. Denton. Not him!"

"You should've shot the other one," Creed growled and twisted toward the stairwell. The sound of boot soles clamoring downward sounded farther and farther away.

He rolled to his feet. The gun centered over him, the man holding it itching to spray him with buckshot. Black grease smeared his baggy pants, and the undershirt beneath the suspenders looked grimy, but he seemed determined to protect Gina, and that was good enough for Creed.

"Stay with her until I get back," he ordered and catapulted down the stairs, two and three at a time, past the second level and onto the first. He searched the long center hall, one side, then the other, before rounding the corner at the end at a full run. Flinging open the tenement's front door, he rushed through and skidded to a stop.

His gaze raked the sidewalk. The street.

Empty, both of them.

Damn it to hell.

He spun on his boot heel and hurried back inside. He had to make sure Gina wasn't hurt, that the scum who'd tried to kidnap her hadn't somehow doubled back to try again, and Creed headed toward the staircase leading to her apartment—

But he spun toward Mrs. Sortino's instead.

He didn't bother to knock. He shoved the door wide open, nearly ripping the hinges from the frame, and found her standing there, just as he knew she would be.

She cried out in alarm. Funny how a woman her size could jump when she was scared.

"Who was he?" Creed snarled.

She squared her shoulders and flung her chin up. "I don't know what you're talkin' about."

"The hell you don't."

"Get out before I call for the police."

Creed took a threatening step closer. "How did he know which apartment was Gina's?"

"She's always entertaining men up there, ain't she? He knew right where to go."

Creed thought of the guilt Gina endured from letting him spend the night. From letting him take her to church and renting a horse and buying her a few lousy groceries, and the fury inside him doubled.

"Don't go thinking you're the only one, mister," Mrs. Sortino declared with a sneer. "And there's that Sebastian feller, too. Oh, no. She's a loose one, she is. You're a fool if you think she's not."

Creed's lip curled. "How much did he pay you to tell him where she lived?"

"He didn't pay me nothing!"

Creed's glance dropped to the hand she kept buried deep in her apron pockets. He clamped his fingers around the thick wrist, the grip strong enough to let her know he meant business.

"Nothing?" he taunted.

Fear flickered in her expression. He yanked her hand out of hiding and found the few coins she kept in her palm.

"Hell of a landlady, aren't you, Mrs. Sortino?" Creed thrust her away in disgust, and the coins clattered to the floor. "You think so little of your tenants that you betray them for pennies?"

"He told me he worked with her at the factory and that he wanted to express his condolences from the fire and all," she said defensively. "Long as he was willing to pay, I figured there wasn't no harm in helping him do it."

"You greedy bitch."

Her bushy eyebrows shot up. "I ain't responsible for the company of the men she keeps, am I?"

He was dangerously close to choking the last breath right out of her. "But you're willing to let one in her apartment to *wait* for her without her knowledge?"

"He said she'd be comin' any minute. How would I know different?"

Creed had heard enough. The woman repulsed him. He spun on his heel and left the room before he did something he shouldn't.

"I heard the ruckus up there, mister," she called after him. "You tell Miss Briganti she's responsible for any damages, y'hear? Mrs. Sortino says so!"

He leapt up the stairs toward the third floor with the same speed he came down and found Gina on her knees gathering the last of the groceries strewn in the hall. Her neighbor, Mr. Denton, held the bag open helpfully, his shotgun set to one side.

Seeing Creed, she halted. "Did you catch him?"

"No." He took the bag and helped her up. Denton rose, too, and from the smell of motor oil on him, Creed guessed he worked on machinery for a living. "Much obliged to you for watching out for her."

Denton gave him a nod. "She had one hell of a scare."

"I'll keep an eye on her from here on out."

The man dragged a wary gaze to Gina. "You got any problems with that, Miss Briganti?"

"No," she said. "No, of course not."

"All right, then. I'll go, but if that hoodlum comes back, I'll have my shotgun ready for him."

She paled a little. "I do not think he will come again."

"You take care, just in case." Denton picked up his weapon and headed toward his apartment. "Good night."

He disappeared inside. Creed nudged Gina into her apartment and lit the lantern in the front room. Lamplight glared over the caved-in kitchen table, splintered beyond repair.

Her fingers flew to her mouth. "Oh, Creed."

He set the groceries on the floor, locked the door and frowned. "Not much left to it, is there?"

"I am sorry." She peered up at him, tears shimmering like black pools.

"For what?" he demanded in a low rumble. "I'm the one who broke it."

She made a sad, negating shake of her head. "He almost kills you."

"And you."

"He almost kills you because of *me*. You never meet him but still he—" she made a tiny sound of sympathy and touched his jaw gently with her fingertips "—he hurts you. Your face, it is swollen a little."

"He cuffed me good." Creed frowned and gave his jaw a few testing wiggles.

"I get you some ice."

He caught her arm before she could hurry to the icebox. "I don't need any."

"But it makes the pain feel better."

He drew her closer. His brain replayed the image of her falling with him in the hall, the sound of her head striking against the floor still gut-wrenching and vivid.

"Don't fuss over me," he said. "You're hurting some, too. I know you are."

"Yes." Her dark eyebrows knitted. She removed her hat and began unpinning her hair. "How do you Americans say it? I have a...goose's egg." Freed from its confines, her shining sable mane dropped onto her shoulders and bounced down her back. Her fingertips delved deep. "Here. Can you feel it?"

His fingers joined hers and found the bump. Thankfully, no blood from it. "A goose egg, all right. You need some ice, too."

"It is not serious."

She lowered her hand, but his stayed in her hair, the fantasy of feeling the strands between his fingers finally true. In the golden lamplight, his gaze lingered over the fine bones of her face, the olive skin smooth as satin. The beauty he found exotic and arousing.

Gina was an innocent to the violence which had erupted in her world. She had no defense against it. No knowledge. No one to keep her from being destroyed by it in the end.

Except him.

"It was Nikolai Sokolov, wasn't it?" Creed asked.

"Yes." She dropped her glance and shivered, as if she relived the scare he'd given her.

Creed cupped her face with both his hands to gently bring it up again, her flesh warm and smooth against his palms. "He knows you saw him start the fire."

"Yes."

"He wants to keep you from talking."

A breath left her. "Yes. Yes, I think so."

"Well, I *know* so." Creed smoothed the pad of his thumb across one delicately-shaped cheekbone. Desperation stirred inside him. She had to know what she was up against. "Men like him are fanatics, Gina. Sokolov will stop at nothing to further his perverted cause."

Her gaze never wavered. "Then I must be careful that he does not find me again."

Creed blinked down at her. "What the hell is that supposed to mean?"

"He is afraid I will keep him from doing his dirty work, so I must stop him before he does any more."

Creed released her. "Just how do you propose to do that?"

She hesitated. "I do not know yet," she admitted finally. "But somehow I find a way."

"You'll find a way."

"Yes."

"He'll kill you first."

The faintest quiver went through her. "It is a chance I take."

"He'll break every law to get to you."

"He is dangerous, yes, but—"

Creed could barely keep from shaking her.

"He'll burn down the damn apartment building, that's how dangerous he is," he roared.

She stiffened.

Her lower lip quivered.

Regret and frustration rolled through him. He gripped her shoulders and brought her roughly against him.

"You know he's capable of it," he said into the hair at her temple. "He'll light the match when you least expect it. In the middle of the night. When everyone's sleeping. You're on the third floor, Gina. Most likely, you won't get out in time."

She drew back, but he refused to let her go until she heard every word he had to say.

"Think of your neighbors," he said. "Mr. Denton. You think it's fair to see them suffer because you're too stubborn to listen to me?"

Sable lashes pressed close together, the reality leaving her shaken, pale.

"No," she whispered.

"Mrs. Sortino would help him do it if she had the chance. Don't think she won't," Creed pressed on.

The lashes parted wide. Gina shook her head in denial. "Even she is not so cruel."

He recalled what Sokolov had given the old crone. Pennies to satisfy her greed. The bribe Gina didn't even know about.

"Ever hear of insurance money? She'd conspire with him if she thought she could make a few thousand bucks off you or any of her tenants."

This time, Gina didn't protest. But she swallowed hard.

"You mean nothing to her," he said more quietly. "And you mean even less to Nikolai Sokolov."

"What do I do? Hide like a little mouse?"

"You're not safe if you don't."

"I will *not* hide!"

He released her. The decision came to him without his conscious thought.

"I'm taking you away from here," he said grimly.

She gaped at him. "What?"

He took the time he needed to work through the plan. The advantages, the disadvantages. He went to the window and yanked back the curtains, braced both hands on the sill and stared down into the street below.

Tails flicking, the palomino and the bay stood next to one another, hitched to the rail, just as he'd left them. All along the dirt street, dreary tenement apartments towered side by side, each structure separated by a few scant feet from its neighbor. Block after block they towered, their existence as bleak as the people who lived inside them.

His gaze lifted to the sky, dimming with the pink-orange hues of the gathering dusk. He thought of another sky, the one he grew up under, a few miles beyond the Los Angeles city limits. A sky that blanketed a different world filled with wide open space, fresh air and clean living. The only world he'd ever known that would be protected and safe.

Call him all kinds of a fool, but there was nowhere else.

He straightened, drew the curtains closed and turned back to Gina.

"Throw your things together," he said. "We're leaving."

Chapter Eleven

Creed had assured her he wouldn't be taking her far, but the longer they rode away from the city, the more uneasy Gina became.

Since the day she arrived from Sicily with Mama, she had never left Los Angeles. The tall brick buildings, the people, the smells and the noise, they were all so familiar. A part of her life, her routine, her thinking, for three long years.

But this, this was different, she mused, her gaze scanning the broad countryside. The land that sprawled green and vibrant for as far as she could see wasn't the California she knew. The vastness, the silence, left her disoriented. Even the air was different. Crisper, untainted from the belching chimneys of factories and restaurants.

Pure and free.

She felt guilty leaving the city to escape Nikolai, no matter how unappealing she found its crowded conditions. She should have remained close to her apartment to wait for word about her mother. Who would know where to find her when it finally came?

Which was why Creed brought her out here, of course.

So no one would know. It was how he intended to protect her from Nikolai. By just making her disappear.

She didn't want to be a coward, but she understood the decision Creed had made. She had to think of the very real possibility her neighbors could be hurt because of Nikolai's vengeance. She had seen what his wrath against Mr. Silverstein had done to all the seamstresses, hadn't she? Besides, what if Nikolai sneaked into her apartment again? Creed would not be with her to help...

Still, she reined the bay to a stop and twisted in the saddle for another look behind her, just to make sure Los Angeles was really not so far away and she could return whenever she wanted to.

Which she did, of course. Soon. She had to.

"Is it still there?" Creed asked.

He halted, too, a little ahead of her. He looked amused at her worry, though he knew it had taken all the trust she had in him to convince her to leave.

"Yes." She shook off the unease and took up the reins again. "How much more do we go?"

"Just ahead into the valley."

He waited for her to draw up beside him before they resumed riding. It wasn't long before a small, coarse-looking dwelling appeared, all by itself, with only a lean-to on one side. At Creed's low-voiced command, they pulled up in front.

She stared.

Whatever she'd been expecting, it hadn't been this.

"You look surprised," Creed said and hooked a knee over the saddle horn. He was completely at ease on the horse. As if he'd been born on one.

"I am." She tossed him a glance. "What is it?"

His mouth curved. "It's called a line shack."

Her gaze returned to the tiny structure, hardly big enough for one person, let alone two. Did he intend to leave her here all by herself?

"I do not know what one is," she admitted carefully.

She prided herself on the English she'd learned when she came to America, but this term she couldn't recall. Could he possibly live here? Or his family?

From beneath the brim of his Stetson, his narrowed gaze swept slowly over the expanse around them. He fell into deep thought, as if he delved into his past and forgot she was there.

"We're on Sherman land, Gina," he said finally. "My father's ranch. He has an outfit that works for him, cowboys who help take care of his cattle and horses. One of the things they have to do is keep the fencing in good shape. So the stock doesn't wander off."

She studied the rough-hewn shack, stark in its simplicity. No flowers to brighten the weathered wood, no grass to soften the dirt and weeds, not even any other shacks around for company. "And this is where the cowboy who checks the fence stays?"

"Yes."

How lonely he would be. "Why does he not live with the other cowboys?"

"Too far." He frowned. "My father owns a hell of a lot of rangeland, Gina. More acres than you can comprehend."

"Oh."

"He has four camps, just like this one, that surround the main spread. North, South, East and West. We're at the West Camp. When the line rider is done checking the fence on this part of the ranch, he moves on to the North one."

"And so the shack is empty until he comes back."

"Yes."

She couldn't imagine it.

"Nothing like your apartment building in the big city, is it?" he asked, watching her.

Her mouth pursed. "No. Always, the tenements are full. One is never vacant long before the rooms get filled again. Mrs. Sortino says she has a waiting list of tenants who want to rent her apartments."

Immigrants like herself, Gina knew, with little money and desperate for a place to stay, no matter how crowded or poor the conditions.

Creed grunted, clearly keeping his opinions of the landlady and the tenement she owned to himself. He slid from his horse to the ground. "The sun's setting fast, Gina. We'd best unload our gear and get settled inside before it does."

His words tripped the rhythmic beat of her heart. Any doubts she might have had about being left alone fled. He intended to stay. It'd be just the two of them, and the cabin was far smaller than she could have imagined, could have possibly known….

She bit her lip. "It is permissible to stay here?" she asked, half hoping it wouldn't be. "You have not had time to tell your father we come."

He flung his saddlebag over his shoulder, hefted their groceries in one arm.

"He'll never know," Creed said in a brusque tone.

Without the city's streetlights, their surroundings would turn pitch-dark quickly. She had no choice but to follow his lead and dismount, too. She peered at him around the bay's long neck. "You will not explain to him?"

"No."

Before she could ask why, he opened the shack's door and disappeared inside. Within moments, a light glowed through the lone window. He came out again.

"There's a water pump out back," he said. "Should be some wood stacked, too. I'll bring in some of both."

Before he'd looked, he'd known the water and wood would be there. "You stay here before."

"Yes." He frowned, as if he thought of the past all over again. "When I was a kid."

Her brow arched. "Alone?"

"My father's idea. He wanted me to grow up fast. Be a cowboy faster."

His resentment gave her pause. Clearly, he hadn't liked the job. The desolation, the solitude, wouldn't be for everyone, especially one so young.

"But you do not want to be a cowboy?" she asked.

"No."

Her curiosity compelled her to prod gently. "What then?"

The frown returned. "A soldier in the United States Army. And wasn't that a hell of a disappointment?"

She wouldn't have thought so, but evidently his father did. From the bitterness in Creed's tone, she knew not to ask more questions, and he offered no further explanation. Her gaze lingered over him as he strode away.

With every hour they spent together, he intrigued her more. Again, she found herself wondering about him. His likes, dislikes. The ideals and dreams that put him at odds with his family but shaped him into the man he was today.

He believed in honor, in patriotism. That much she knew. A belief so strong that it inspired the respect of a man of Graham Dooling's prominence in the American government.

Her instincts insisted she could trust him, and yet…

She could not forget he was still a stranger, and she would be staying with him in this desolate place. A stranger, rugged and virile, who made her mind jump at the prospect, who made her blood warm from a curious unease.

And from anticipation.

But she drew herself up with resolve. It was silly to dwell on such foolishness when her predicament allowed her no other recourse. Carrying her valise in one hand and clutching the sketches she'd refused to leave behind against her chest, she entered the line shack. Her curious gaze took in the table and a pair of chairs, a cast-iron stove and small cot.

She laid her valise and sketches on the straw mattress, along with her coat, and she turned her thoughts to tidying up the place. By the time she gave the floor a hasty sweep with the broom she found tucked in a corner, Creed returned.

He set a bucket of water down, then squatted next to the stove, opened a side door and began to fill the fire box with the wood he held cradled in his arm.

She reached around him to put the broom away. He shifted, giving her as much room as he could.

"The shack is stocked with some supplies." After he lit the stove, he straightened, took a skillet and box of utensils off a nearby shelf, and set them next to their groceries on the table. "Nothing fancy here, but help yourself to anything you need."

She regarded him. "I do not need fancy, and you are sure we can come in here and use your father's shack without his permission?"

Creed fisted his hands on his hips. "We have an unspoken agreement out here on the range, Gina. A man is welcome to the hospitality a cabin like this can give. All that's expected is that he leaves it in the same condition he found it. My father's permission doesn't matter."

Puzzled by his strange explanation, she found the veal cutlets and tore open their paper wrapping. "There is no lock on the door."

"Don't need them out here."

Her eyes widened in surprise. "And no one steals?"

This she couldn't believe. Never had she or Mama left their apartment without securing the lock firmly. They would not dare be so careless.

"Can't say it wouldn't happen, but it doesn't as a rule."

She eyed him doubtfully.

"Not many folks know the shack is here. We're out in the middle of nowhere." His expression turned grim. "That's why I brought you here. So the Sokolovs won't find you."

The words were a cold splash of reality, a reminder of his intent to keep her safe. She found a pot and filled it with water for heating. "But still they look for me."

"Yes. Until I can arrange their arrest."

"And if you cannot?"

"Don't underestimate me, Gina." He headed to the door. "I'll see to the horses, then come in and help you with supper. It's getting late."

His avowal for justice lingered in her mind after he left. She wasn't so foolish to think Nikolai would let himself be put into the Americans' jail easily. And Creed was only one man. Why would he think he could fight the brothers' violence alone?

Darkness had all but fallen. The anarchist meeting would start soon. She refused to have Creed whisk her away to a remote section of his father's ranch and expect her to do nothing while he tried to make his arrest, no matter how skilled he thought he was.

She had to find a way for revenge. For Mama's sake.

But mostly for her own.

Gina perched cross-legged on the cot and watched him put on his disguise.

His transformation amazed her. He wasn't the Creed

Sherman she knew before supper. Instead, he became a different man after, one Nikolai would never recognize. Or Graham Dooling. Or herself, if she hadn't seen him do it.

He sat at the table with his shaving mirror in front of him. Using the lantern light at its brightest, he worked carefully to apply a crepe wool beard to his chin and cheeks, tacking it in place with spirit gum. He did the same with a moustache and thick brows, all in deep burnished brown, the color of his own facial hair if he had had the time to grow it out.

Already, he wore a crumpled black suit pulled from his saddlebags, and he'd traded his new Stetson for a felt bowler, which wasn't so new.

He looked like one of America's poor. Someone who would understand Nikolai's view on capitalism. A man who would fade into the crowd at one of his meetings.

And he excited her like no other, stirring her blood from the kind of man he was. The illicit plan he intended to carry through left her fascinated from the sheer courage he'd need to see it done.

Yet his recklessness frightened her, too. If he failed, if Nikolai discovered Creed spying on him for the American government, he'd be furious. Creed would certainly be killed. It was the way of the anarchists to meet in secret to plot their revolt against authority, always with the use of violence. Assassination, bombs and tyranny. They wouldn't think twice about murdering Creed for interfering.

He'd explained their strange beliefs to her at length while they ate. Their hatred of the way of life in the United States. Their dreams of free living without interference from the government. Their intent to transform society to conform to their ideals.

A sobering conversation, for sure. But one she had needed to hear.

He turned his head one way, then another, for a final inspection in the glass. Giving the beard a pat of satisfaction, he set the mirror aside and swiveled toward her. He waggled his wooly brows with a reckless grin. "What do you think?"

Her heart skipped at that grin. "I think you enjoy yourself too much."

He shrugged and set the mirror on top of his shirt, folded neatly over his denim Levi's, both stacked on one side of the table. "Going undercover appeals to me."

She thought again of his courage and all that could go wrong, no matter how fearless he was. "It is dangerous."

"If I'm not caught, it isn't."

He rose from the table and slipped his deadly-looking knife into its sheath at his hip. She shuddered at the blood that would've spilled if he'd been forced to use it at her apartment this afternoon.

"Know how to shoot a gun?" he asked.

He produced a Colt pocket pistol with a gleaming silver barrel and held it out to her.

She didn't take it.

"Papa taught my mother and me when his troubles with the Black Hand begin. I do not use a gun since." She held his gaze. "Why?"

"You'll remember how, if you have to." He laid it next to her on the thin mattress. "Keep it by you while I'm gone."

Now that the time had come, apprehension rippled through her at being left alone. Far away from anyone on his father's ranch. And the night was so dark.

"A few hours. No more," he said, watching her.

She uncoiled from the cot. "Why can you not take me with you?"

It'd been there all long, she realized suddenly. Her need

to see Nikolai again, to learn more about him so she could take her revenge when he least expected it—when she had the advantage.

Thunder brewed in Creed's expression. "No."

"You can disguise me. Make me look like a man, like you," she said, the idea of infiltrating the meeting with him taking root. "No one knows I am Gina Briganti."

"Are you *crazy?*"

"He must pay for what he does to my mother and to all of us at Premier. He cannot get away with the terrible thing he has done."

"You think I don't know that?" he demanded.

Gina pushed on, relentless. "So I must do everything I can to see that he is punished, and if I go to the meeting I can—"

"I'll handle the Sokolovs."

Defiant, she stood. "I do not want to stay here!"

"You don't have a damn clue what you're up against."

"I think I do!"

"Nikolai will get what's coming to him. But he'll get it my way." Creed pulled a Smith and Wesson revolver from its holster and stuffed it into his waistband. Beneath the ill-fitting jacket, its bulge wasn't noticeable. "And I won't have another word from you on it."

She pressed her lips together in frustration and glared at him.

He glared back. "Understand?"

She made him wait for her response. "Yes."

"All right, then." He took up the last of his weapons, a slim Remington rifle he kept in one hand. With the other, he pushed the battered bowler onto his head. "I'll get back as fast as I can."

"Fine."

"Try to get some sleep or something until I do."

She flashed him a look of annoyance. Like she was a baby to be hushed?

He sighed at that look. "Gina. I can't risk taking you with me. It's out of the question."

"So you say."

His mouth tightened under the moustache. "Exactly."

He strode to the door, cast her a final glance, then left without saying goodbye. Within moments, the sound of the palomino's hoofbeats faded away.

Gina stood stock still. The silence in the little shack closed in on her, the knowledge she'd be spending several hours without him with nothing to do.

Her glance swung to the shiny Colt lying small and unobtrusive on the cot. Papa had taught her how to shoot for good reason. He would want her to use the little pistol to avenge Mama. He wouldn't want Gina to be weak and let Creed do it for her.

Nikolai was no better than the Black Hand. Both struck against the vulnerable and the innocent to further their own demented causes. Each as ruthless as the other.

Nikolai had to be stopped.

If she didn't fight, he would destroy her hopes and dreams, just like the Black Hand had destroyed Papa's.

Her veins surging with resolve, she flung open her valise and pulled out a dark fringed scarf. Quickly, she knotted it under her chin, hiding her hair in case some slipped from its pins. She threw on her coat, stashed the pistol securely into her pocket and flew out the door.

Within moments, she mounted the bay and rode hard out of the valley toward Los Angeles.

Chapter Twelve

Creed listened to Nikolai's ramblings with gritted teeth. Only sheer willpower kept him from bolting from his seat and stuffing his fist down the man's throat to shut him up.

The Russian had no remorse for what he had done to the Premier Shirtwaist factory. While he stopped short of admitting his guilt in setting the fire, he praised the results, seeing the building's destruction in a positive light so that better things might come from it. He preached of a Golden Age in the near future, one without police or judges, no administrative authority and pure freedom. Through it all, he encouraged each man in attendance to apply complete devotion to his cause, even martyrdom if necessary, in pursuit of it.

And, of course, to be generous with their donations to help him lead the fight.

Even more disturbing, he had managed to scrape together a following, a ragtag group of America's poor, troubled and dissatisfied. In their desperation for a better life, they gathered in anger and blind faith, as hungry for vengeance against their plight as they were for bread on their tables.

Hell, they *filled* the room, once used as an office for the defunct warehouse. Nikolai stood at the front, an imposing figure with his thick moustache and burly shoulders. Beside him, sitting behind a battered desk, his younger brother, Alex, half his size, silent and pale.

From his back row seat, Creed studied him. The two brothers couldn't be more different. Alex was content to let his older sibling rant while his gaze meandered over the group, as if he had nothing better to do except distribute the propaganda stacked neatly on the desktop. Yet he was as guilty as Nikolai in starting the factory fire. He didn't look strong enough to survive in the harsh world of an unemployed factory worker, but that's where he was, and all from his own doing.

It didn't make sense to Creed. Not that it should. All that mattered was setting the trap for the Sokolovs' arrest and getting them both off American streets.

And fast, before President McKinley arrived.

The sensation of cool air dissipated his thoughts. Alex's gaze idly lifted toward the room's back door; Creed's followed to see a woman slip through and take the last empty chair in his row.

With a half dozen men between them, he couldn't see much of her beyond the scarf she wore low over her forehead. Why she'd want to get involved in the male-dominated anarchist world, he couldn't fathom, and it rankled that her arrival left standing room only for Nikolai's tirades. How many more of his godforsaken followers would arrive tonight?

The Russian's current diatribe ended, and he gestured for a drink to wet his throat. Alex handed him a glass of water, and Nikolai drained it dry; when he handed the glass back, Alex bent close and whispered something in his ear.

Nikolai's gaze lifted to the woman in the back row. A mix of wary astonishment flickered in his expression. He straightened, and a faint smile formed on his lips.

"Well, comrades, we have an unexpected surprise. A woman has joined us," he said. "We are fortunate she is interested in helping with our cause, eh?"

She didn't move. Every head turned toward her. Including Creed's.

"Share with us your ideas," Nikolai said.

She remained silent, hunched in her chair. It seemed to Creed her breathing had quickened, as if it mortified her to be the center of attention.

"Do not be shy." Again, the Russian urged her, but his voice had taken on a slight edge, as if it annoyed him she didn't obey him in front of his followers.

"Leave her alone," Alex said with a shrug. Clearly, he thought the tongue-tied woman was unworthy of the time it took to prod her. "It is only her first meeting with us. She does not know what to expect."

A moment passed while Nikolai considered whether to press the issue. In the end, he gave a relenting nod.

"Maybe later we will get to know her better," he conceded. He picked up a piece of paper and shifted his stance, his attention once more on his audience.

But Creed's remained on the woman. The profile he could barely discern through the scarf. That little hook to her nose…

"…received word that someone important to the Americans, someone of the highest authority, is coming—"

Creed's thoughts jerked back to Nikolai.

"—by train very soon."

Ominous murmurs went up amongst the men, the seeds of revolt, planted by Nikolai, budding in their minds.

"And what an opportunity for us, eh, my comrades?" He smiled, cold and calculated.

Creed's stomach clenched.

This was it. The intelligence Graham had received about the president. Somehow, via someone, the top secret information had sailed all the way from Washington, across the country, to land here, in California.

Into this room full of misguided zealots, thirsty for blood.

"You do not know when, Sokolov?" someone with a thick Polish accent demanded.

"We know only that he is coming."

"Ain't no good if we don't know when," another called out.

The Russian's ice-blue eyes locked over him. "Do you think I do not understand that exact thing?"

An arm waved, capturing his attention from the other side of the room.

"Your friend going to let you know when he finds out?"

"He is."

"What if he don't find out soon enough?"

"I am prepared for that as well."

An expectant silence fell over the men.

Again, that ghost of a smile. "No one has asked who is coming. Only *when* he is coming."

They exchanged glances among them. Clearly, it hadn't mattered.

"You're sayin' someone of the highest authority?" one of the more astute among them asked. "As high as McKinley himself?"

"It is him."

Instant cheers went up, the sound deafening in the packed room. Nikolai let them enjoy the moment before he raised his hand, commanding their silence again.

"We cannot allow this precious opportunity to be lost,"

he said. "We must show America we demand deliverance from oppression!"

"Yes! Yes!" they roared.

"We must lay the misery of thousands of laborers at the president's feet!"

"Yes! *Yes!*"

"We must destroy the hypocrisy!"

Emotions whipped into a frenzy.

"We must destroy the tyrant responsible. We must destroy President McKinley!"

Fists shook. Voices chanted.

"Death to the president! Death to the president!"

Rage bubbled inside Creed. Sheer self-control kept him in his chair and clinging to his cover. Never had the need to defend the United States against vermin like these burned so hot inside him. Only years as a mercenary soldier, hard-won years of experience infiltrating hostile countries, kept him from doing some pretty strong yelling of his own.

Because key information was at stake. Revealing himself now, giving in to the patriotism surging through him, would destroy what he needed most.

The knowledge the War Department would use to protect their leader. At all costs.

Including the lives of these men, if necessary.

"Does anyone among us work at the train station?" Nikolai called out.

The room quieted. Heads shook in negative replies.

Sweat glistened on the Russian's forehead, the exhilaration coursing through him. "We must be there when McKinley comes. We must be ready."

"Yes, yes!" the men cried.

"But we need information. The day, the time, of his

train. They will try to keep it secret from us until the last possible moment."

"Then how will we get it?" someone sounding French asked.

"From the inside," he said.

"But *how?*"

For the first time, Nikolai hesitated, the solution evasive. "We will find a way. We will use someone they will not suspect."

"A woman," Alex said suddenly.

His sibling's blond head whipped toward him.

"A *cleaning* woman," Alex rushed, leaping from his chair in excitement. "No one will think to suspect such an insignificant laborer. Yet she would have access to the itineraries when no one is looking. When they are gone from their jobs for the day."

"Brilliant, Alex," Nikolai breathed, his pride shining.

"She must be one of us. Someone who believes as we do."

"Yes…"

For a moment, no one spoke.

Then, as if the idea dropped into their brains at the same time, everyone turned to the only woman in the room, the one draped in a dark fringed scarf in a far corner.

And Creed's heart forgot to beat.

The color drained from her cheeks. She shook her head in vehement refusal.

"You have sympathy for our cause, comrade," Nikolai noted softly. "That is why you are here, is it not?"

She didn't move but for the hand that slipped slowly into her coat pocket….

"Stand so we can see you better," he commanded.

Every muscle in Creed's body tensed. Gina, the crazy, *crazy* fool—

He had to get to her before anyone else did. Before Nikolai, especially, and his legs braced to bolt, his instincts wired for the precise moment...

She stood, and Creed could taste the courage it cost to reveal herself to these men who were no better than a band of cold-blooded assassins.

She showed no fear, but damn it, she looked small among them. Vulnerable. Utterly defenseless.

One ice-blue eye narrowed over her, as if Nikolai strove to see past the fabric that shielded part of her face. As if something about her nagged at him.

"Speak, woman," he ordered.

Still, she said nothing. Her fingers lifted to the knot under her chin.

"We ask for your help," he grated, the hard edge back in his tone. "Are you willing to give it for our cause?"

The scarf fell away, and Gina stood defiant before him.

"I will do no such thing, Nikolai," she snapped, the Italian accent in her words a sharp contrast to the guttural Russian in his. "Do not ask me again."

"She is from the factory!" Alex exclaimed. "I remember seeing her there."

"I have seen her, too. Many times." Nikolai's voice had turned soft, lethal. "Her name is Gina Briganti, and she is much more beautiful when she is not trying to hide her identity from us."

The mood shifted in the room. From revolution to unease.

Creed carefully parted his coat, his hand only inches from the Smith and Wesson tucked into his waistband.

Tension emanated from Nikolai, the trouble he could sense coming. "So you have learned about the secret meetings of the anarchists from our friend, Sebastian."

"He wants nothing to do with your crazy ideas. I do not, either."

His burly shoulders lifted in a careless shrug. "Then it is a shame. The revolution will come. We will change society for the good of everyone, but especially the laborers who must work like animals."

"There is no shame in working for an honest wage, Nikolai," she said. "You come here, like me, to live in America. You want to prosper and succeed, and why not? It is the Great Land of Opportunity. But you have no pride in learning new skills. You want only to hurt the innocent with your wild ideas!"

He jerked as if she'd slapped his face, the insult she hurled at him for everyone to hear.

"That is enough!" he bellowed.

"So you start the fire at Premier, then you run like a coward." Her fury fueled the accusations. "You leave behind death and pain. Yet you feel nothing. You *suffer* nothing."

Startled murmurs rippled through the men. Their reaction to his guilt, the implications from it.

Gina flashed a contemptuous glance over them. "He does not admit to you what he has done? Maybe you do not care? Or maybe you would do as he does, if you have the chance."

Backs stiffened. The unease in the room shifted to hostile indignation.

"You got nerve with your sass, lady," a Polish man called out.

"Someone must help us," a Frenchman claimed. "Sokolov is the man to do it, and if he thinks setting a fire at Premier will get society to change their thinking, then so be it!"

"Yeah. Get out! You ain't got no right sneakin' in here anyway. We got freedom of speech. We can meet and talk, same as anyone else."

"But I have a right, too," she said with chilling calm. She pulled out the little pistol Creed had given her. Steadying her aim with both hands, she leveled the barrel right at Nikolai. "He must not get away with what he has done."

No one moved. No one breathed. No one went for a weapon.

Except Nikolai.

A revolver, hidden behind a stack of flyers on the desk, a Russian Army .44 more deadly, more powerful, than her derringer could ever be.

If he pulled the trigger, if his aim was true, she'd never have a chance.

And Creed died a thousand deaths.

Nikolai's gaze hardened. "I would not have thought a woman with such beauty and talent would be so foolish to try to kill me in front of so many."

"No, Nikolai. Not that. I want only to see you rot in jail the rest of your life, and Alex, too, if it is the last thing I do." Her voice quivered with the avowal.

Suddenly, one of the men jumped from his chair.

"She's a spy for the police!" he yelled in panic.

"It's a raid!"

"Let's get out of here!"

Pure chaos erupted.

Creed burst into action. He shoved aside the man next to him, then another and another, barreling his way toward Gina with a clatter of chairs and bodies. He tackled her to the floor, and the derringer went off on their way down, the sharp report masking her startled scream.

Nikolai yelled. Alex, too. The Army .44 fired. Thwap! A bullet lodged into the back of a nearby chair. Thwap! Another, somewhere over their heads.

Creed sprawled on top of Gina, protecting her from a stray

shot. No more came. He stabbed his gaze through the chair legs surrounding them. Raked it across the front of the room.

The brothers weren't there.

He caught sight of a leather boot sticking out past the edge of the desk. Nikolai's. Either he was hurt or hiding or dead. Creed didn't care which. He had to get Gina the hell out of there.

"Get up," he said and hastily helped her to her feet.

The doorway was crammed with panicked, fleeing men. Creed grabbed the nearest one by the front of his grimy shirt, shoved the nose of the Smith and Wesson into the man's throat and sandwiched Gina between them.

"You're going to be a shield for us, y'hear?" he hissed between his teeth. "Just in case Nikolai starts shooting. Your back before us."

"I ain't done nothin'," the man said, raw fear in his eyes as he stared down at the gun. "I swear it."

"Yeah, well, you'll get us out of here. C'mon. Move it!"

Creed's grasp stayed tight on the man's shirt, and the pressure of the revolver against his throat even tighter. He yanked the man forward, forcing Gina to walk backward with him. They managed an awkward but quick escape by squeezing themselves through the doorway, down a single step and into the night outside. All around them, men scattered like cockroaches in the dark.

"Where's your horse, Gina?" he demanded.

"Over there. By the fence."

On the far side of the warehouse. The palomino was closer. Creed shifted direction, headed toward his mount first, tethered to a tree near the corner. When they drew alongside, he released his grip on his captive's shirt to give her a firm nudge toward the horse.

"All right, *comrade*." He lifted the Smith and Wesson from the man's throat. "Get out of here, and don't look back. Y'hear me?"

The man didn't need to be told twice. He broke into a full run in the direction they just came. Creed watched long enough to see him disappear into the clutter of fleeing horses and wagons.

He tucked the revolver back into his waistband and vaulted into the saddle behind Gina, then reached around her and pulled the Remington from its scabbard. He felt better having a more accurate weapon, one capable of rapid fire. He knew only too well what the Sokolovs were capable of.

"Let's go," he ordered.

She gripped the reins and took control of the ride, freeing him to defend them if necessary. As they rounded the far side of the warehouse, approaching the bay, Creed ordered her to pull up, deep in the building's shadows. The office light was still on; he didn't want to take any chances before they claimed the mount.

His glance searched the road in front. The anarchists had wasted no time escaping, for sure, but a couple of horses remained. He had a pretty good guess to whom they belonged.

The office light went out. Except for the silvery sheen cast from a half moon, the area around the warehouse plunged into darkness. Two men emerged, each carrying bundles, the propaganda so important to their cause, neither was willing to leave it behind.

They cast cautious looks around them and went straight for the horses. Alex mounted; his brother managed it eventually, and ugly realization swept through Creed.

Seemed Nikolai would take a memento home with him tonight. He'd be more dangerous than ever because of it. Worse, there'd be no telling how he'd retaliate. Or when.

But one thing was sure. No one was safe if he did. Especially Gina and President McKinley.

Chapter Thirteen

He was angry with her.

Gina knew it from the hard set to his mouth, the clipped way he moved, the grim look on his face...but mostly she knew from his silence.

She sat on the cot and clasped her hands tight in her lap. He hadn't spoken during their ride back to the West Camp's line shack, not even at the warehouse to suggest that she switch to her own horse after the Sokolov brothers had ridden off.

Instead, Creed had shared the sleek palomino with her. Maybe he felt it was faster and safer to do so. Or maybe he hadn't wanted to lose sight of her in the dark night. But the anger had been there in the tautness of his body and in the aloof way he held himself against her in the saddle.

She could feel it.

She didn't like it.

She kept thinking of the first time they'd ridden together, when he'd taken her back to the tenements in hopes of finding her mother after the fire. How careful he'd been to keep her warm. How their conversation had been intimately hushed while they rode on the deserted streets. The feel of his chin against her hair...

Now, he was at the table again with the mirror propped in front of him, peeling the fake beard from his cheek. His lean fingers worked deftly to dismantle the disguise and turn him back into the man he truly was.

And she didn't know who that might be. Not really. A score of questions swam in her mind as she sat watching him, the curiosity she didn't dare satisfy.

Yet.

It'd be up to her to clear the air between them first, she knew. He had his reasons for being upset with her, but he had to understand her side of it. Why she'd done what she'd done. Not for herself and her dream for prosperity in America, but for her mother and all the other seamstresses at Premier.

She drew in a breath, let it out again, bracing herself to meet his wrath head-on.

"You want to be angry with me, Creed, but I do not apologize," she said finally.

His glance found her in the mirror. "Not even if I told you barging in on that meeting was one of the most stupid things you could've done?"

Her hands clasped tighter. She did not "barge," but she declined to clarify the point. "No."

"Or that you could've gotten yourself killed? And me right along with you?"

Her heart fluttered against her breast. In that regard, he might be right. "I never want to put us in danger tonight."

He tossed aside the beard and set to work on the moustache. "Well, honey, that's exactly what you did."

"I want only to avenge my mother. I cannot sit back and do nothing."

"You damn near destroyed any chance of getting the brothers behind bars anytime soon."

"How?"

The moustache came off. He went for a brow next. "By sending them into hiding. Until they're ready to come out, they'll be more elusive than ever."

She rejected his logic with a firm shake of her head. "I do not think Nikolai hides for very long. The anarchism is too important to him."

"He'll fight for his cause just as easily underground." He dropped the second brow on top of the hairy pile in front of him and turned toward her, Creed Sherman again. "And you know what else?"

She hesitated to answer. "What?"

"He'll come after you next."

She sucked in a breath. Was this his way of punishing her for confronting Nikolai? By trying to frighten her?

"You don't believe me?" He rose, took off the baggy coat and tossed it over the back of the chair. He proceeded to unbutton the cuffs of his shirt, as casually as if they only discussed the day's weather. "The brothers know who you are. They know you witnessed their crime. You think either of them want you going to the police and spilling your guts?"

"I do not regret telling the Sokolovs what I see," she said, rising from the cot. Suddenly, she was cold. Shivery cold. "Can you not understand why it is important for me to get revenge for all they have done?"

"Revenge? How the hell did you think you'd manage it with that little pea-shooter I gave you?"

Her brow furrowed at the unfamiliar word. "The pistol? I never intend to kill Nikolai."

"No, but you wounded him." He yanked the shirt from his pants waistband, little savage movements that indicated his anger with her. "That was enough. Now he'll want to get even for it."

She crossed her arms under her breasts and swallowed. Hard.

The shirt landed on top of the coat. Creed stood bare-chested and muscular and so vibrantly male that he unsteadied her already unsteady breathing.

"You have any idea how much that scares me?" he asked roughly.

She turned away. Her eyes closed. She couldn't think when he looked like this, half undressed, frowning, blaming her for what she had done when she thought it was the right thing to do.

"Maybe I begin to," she admitted.

"It does. Plenty."

Clothing rustled as he exchanged the pants he wore for his Levi's. She tilted her head back and stared at the shack's rough-log ceiling. She didn't want to imagine what he looked like, all but naked, unbothered by modesty. Or that she was alone with him, in this tiny house. And he distracted her from matters far more troubling.

"Gina."

His voice came from right behind her, sending her thoughts scattering. His hand grasped her shoulder, his touch both firm and gentle. He turned her toward him.

"You should've trusted me to take care of the Sokolovs without you," he said.

Unexpected emotion pushed into her throat. The risks he'd taken for the justice she craved. "Why should I let you?"

"Because you had no idea what you were doing. I did."

"Louisa Briganti is my mother. Not yours. I do not believe you can care about her as much as I do."

A storm gathered in his eyes, darkening their depths like

burnt almonds, reminding her of the groves that grew them in her beloved Sicily.

"You think I wouldn't have done the same for my own mother?" he grated.

She tried to imagine him as a loving son. She tried to imagine the woman who gave birth to him, too, and raised him from a small boy into full-fledged manhood. His mother would've helped shape his ideals, his strengths, the honor so much a part of him.

Yet he warred with his father, clearly a man with ethics, who worked hard to build a ranch this size, too huge to see in one day. A great accomplishment in itself. A man who had different dreams than his son about who he should be.

Gina knew these things only by the words Creed didn't say. The resentment he wasn't always able to hide.

"I would have." He stepped back, as if offended she might think otherwise. "If it was the last thing I ever did for her."

"Yes." In the small confines of the little shack, her voice was hushed, subdued. She contemplated him, his family, his life, and the curiosity unleashed in torrents inside her. "Who are you, Creed?"

His hard gaze held hers, as if he probed into her reasons for asking. "Maybe you shouldn't know."

"Maybe I should."

A muscle moved in his jaw. Eventually, he nodded. "All right. I'll show you."

He took the pocket pistol from where she'd laid it on the cot and put it on the table, next to his disguise. Beside it, stretched out full length, he laid his holster, displaying two Smith and Wesson revolvers. He added the Remington rifle, several boxes of cartridges, the wide-bladed knife, a switch-blade, a set of nickeled handcuffs and brass knuckles.

The lantern light glinted over all of it. His personal

armory of deadly weapons. And the blood pounded heavier in her veins.

"That's who I am, Gina," he said.

Her stare lifted. She was almost afraid to ask. "Are you with the police?"

"No."

Her dread deepened. "Someone in the Mafioso? Or—"

"Nothing like that."

She believed him and felt a little better. "You are with the American government." The memory came back, the reason Graham Dooling needed him. "A soldier."

"More than a soldier, Gina. A mercenary."

Her fingers pressed against her lips from what that might entail. "Oh."

"I work for the War Department. They hire me to do what ordinary soldiers can't." He paused. "Or won't."

"I do not know what you mean."

"I have skills you don't even want to know about."

"To protect the United States."

"Very good." He gave her a cold smile.

She needed a moment to absorb it all.

"I've fought on foreign soil to protect the freedoms you use every day, Gina. I work undercover to collect intelligence for the War Department. They think no price is too high to pay for my services." One broad shoulder lifted in a careless shrug. "I'm that good."

"Oh. I see."

He regarded her, as if he wondered if she really did. "I planned to retire. Lead a normal, civilian life. That's why I came back to California."

She recalled his elaborate disguise for Nikolai, his skill in infiltrating the secret anarchist meeting.

"But you do not retire yet," she said.

His gaze remained on her; the air between them shifted. "I met you and my plans changed."

"I think it is Graham Dooling who changes your plans," she said quietly. "Not me."

"Let me explain something to you." He spoke in a low, rough tone in deference to the confidence he was about to share. "Graham works for the Secret Service. It's part of his job to keep the president of the United States safe. The War Department ordered Graham to contact me to help him protect McKinley when he arrived. Originally, I told him no."

The words rolled through her. Creed's importance, the power he held in the eyes of his government. Their respect for him.

Their need.

And yet he'd chosen not to protect the most important man in the country?

"Like I said, I had plans of my own," he said, as if he read her confusion and understood it. "I'd intended to leave America to fight abroad. But after I saw how much you and scores of others were hurt from the fire, I knew I had to hold the Sokolovs accountable. I delayed my plans to leave. I couldn't walk away."

Instead, he'd risked his life, again and again, for her. For everyone. The realization moved her.

"Until Nikolai announced the news at his meeting tonight, President McKinley's trip here was top-secret information," he continued. "But whoever informed Nikolai committed a serious breach of confidentiality. In the mind of the military, Gina, the brothers and their informant are guilty of treason for planning to assassinate McKinley. Their behavior is inexcusable."

"Yes," she said quietly.

"It can't be tolerated."

She drew in a slow breath. "No."

"If necessary, I'll kill them."

She let it out again with a shudder. "Oh, Creed."

"Does that scare you about me?" he asked.

"I think it does."

"Don't let it." He took a step toward her. "I'd never hurt you."

A few more steps, and he was right there. In front of her. He terrified her and excited her, all at the same time.

"Nikolai will hide until the day McKinley arrives," he said. "Then he'll show up with guns blazing. By then, it could be too late."

"I hope you are wrong." She *prayed* he was.

"I'm not. That's why I have to find him. I have to keep him and the rest of his band of fanatics from assassinating our president." He reached out a long, muscled arm and knuckled her chin upward. His whiskey-colored eyes smoldered over her. "And I have to keep him from hurting you."

Her world tilted from his nearness and all he'd told her. The implications of what she'd done—the regret from it, most of all.

"Do you understand, Gina?" he asked.

"Everything you make very clear, yes."

"Hell of a predicament you've gotten yourself in, isn't it?" he murmured. His fingers, slow and sure, slid under her hair to curl around the back of her neck. "Nikolai wanting revenge on you."

His tawny gaze held hers. She couldn't look away from him if she tried. Which she didn't. "It is not a good thing, no."

"You need my protection, for sure. He'll kill you if he finds you." His glance drifted downward, unhurried and male, and settled over her mouth. "Should I exact a price from you for my services?"

Warmth pooled deep in her belly from the game he played. A strategy meant to entice a woman.

And if she wasn't very careful, he would win.

"Only if it is one I think I can pay," she said, her tone amazingly cool.

"You can. Rather well, I suspect."

The heat in his eyes was like a caress that lingered on her skin. She craved more. Only the fear of what she would lose kept her from it.

"But I am only a poor Italian immigrant," she said, her tone demure. "I have little to give, so the price, it must be one I can afford."

"I'm sure we can come up with something…beneficial for both of us."

It was all she could do to continue his ploy without giving him the advantage. "I have learned not to make the bargain until it feels right—" she laid a hand over her breast "—in my heart."

A faint layer of surprise flickered over his shadowed features. After a moment, he inclined his head, giving her the win, after all.

"I'm a patient man, Gina." He released her and stepped back, robbing her of his warmth, the awareness that came with having his body close to hers. "Get some sleep. You've had a hell of a day."

She breathed a little easier at the reprieve he'd given her. "So have you."

"I've had worse. Believe me."

A few steps took him to the table. He repacked his weapons into the saddlebag, keeping their ugliness from her. The reminder of who he was.

Her glance trailed over him. The shape of his strong body. How his shoulders tapered to a narrow waist. The sun-bronzed skin stretched lean and sinewy across his broad frame. The muscle that rippled with every movement he made.

His power.

Pure, unadulterated male, this Creed Sherman. He would know the ways to make a woman appreciate being female.

What would it be like to be kissed by him?

He turned back to her and caught her staring. He knew what she was thinking, of course. He had cleverly manipulated her so she would. He pushed his arms into his shirt, giving her a glimpse of the dark thatch of hair under each.

"Damn shame the cot's not big enough for both of us, isn't it?" he asked.

Her pulse leaped. "It is a good thing it is not."

His mouth curved. He found his bedroll and headed toward the door. "I'll be outside if you change your mind."

Giving her a final, lingering glance, he left.

She stared at the closed door.

Not only kissed, but to make love with him, too?

She sighed....

And chastised herself for thinking of him in ways that could never be. He'd told her he wouldn't be in America much longer. Days, if that. Only until President McKinley no longer needed his protection and the Sokolovs were captured.

She had to barricade her fickle heart against her attraction to him, and she forced her thoughts down a different road.

Obviously, being a mercenary had accustomed Creed to sleeping outdoors. Still, the night was chilly, and a guilty worry niggled at her while she changed her dress for her nightgown, unpinned her hair and gave her face and teeth a thorough wash. After dousing the lantern, she tugged the cot's wool blanket free from the mattress and climbed beneath it, then settled against the lumpy pad and thin pillow to get comfortable.

In the silence of the darkness, she couldn't stop thinking about him. Outside and alone.

Or that she would never forget him, no matter what happened with Nikolai.

Gina shifted to her side, and the mattress crackled. A few hours ago, she was sure she'd done the right thing confronting the Russian with a weapon in her hand, vengeful enough to use it.

Now, she wasn't so sure.

Creed had every right to be angry with her. If not for him, she'd be dead right now, felled by Nikolai's gun. If Graham hadn't asked Creed to change his plans, convinced him he was needed here in Los Angeles, he could've been anywhere in the world tonight. Wherever the War Department needed him to be.

Instead, Creed chose to stay with her. To protect her from Nikolai.

She owed him for that. Just like he said she did.

Resolutely, Gina got off the cot and pulled the blanket with her. Hardly noticing the cold against her bare feet, she flung the covering around her shoulders, opened the door and stepped outside.

Chapter Fourteen

He heard the faint creak of the hinges, and he went still.

Her feet padded closer, then halted beside him. Anticipation erupted within Creed. The satisfaction from why she'd come.

He glanced up. Starlight glinted on her hair, a halo of sable silk flowing down her shoulders. She stood over him, swathed in a blanket, slender and beautiful.

She said nothing, did nothing. He sensed her uncertainty, her unwillingness to make the first move.

Coming out had been enough. He'd take it from here.

He threw back half his blanket. Her hesitation seemed to melt, like morning dew under a hot sun. She unswathed herself from the wool and draped it over him, adding it to his own.

She came to him, then, Venus herself, unfolding her body to lie beside his. He covered her up to her neck, but already her warmth soaked into him. He raised himself up on his elbow to see her better. And waited.

A moment passed. Her head swiveled toward him. "I come because of what we talk about tonight."

His manhood stirred. So did his imagination of how her lips would taste against his. "The fee for my services."

"Yes."

"You're ready to haggle a price?" he asked, hopeful.

"Not yet."

He forced himself to be patient. "What then?"

"I come out to tell you I am sorry."

"For what?" he asked, making her say it.

She tore her glance away. "I should have listened to you and not go to the anarchist meeting."

He grunted. Cost her some pride to admit it, he knew. The apology she refused to give earlier.

"If I have a disguise as clever as yours, then Nikolai would not know me, and I would not have made the mistake." She bit her lip. "Now it is done and I cannot change it."

"We're stuck with the consequences, aren't we?" he said, not giving her an inch on it.

"Yes." She stared up at the stars. "And I cannot shoot Nikolai in cold blood."

"Things would've turned ugly if you had."

As it was, he'd barely had time to get her out of there before both of them were shot for their trouble.

"Yes," she admitted.

"You could've been thrown in jail, and then what would you have done?"

Or him, for that matter, besides go crazy with worry? Would've taken some legal wrangling to get her out again, for sure.

"I think of those things, yes."

So had he. Over and over.

She shifted to her side, rustling the blankets to face him, their bodies a feather's breadth apart. Embers stirred, deep in his groin, the desire to feel her pressed full against him. Soon, he hoped, he would.

"But now we know the brothers plan to kill the president. They are guilty of two things," she said.

He nodded. "Arson and an assassination plot. Both of them are damned serious crimes."

"I want to help you arrest them."

He refrained from explaining he was a soldier, not a policeman, and that she had no business trying to arrest anyone.

"They'll get their justice due them," he said. "As soon as possible." His mind sifted through the judicial process. The solid evidence they'd need for a jury to convict the brothers for either vindictive act. Evidence he lacked. "But not yet."

"When?" she asked.

"Right now, it's their word against ours. I'm going to make sure we have everything we need to throw them in prison a long time."

"I am a witness for you. Is that not enough?"

"No. There's more to their plotting, Gina. I have to dig deeper to find it."

He could feel her disappointment. He laid his thumb against her lips and traced their shape, one side to the other, coaxing away the pout, learning their fullness. Liking it.

"About the only good thing that happened tonight is that we gleaned some valuable information," he said. "I'll pass along every piece to Graham first thing tomorrow. He'll want to get some safeguards in place before McKinley's arrival." Creed was reluctant to open a window into the twisted minds of fanatics, but there was no help for it. Under the circumstances, she needed to understand. "Nikolai is working with someone in Washington. Someone on the inside. I have to find out who he is. McKinley won't be safe until I do."

She made a little anxious sound with her tongue. "It is my fault the brothers hide and you cannot find them in time to get this information."

"Gina." He rolled to his back and brought her with him, settling her on top of him, her body soft and supple through her nightgown. "We've discussed it enough. What happened tonight, happened. Worrying about it isn't going to change a thing."

"Maybe this is true." Her body relaxed into his. She stacked her hands on his chest, rested her chin on them.

"Main thing is you didn't get hurt. I aim to see that you don't. Ever. Same with the president."

"I know."

"So from here on out, let me take care of the Sokolovs. I'll take care of you, too."

"I do what I can to help you," she said firmly.

Like hell she would.

But he kept his mouth shut. Her stubborn pride would only fight him on it.

Then, while his mind was furthest from it, she cupped his face between her hands, lowered her head and touched her lips to his.

"Thank you," she whispered.

The kiss was over before he'd had a chance to know it was coming, much less enjoy it. She slipped off him, but Creed switched their positions and pinned her beneath him.

"You want to kiss me?" he demanded gruffly. "Then you'll do it proper. The price for my protection, remember?"

Startled laughter erupted from her. "I only want to thank you for all you must do for me and my mother, the president and for *everyone* in America. You do not like the payment I offer?"

"I'm charging you the full amount, woman. Not a penny less."

It'd been a long time since he kissed a woman. A noble and incredibly stupid decision to save his affections for Mary Catherine, since he was planning to marry her and all.

And what a waste that proved to be.

He had some catching up to do, and there wasn't a finer, more desirable woman than the one he had right here, sharing the blankets with him.

"So kiss me again," he growled. "And do it right this time."

He took her mouth before she could barter with him further, and the need in him grew needier as the kiss lengthened. A hunger that swept through him, consuming his every thought. Holding him prisoner.

Firing up his blood.

Her arms lifted, wrapped around his neck. Creed fisted his hand in her hair. Angled his head. Hardened the kiss. He craved more, the taste of her only the beginning. Her mouth opened under his, allowing him the sweet delights waiting for him inside.

Her breathing turned ragged, the passion in her building. Matching his. He craved still more, and his hand left her thick mane to splay down her back, pulling her closer, wanting to absorb her into him.

Man into woman.

Her nightgown was a thin barrier to the pleasures of her body. His palm dragged along the curve of her hip, the dip that formed her waist, upward to her breast….

And the fire raged hotter.

His fingers flexed around the full, pliant globe. Pure, delicious female, this Gina Briganti. She quivered, and a shredded little moan left her throat. Damned if she didn't have him all but aching and desperate at the sound of it.

He reached down to her thigh and grasped her gown to pull it up. Unexpectedly, her hand flew to his and stopped him before he could.

"Please," she said in a jagged whisper.

He needed a moment to drag himself out of the flaming lust...

"I cannot," she whispered and pushed against him.

...the reality of what she denied him. His head lifted, his ardor cooling fast.

"Gina," he said, his voice husky, her name suspiciously on the brink of a plea.

"The price you charge me, it is too much," she said and pressed her fingers to his mouth, stopping the kisses. An attempt to regain the composure she'd all but lost. To be strong enough for both of them.

In the shadowy moonlight, he glimpsed her lips, wet and swollen from the ravaging he'd given them. The passion and desire still on her face.

He'd expected more than he should have. Wanted more than she was ready to give. She was too vulnerable yet. Her world fragile. And what right did he have to plow his way into it?

"Okay." Reluctantly, he drew back. "Sure." His palm rested on her belly, flat and smooth, his restraint admirable as he kept himself from fondling those luscious breasts only a short trip farther up. "But you'd best know I'm going to keep on protecting you. The price won't be paid in full for a while yet. I'll wait as long as it takes until it is."

It'd been part of his success as a mercenary. Being ruthless and patient. Waiting until the precise moment. Then making his move. Taking what he wanted.

And he wanted her. She was worth waiting for. He

couldn't scare her away, not when she'd begun to mean something to him.

"It is time for me to go inside," she said and lifted the edge of the blanket to rise.

He nudged it back down again. "Stay with me, Gina."

"Sleep with you?" She appeared surprised.

"Yes."

"Nothing else?"

"I swear it."

Her lips softened knowingly. "I do not think you will let me do such a thing."

"Try me. I'm lonely out here."

She laughed again, and something moved inside his chest, something deep and warm. Her amusement faded, and she touched his cheek gently. "I think I will be lonely on the cot, too. So I will stay with you. But only if you do not—how do you say?—charge me too much."

He grinned like an idiot at his victory. "Fair enough."

She rolled over, then, as easy as that, wiggled a bit backward, fitting her bottom casually to his groin, like it was meant to be there.

He pulled her closer. The scent of her hair surrounded him. The warmth of her body. The prospect of being with her the whole night through, especially.

For now, it was enough.

Creed sipped his coffee in the shade of the line shack and watched her sleep. The morning sun kept her relaxed and comfortable under the blankets without him.

She was a snuggler, for sure. A female tangle of arms and legs. She was born to spend her nights with a man. Curl herself around him without even knowing she did. Give him pleasure from it, too.

Contentment.

He stared down into his brew. Trouble was, he couldn't feel content about anything right now, including a woman. Gina. Time was ticking. Once the Sokolovs were captured, he'd be heading off America's shores. South, most likely. It was inevitable he'd have to leave her behind.

But it was going to be hard.

Real hard.

He couldn't give her anything more than a brief, passionate affair. A lusty roll in the sheets. Hadn't the desire he barely held in check last night proved he'd wanted that very thing?

He would've taken her if she'd let him.

Good thing she hadn't. She would've only been hurt by him in the end.

After the horrors of the past days, she deserved happiness and stability in her life with a man she could depend on to be right beside her. Every day. And night. Forever.

It wouldn't be him.

He was a soldier. He had to leave, to fight, no matter how much he'd miss her. He *wanted* to go. It was who he was.

So why did he feel like a part of himself would stay behind with her?

Grimly, he shook off the melancholy. Wasn't like him to feel like this. He reminded himself he had a job to do, the next step of it being a ride into Los Angeles. And the morning had already crept too far past dawn.

Determined to be more focused on the battle he had to fight, he strode into the shack and refilled his cup. He did the same with a second and brought them both outside.

He hunkered beside Gina, making sure his shadow shielded her. He'd learned she was slow to start her day without coffee to get her going first. Waking to bright sun wouldn't make it any easier.

She stirred, then rolled away from him, covering her face with the blanket. His mouth curved; he set one of the cups down, reached over and pulled the blanket back down again.

"Hey, Gina," he said.

One dark-lashed eye peeped at him. "You are up already?"

Her voice sounded husky, slumberous. Stirred his blood hearing it. Bothered him, too, that another man someday would have the privilege of hearing her like this every morning of his life.

"For a while now. Here."

She glanced at the brew, sat up, arranged the blanket over her lap. He handed her the cup.

"Thank you," she murmured and sipped.

"You're welcome."

His gaze riveted on her. The way she looked all tousled from sleep.

She drew her knees up and tilted her face into the sun. Her expression turned so pensive, Creed had to find out why.

"What do you see up there?" he asked.

"I see the new day." She pulled her gaze back to him. "When I first open my eyes, it is there. On my skin."

He recalled her dreary apartment, the lone front window she valued so much. He thought, too, of how dark her bedroom at the back would always be without one. And how he'd always taken something as simple, as basic, as a bright morning sun for granted all his life.

"Have you never slept outside?" he asked.

Her gaze held his, soft and alluring. "Not with a man before."

A peculiar satisfaction settled over him at that. "Ever?"

"A few times, yes, when I am a young girl. In my Aunt Rosa's yard in Sicily." She smiled at the memory. "My cousins and I think it is an adventure."

An adventure. So many times for Creed, it'd been a necessity, when he'd been on the move, hunting for an enemy. Or on the run from one.

Her smile faded. She stared into the black liquid in her cup. "I had another *visione* last night, Creed."

"Did you?" he asked, curious in spite of himself.

"Again, my mother is in a dark place. I cannot see her face, but I know she is there. I hear her crying, and my heart, it breaks. She tells me she is afraid for me. She tells me again of the evil." Gina lifted the cup to her lips but didn't drink. "I believe she warns me about Nikolai. And because she helps me believe this, I know she is alive."

Creed fell silent. Real easy for her to get caught up in her visions and interpret them against what was happening in her life. Made sense she'd think the evil applied to the Russian brothers, too. They were trouble all right.

If nothing else, the dreams gave her comfort in a peculiar sort of way. They helped her get through the worry about her mother, and who was he to tell her anything different?

She seemed to pull herself from her reverie, and her brows furrowed. "What day is it? Monday?"

"Yes."

"It is strange I am not at the factory. Every Monday, I am there."

"Yes." Given her routine existence, he knew she would have been.

Her expression grew troubled. "I must go back into the city." She tossed aside the blanket, careful not to spill her coffee. "I should have been ready to go there by now."

Creed braced himself. "I want you to stay out here."

A tempest brewed in the depths of her eyes. "No."

"It's not safe for you to go back."

She made a negating gesture. "Maybe my mother is found by now. Maybe there is word about her."

"If there is, I'll hear it. And I'll tell you."

"What? You?" She stood, her coffee forgotten, her nightgown rumpled, her dismay building. "You go into the city, and you do not want to take me with you?"

"That's right."

Aghast, she pressed a hand to her breast. "I am her daughter. I should be there."

"Under different circumstances, yes."

"Then I go without you."

"Damn it, Gina!" He tossed aside his coffee and stood, too.

"I should be keeping vigil for her. Serafina, Sebastian, they will all be shocked I am here with you instead."

"Well, they don't have a bunch of lunatics after them, do they? Have you forgotten what happened last night? Every man who was in that warehouse office knows your name. They know you're a seamstress from Premier. And you know they're plotting to assassinate the president. You think any of them will have any trouble tracking you down to keep you from talking?"

Her teeth sank into her bottom lip.

"What good would you be to your mother dead?" he persisted, his tone quieter but no less fierce.

"I do not want to stay here and do nothing. Maybe she needs me somewhere."

He stepped toward her, hooked an arm around her neck and pulled her roughly to him. "I know. But you'll just have to trust me to do what I can for you alone."

Her arms curled around his waist and to his back; her forehead dropped to his chest. "How long will you be gone?"

"The afternoon. No later." He hoped.

"You will talk to Graham? Tell him what we know?"

"Yes. First thing. I'll go to the infirmary to see if there's news about your mother right after. I promise."

For a long moment, she didn't say anything, taking the time she needed to convince herself. "Then I hold your promise in my heart." She pushed away and squared her shoulders. "I can make a soup for us while you are gone."

"Good." He slid a finger under her chin, tilted it up slightly, making sure he had her full attention. "But if you take off after me like you did last night, I swear I'll find you again, and you'll be damn sorry when I do. You hear me?"

She rolled her eyes. "How can I not? You almost shout at me."

He grunted. She had no idea what he could do. He'd track her down or die trying.

He headed toward the palomino, already saddled and ready to ride. He mounted up, but his worry lay in the bay, tethered in the lean-to. Free for the taking.

And he gritted his teeth with the hope Gina and the horse were still there when he came back.

Chapter Fifteen

It didn't take Gina long to freshen up, change back into her good Sunday dress and tidy up the line shack. After a light breakfast of bread and canned peaches, the day stretched ahead of her with little to do but wait for Creed to return, and the hours seemed like forever.

She was unaccustomed to having so much idle time. Always, it was important to work, all day every day, week after week, to make the money she needed.

And to save for her dream. The most important thing of all.

Had it all been for nothing?

Again, the fears came and churned in her stomach. The haunting knowledge of the deplorable life she'd have without Mama and their menial jobs at the factory. Would it be worth living?

Her gaze snagged on her sketches, lying neatly on the cot. They were all she had to keep herself from drowning in worry and despair, and tendrils of hope, of renewed determination, budded inside her. She clung to the hope and refused to let go. Until she found her mother again, as her *visione* promised, her designs would keep her from going crazy.

She must keep her dream alive. She couldn't give up, not now when she needed more than ever before to be strong, focused, and, resolutely, she took her sketches and went outside.

She settled herself on the blanket still spread on the grass and busied herself with putting the finishing touches on her newest design, an elaborate tea gown in *la maison Rouff* style, newly popular in Paris.

It was Gina's favorite. She envisioned it made of the most expensive of fabrics, peau de soie perhaps, in a shade of old-rose and brocaded with delicate pink and blue flowers. The sleeves, luxuriously shirred, fuller at the shoulders, and the skirt split to boast of an apron of crisp pink mousseline de soie. She penciled in a large bow on the left waist, which would be in blue, trailing the ends clear to the skirt's hems.

Elegant. Glorious.

A woman couldn't help but feel beautiful wearing such a creation, she mused, darkening the edges of a row of small ruffles with the tip of her pencil, the black satin which would be sewn on as a finishing touch. Regal and pampered, too.

Slowly, her coloring strokes halted. She studied the design again, the extravagance of it.

Creed had made her feel beautiful when she wore something not nearly as special—the dress she wore now. Her navy one with its simple little flowers.

The dress of a seamstress, that was all.

She remembered the look in his tawny-brown eyes when he first saw her in it, as she rushed to get ready for Mass. They had smoldered, warmed her blood like hot whiskey, and she had known.

For him, an expensive tea gown didn't matter.

Gina's spine straightened. For her, though, it did. The gown would make her someone special. No longer a poor Italian immigrant, but a success with her designs in her very own dress shop. With them, in time, she would profit in America.

She refused to be poor forever. Her pencil resumed its shading with more purpose, but her mind continued to think of him, and soon, her pencil slowed again.

Not only did he warm her blood with his eyes, he warmed her with his kisses, too.

Her fingers touched her lips, and a fluttering began, deep in her belly. Last night, his mouth had been both rough and gentle. Thorough and intoxicating. A man's passion, meant to seduce a woman.

He had almost succeeded.

How she'd managed to stop him, she didn't know. But she couldn't allow him to sweep her away, to steal her heart and body, only to carelessly toss her aside when he was through.

In that, she must be strong. He lived the exciting, dangerous life of a soldier of the world. A mercenary. He claimed to want to retire, but how could he ever be happy settling down in one place?

And certainly not with a boring factory worker, like her.

He would never stay. This she knew for sure. His government, the War Department he revered, needed him too much.

Her concentration lost, she set aside her pencil and sketch with a bemused sigh. Compelled by an inner need to be soothed by the peace of the land around her, she rested her chin on her knees.

Her gaze dallied along the horizon. The Santa Monica Mountains towered over the city with their majestic tips whitened from snow. Lower, the chaparral with its pines and brushes. At their foot, the sprawling rangeland of the Sherman ranch, alive with its oak woodlands and range grasses and wildlife, too many for Gina to name. All of it, open and free.

With not a single dingy tenement in sight.

How easy it would be to live here. To thrive and be happy. How could Creed want to leave such a place behind? His home, cut out from his life. Did he not know how fortunate he was to have such a legacy?

She couldn't understand, and the sadness swept through her. She had nothing so valuable, not since she left Sicily, and why should it bother her what he had and didn't want?

She stood up. She had to stop these restless thoughts. The self-pity. It wasn't up to her to decide what Creed should want and not want, and it was only because he left her alone with so much time on her hands that she tortured herself from thinking about it.

She strode into the shack. Better to busy herself with the Stracciatella, the simple soup of her people, and one Mama had made many times. Gina chopped the last of the veal cutlets into chunks and added them to the broth. The soup would be a hearty lunch for them.

And making it would keep her from thinking so much.

She had just finished spooning semolina into an egg and parmesan cheese mixture when she heard the leisurely staccato of a horse's hooves. Her head lifted in surprise.

Creed had returned already?

Quickly, she beat the thickening mixture until it was the right consistency, then stirred the mix into the boiling broth. All the while, her pulse sang with anticipation from seeing him again, hopefully with news about her mother.

Leaving the pot simmering, she hurried to the shaving

mirror he'd left on the table. The glass showed her cheeks flushed from the stove's fire, and she fanned them as best she could. A quick check of her hair showed her pins intact, at least. She rushed to the door and flung it open.

But it wasn't Creed's palomino outside, reins dragging. And it wasn't him striding in her direction, either, with a puzzled stare at the blankets and sketches she'd left on the ground.

Instead, a cowboy, not yet twenty, dressed in dusty Levi's and a beige shirt, bandanna and Stetson, with a face tanned from the wind and sun.

She froze in her tracks. "Oh!"

His stare whipped toward her. He took a startled step backward. And yanked off his hat, crushing it against his chest.

"Ma'am?" he choked.

He looked so surprised to see her, instant guilt surged through Gina for being there, even though Creed had assured her she could.

"I am sorry. My name is Gina Briganti," she said, lest the young man think she had something to hide. Immediately, she extended her hand.

He glanced down at it, then hastily reached out and clasped her fingers, revealing his own to be rough and callused.

"Marcus Sherman, ma'am," he said, releasing her. "Pardon me for acting like my talk-box is busted. I've just never seen a woman out here before is all."

She blinked. "Your name is Sherman?"

It was her turn to stare. She could see it now. The resemblance. The same almond-colored eyes. The same hair of burnished gold. The same angular jaw and strong chin.

Though he wasn't the same size, she decided, remembering the breadth of Creed's shoulders and his tall, lean build. And this man didn't possess Creed's impression of confidence, hard-won from the experiences in his life, the danger of fighting America's enemies.

And maybe Marcus never would. But the similarities were there. From the sire they shared.

"You are his brother," she breathed, amazed.

He stiffened. "Creed?" His glance shot toward the lean-to, her horse tethered there, the unfamiliarity of it. "He brought you out here?"

The tension in his tone made her uneasy again.

"Yes," she said carefully.

His lip curled. "Well, he sure as blazes works fast, don't he?"

"What?" she asked, taken aback.

"And now he's drowning his sorrows in you."

She didn't understand why he sounded so resentful. "We come because he wants to keep me safe."

"I'll bet he did."

"It is true!"

"You're a right pretty piece of calico. He's just havin' a little fun, that's all." He snorted in derision. "Ma'am, you can have him."

He kicked the ground in disgust, spun on his boot heel and headed back toward his horse.

Gina realized she'd just been insulted. Creed, too, and she sucked in an indignant breath. A few quick steps planted her between Marcus and his horse. She set her hands on her hips and glared.

"Why do you talk of him like this?" she demanded. "You do not understand his reasons."

"I've known him a hell of a lot longer than you have, ma'am. I understand plenty."

He attempted to step past her, but she would have none

of it. Creed didn't have the opportunity to explain, and so she must, for both their sakes.

"You will listen to me to learn the truth from the beginning," she snapped. "I already tell you I am Gina Briganti. I work in the city, at the Premier Shirtwaist Company factory. I am a seamstress there. There is a fire, and your brother saves my life. I think you did not know that, eh?"

A moment passed. His expression shifted. "No. News is slow sometimes—"

His excuses did not matter.

"I see the man who starts it," she grated. "He commits arson. Creed brings me here because the man, he tries to kill me."

Color drained from the tanned cheeks. "Kill you?"

"And I tell you more." Her chin lifted, the news she was about to impart. "This man, he wants terrible things to happen to the American people. But mostly to the president."

Marcus's jaw dropped. "McKinley?"

Her eyes narrowed. "It scares Creed very much. He does everything he can to protect him. Like he protects me."

Marcus nodded, but only once, as if he began to comprehend.

"So he's off fighting another of his wars." He spoke with some annoyance, but not so much as before. "What's he thinking? That he's a one-man army or something? Has he gone to the police?"

Gina shook her head. To all his questions.

Marcus tightened his mouth. The disapproval he didn't say, but Gina could hear as plainly as if he did.

This rift between them troubled her. They were brothers. Family. Had her being here made it worse?

There was little she could do to make things right, but she had one small attempt left.

"Come inside," she said, sweeping past him. "There is something you must see."

His hesitant glance slid toward the shack. "What is it?"

"Come." Giving him an impatient gesture to follow, she went inside.

In a few moments, he joined her. She stood next to the table; Creed's saddlebag still lay on top. Wordlessly, she removed the assortment of weapons inside and laid them all out, side by side, to show Marcus the man Creed was.

But the look on his face said he already knew.

Somber, he trailed his fingers over the rifle, the derringer, the knives. He picked up the brass knuckles and nickeled handcuffs, then examined them, only to frown and set them down again. He had to read the label on the container of spirit gum to discover its use, to know that it was a deceptively crucial part of the disguise Creed was able to create. And finally, the disguise itself, the woolly mass of beard and brows lying in a heap.

"He is a master at what he does," Gina said softly.

Marcus's throat worked. "Reckon so."

"Maybe now you respect your brother a little more, eh?"

He raked a hand through his hair. "He was gone a hell of a long time, ma'am. He never told us what he did. His work. That it—"

He drew in a long breath. And Gina understood.

"Means so much to him that he will die so you—all of us—have freedom," she finished firmly.

"Well, why didn't he say something?" he demanded. "It would've made things easier between us if we knew."

"And then you worry for him. Or maybe praise him." She shook her head slowly. "I do not think he wants that from anyone."

Marcus's hand tightened on the brim of his Stetson. "I reckon not."

"An honorable man, your brother. There are not many like him." This she had seen for herself, again and again.

Marcus angled his head away, keeping from her his struggle to shed the resentment too long inside him.

Gina marveled that he wanted to. And tried. She knew, then, she had done all she could.

Her head cocked in consideration. "Now, maybe we can be friends, eh?"

He looked at her with uncertainty. "I think I'd like that, ma'am."

She thought of Creed, that he'd be back soon. "I have hot soup. We will have lunch."

Marcus's uncertainty faded with his smile.

"I'd like that, too," he said.

Nikolai rode toward the log bathhouse, nestled in the sprawling hills outside Los Angeles. Anticipation curled through him. There wasn't a finer place in America than the hot mineral springs enclosed within.

In the soothing waters, he could forget the despair in the city. From their serenity, he could immerse himself in his dream, plan the many ways of revolution. And he could nurture his hate.

At first, he came for Alex, so often plagued by the pain in his stomach and in his bones. The bubbling waters provided relief from the ulcers he'd battled most of his life. They helped him breathe, to move as free as a child, and Nikolai marveled at their healing magic.

But today, he came for himself. For the fire in his thigh.

He hadn't expected to see her at one of his meetings. The beautiful Gina Briganti. Her courage had astounded him. Her daring infuriated him. Driven by her passion and ideals, she had defied him in front of everyone.

Then, she shot him.

His lust stirred. A woman of valor. A shining example for the rest of his comrades on how to rise up from the masses.

And act.

He might've hated her for what she'd done if it hadn't been an accident, an unfortunate result of the panic of the spineless men who'd run away from their own wild imaginings.

A spy for the police, they said.

He would've known if she was. For many weeks, he watched her in the shirtwaist factory. Each time, he saw only a dutiful daughter and a hard worker—one of Silverstein's best.

She could be one of Nikolai's as well.

He had only to convince her of the merits of anarchism. Teach her to be strong against the crush of authority and their hypocrisies. With her intelligence, her impassioned way of speaking, and most of all, her bravery, she would be his very own Emma Goldman.

Together, they could accomplish amazing things. The reform so necessary in America.

The distinct smell of sulfur roused him from his fantasies. Reminded him he'd come here to be strong again. That the infection festering in his thigh must be healed.

It had been up to him to remove the bullet last night. He didn't dare go to the Los Angeles Infirmary, not for the money it'd cost or the suspicions it'd raise. And Alex couldn't do the surgery for him. He'd paled and clutched his stomach at the idea of it.

So Nikolai downed the last of his vodka and managed it on his own, though not without great damage to the muscle inside. He couldn't sleep from the pain afterward, and this morning, the raw, angry flesh told him he must sit in the magic waters for a while.

He pulled up in front of the bathhouse but didn't dismount. He scrutinized the rangeland around him, more acres than he could count. All of it, owned by one man.

Gus Sherman.

Nikolai had taken care to ask questions before they began using the waters. He'd learned Sherman was a powerful and wealthy cattleman, and his greed filled Nikolai with contempt. The rancher had more land than he could ever use, yet thousands lived crowded lives in dingy tenements in the city, many of them children who craved fresh air and the brightness of the sun.

Nikolai and Alex helped themselves to the bathhouse whenever they wanted. In this small way, Gus Sherman would share his riches with the poor and downtrodden.

Nikolai smirked at the thought, but the ache in his thigh reminded him his need was real. The solitude of the morning assured him he was completely alone. Today, not even Alex was with him. Nikolai was expecting a letter from Washington and had sent him into the city to wait for it.

Nikolai dismounted awkwardly, and his teeth clenched from the effort. After the pain subsided, he untied his knapsack from the saddle and limped toward the structure.

The dim interior provided a safe, private haven. Flat rocks encircled the gurgling spring, their surfaces moist, like the air. Buffalo skins covered the ground, offering protection for bare feet. He stripped naked and delved into the knapsack for a towel.

His fingers closed around her dark fringed scarf instead.

The beautiful Gina Briganti had left it behind in her haste to escape the chaos of his meeting, but Nikolai found it, forgotten between the chairs.

His eyes closed. He pressed the soft *babushka* to his nose and inhaled deeply, his mind alive with the smell of her hair within the delicate threads. The fabric draped around his wrist and down his arm, inciting his senses; he trailed the cloth around his neck, floated it over his face and across his head, as if the scarf were Gina herself, her body an undulating wave of sensuality and motion, her desire only to pleasure him.

Love him.

His eyes opened, and the illusion shattered.

Twice, she had escaped him.

With the help of the men who protected her.

Suddenly furious, Nikolai tossed aside the *babushka*. He stepped into the warm, swirling waters, immersed himself in their depths. Something in his memory nagged him. Persistent and foreboding.

The first time, at her apartment. The tall American, then. The one who swaggered with authority. And the second, at Nikolai's meeting, this one bearded and poor.

Each had pounced to defend her. Each fierce and dangerous, like the powerful tiger in Siberia.

But both different.

Or were they?

Chapter Sixteen

Creed hunkered in the grass and chewed absently on a slender stem of foxtail. The park across from Premier, the one where he'd taken Gina to escape the horrific fire, was a good place to meet Graham. Except for a few children playing ball at the far end, there was no one else around to hear what Creed had to report.

He'd decided leaving a message with Collette was the most efficient way to contact the Secret Service agent. She recognized Creed's urgency and promised she'd send word to her brother; Creed had trusted that she would, and Graham was due any minute.

Creed used the time in between to make a few inquiries. The Los Angeles Infirmary first, in hopes of information on Louisa Briganti, but the tired-looking nursing nuns could offer nothing, claiming she was still listed as missing.

It troubled him they were no closer to finding her. His gaze tarried over the deserted, soot-blackened factory building across the street. Where could she be, if not the infirmary?

Puzzled, he shook his head. While there, he'd taken the opportunity to ask about Nikolai. The Russian had been wounded last night. Might be he needed medical attention, and with the infirmary located closest to the abandoned warehouse, he might have gone there. But no one with an injury like his had been registered.

Creed went next to the police station, his mind on the factory bookkeeper's list of names. A few discreet questions yielded the Sokolovs' apartment address. A visit *there* revealed nothing from the landlord except that the brothers hadn't been seen since several days hence. The day of the fire, to be exact. Creed had gone a step further, padded the landlord's palm, and had himself a good look around their rooms. The search produced nothing, except that they'd all but packed up and left.

Creed rubbed his hand over his face in frustration. Hours of work, and nothing to show for it. Added to that, it was late. He'd already missed making it back for lunch with Gina.

He spied Graham striding toward him, dressed in his dark suit and shiny shoes, as always. Relieved the man was punctual, Creed tossed aside the foxtail and stood to meet him.

Graham drew closer, his arm extended. "When Collette said you needed to talk to me, I figured it must be important."

They shook hands.

"It is," Creed said. "I infiltrated an anarchist meeting last night. Learned some solid intelligence on the plot to assassinate McKinley. The Sokolovs are spearheading a plan, at least here in Los Angeles."

"Nikolai and Alex. The brothers you told me about. Your information fits with what we've learned so far," Graham said grimly.

"The news of the president's impending arrival has leaked," he added. "They know he's coming. And how. They just don't know when."

Stunned, the agent stared at him. "The news has been top secret. I only received word myself yesterday. And it's already being distributed?"

"To a bunch of crazy zealots. They're planning to meet him at the train station with bells on."

Graham paled and reached into his pocket for paper and pen. "I'll arrange to have a detail of agents ready."

"You could arrange a dozen of them, and they wouldn't be enough," Creed said, suddenly impatient with the man's thinking.

"Sir?"

"It only takes one bomb to kill the president and scores of people besides. A detail of agents won't do a damn bit of good."

"Yes, sir." But Graham appeared unsure.

"The one thing in our favor is the Sokolovs don't know when he's coming. We have to keep that information confidential as long as possible." His mouth tightened. "In other words, we have to find the source of the leak."

"Our intelligence efforts are our best. But it takes time to counter espionage such as this."

"Time we don't have."

"I'm afraid so, sir."

"I have a theory." Creed had torn apart the possibility, piece by piece. In the end, he'd become convinced. "There's a spy in the War Department. Or the Secret Service. Maybe both."

Graham blanched.

"I'm certain General Carson recognizes the threat," Creed continued. "That's why he ordered you to contact me. Someone with access to the White House has inside information to the president's whereabouts, and he's passing it along to the enemy." His mouth tightened. "The Sokolovs."

"I hope you're wrong, sir."

"I'm not. There's no other explanation."

Graham drew himself up. "Then we must proceed as such."

"Exactly."

"What's next?"

Creed reached inside his pocket, withdrew a folded letter. "Send this wire to Jeb Carson at the War Department in Washington. Pull some strings if you have to. I want it delivered within the hour." He squinted an eye along the city's horizon. "It's written in code. Only Jeb will know how to decipher it. He'll relay my message to the general."

Graham tucked the missive into an inside pocket of his suit coat, his actions protective, as if the words were priceless gold. "Consider it done."

"In the meantime, I'll do what I can to track down the Sokolovs." Since the matter was top secret, he couldn't risk informing the police. "The brothers are the spy's contact. It's imperative that communication between them is cut off."

Looking overwhelmed from it all, Graham blew out a breath. "Anything else I can do, sir?"

"As a matter of fact, there is." He lifted his hat, threaded a hand through his hair. His inability to locate Gina's mother was as much a concern as the espionage. For Gina, maybe more so, and time was against them both. "Check the surrounding infirmaries to see if Louisa Briganti was brought in. Hell, check all of them in the city."

He had to extend the boundaries of their search beyond the general area of the shirtwaist factory. There was no other answer for it, not after the checking and rechecking they'd already done.

"And Miss Briganti, sir?"

An instant image of her formed in his mind. How she

looked last night, sheathed in silvery starlight. An urgency went through him, a longing to be with her again.

"I've put her in hiding," he said finally. "On my father's ranch. She's safe, for the time being."

"Of course. You would see that she was. Very good, sir."

As if they both had the same thought, their work waiting for them, they quickly shook hands and parted.

Creed headed toward the palomino, his steps lengthening as he drew nearer, his need to see Gina consuming him. Now that he was ready to head back, he couldn't get there soon enough.

He made it a fast ride out of town and onto Sherman land, but as he approached the West Camp's line shack, the sheer quiet of the place shot dread up his spine.

If she was here, she would've heard him ride up. Come out to meet him.

But she didn't.

Their blankets were still outside, her precious sketches on top, their edges fluttering in the breeze. The peculiarity of the sight gnawed at him. Wasn't like her to be careless with her designs, and she sure as hell wouldn't leave them behind.

Voluntarily.

He dismounted, unshucked a revolver, and went inside. His gaze clawed the perimeter of the shack, his senses fine-strung to what he'd find. His weapons, each accounted for, lying on the cot. Her soup still hot on the stove, a plate holding a few slices of bread, and two tin bowls with remnants of broth inside on the tabletop.

She'd been with someone. Who?

And where was she now?

He bolted outside. The tracks in the dirt, the trampled grass, told him that a lone rider had been here not long since. His dread deepening, his gaze lifted to the crude lean-to, and his worst fear came true.

Gina's horse was gone.

He headed toward the palomino with a curse, the vow strong within him to search the far corners of Sherman rangeland until he found her, but the muted sound of voices told him he didn't have to go far.

By the time he could figure where they were, somewhere behind the shack and getting closer, Creed was mad enough to peel a rattlesnake. He'd given Gina strict orders to stay put. What if her whereabouts got back to the Sokolovs somehow?

He waited. Refused to go to her first. He kept his Smith and Wesson cocked, just in case, but his curiosity raged. The line shack's location couldn't have been more remote. Who would have found her all the way out here?

She appeared, then, side by side with another rider. In no hurry. Oblivious to Creed's presence. The man kept her engrossed with their talk, and at first, only their profiles were discernible.

Until they realized he was there.

They pulled up in surprise. And Creed recognized Markie.

The last person he wanted to see, with the sole exception of the Old Man himself.

"You are back!" Gina exclaimed.

He dragged his gaze to her. She looked feminine sitting there on the horse. Sophisticated, too, with her hat and Sunday dress. Their outing had colored her cheeks fresh-air pink and sparkled her eyes like black diamonds. Gotten rid of some of her worry, too. Creed had never seen her so relaxed.

No wonder Markie couldn't keep from staring at her like a pie-eyed greenhorn. And why did it rile Creed that he did?

"I told you to stay here, Gina," he growled, sheathing the revolver.

Her surprise shifted to wary defensiveness. "You tell me not to follow you. I do not follow."

"You up and left without a care. Didn't even bother to arm yourself, did you?"

"We didn't go far, Creed," Markie said. "Quit yelling at her."

His teeth gritted. He wasn't yelling. Only on the brink of it.

"What are you doing here?" he snarled.

Markie leaned forward on the saddle horn. He looked relaxed, too. Unruffled by Creed's lack of hospitality.

"Just happened to be taking my turn checking fence, that's all," he said. "Saw smoke coming from the shack's chimney. Decided I'd have a look-see."

"We do not expect to find each other," Gina concurred. "But it is nice that we do. Did you learn any news about my mother?"

"No, but I've got Graham checking on it," he said, shifting the conversation's gears with her.

"There is nothing? Again?"

She appeared crestfallen, and it tugged at him hard.

"He'll check every hospital in the city. We're doing everything we can." He realized how trite the words sounded, but he meant each one.

Her throat worked, and she squared her shoulders, the strength he admired about her. "Yes. This I know."

"Gina told me you've got a hell of a fight on your hands," Markie said, shifting the conversation again.

Creed's attention swung back to him. That riled, too. Gina confiding in him. His kid brother knowing, seeing the unpleasantness of war, even one brewing right here in America.

Beginning from his early days at West Point, it'd been that way for Creed, a curious kind of protectiveness of his family. Shielding them from what he did. Killing and deceiving. The ruthless life he lived for six long years to defend them from the enemy.

"She did, did she?" he demanded.

"I want him to know," Gina said. "It is important. Too long, you are gone, and your family does not understand why."

"If I'd wanted them involved, I would've done it by now," he bit out.

"Don't blame her, Creed," Markie said. "I kept flapping my jaws at her, asking questions. A whole string of 'em."

Creed's attention bounced between the pair, both of them looking down at him from their horses, sides drawn. Made him feel like he was on the losing one.

"Bring her out to the main house," Markie said quietly. "She'll be safer there."

Creed stiffened. Run to the Old Man for help? Face Mary Catherine again? "No."

His brother sat back in disgust. "That pride of yours might just get her killed, then, and you along with her."

"Don't recall asking your opinion, Markie."

"Well, I'm giving it. This time, your fight's close to home. No shame in going back if you need to."

Creed gritted his teeth. He'd left there once, twice, and he refused to return. Not for a good long while, and sure as hell not now, when going would put the whole outfit in danger.

"What do you expect her to do out here, anyway?" Markie persisted. "No one's around for miles. You'll just hide her away while you go off to fight your little war? You may as well dig her a hole and cover her up in it."

"She's my problem. Not yours, damn it. And it's not a little war. What would *you* know of fighting one?"

"Stop!" Gina flung her hands up in exasperation. "You argue like schoolboys! Both of you, stubborn bulls!"

"He's as bullheaded as they come, for sure. Always was, as I recall." A muscle twitched in Markie's tanned cheek, the annoyance he held in check. He took up his reins and touched a finger to his hat. "I'll be moving along. It's been a real pleasure, Gina. You're a fine woman. I'd like to see you again soon, if that's all right."

"Thank you, Marcus. I would like that, too."

He gave her a quick nod of acknowledgement before his glance turned back to Creed.

"You know where to find us when you smarten up," he said.

With that, he turned his mount and rode off.

Creed stood stock still and watched him go.

His brother had some starch in him, for sure. Something he never had when he was twelve. It unsettled Creed how much of a man he'd become. No longer afraid to stand up and speak his mind.

And Creed had missed every bit of it. Six years' worth of growing up. Learning starch. Gone.

Gina dismounted. "You are not very nice to him."

Creed grunted.

"He wants to help us, but you spit in his face." She strolled to the blankets, picked up her sketches.

"The hell I did."

"He admires you, and that is how you treat him."

The sting of her scolding rolled through Creed. He tried hard to be unaffected by it. And failed.

"A high and mighty soldier you are, eh?" she taunted. "Too important for your family?"

"Gina," he grated.

She rolled the blanket into a tight ball, held it beneath her arm and stood stiff before him.

"And then you say *I* am a problem to you." She sniffed. "I do not want to be your *problem,* so I will go back to my apartment."

His eye narrowed at her threat. Did she really believe he'd let her go? After all that had happened between them?

Besides, how could he explain he'd tangled horns with his father almost from the time he'd been able to think for himself, that too many hurts and disappointments had wrenched them apart, taking Markie with them? Maybe forever?

And throw a woman, Mary Catherine, into the mix...

"I didn't mean it the way it sounded," he said, scrambling to save himself. "You know I didn't."

Her wounded silence challenged him to try harder, a warning he was sinking fast if he didn't.

"I'll protect you the best way I can under the circumstances," he continued. "I *want* to."

"So does Marcus."

She headed toward the line shack. Creed clenched his jaw and caught her arm before she could pass him. If she thought she could goad him into a little jealousy, she'd damn well succeeded.

"You two were acting mighty friendly for having just met," he rumbled. "First-name basis. Going riding together. Guess he knows a pretty face when he sees one, doesn't he?"

Eyes flashing, she yanked free. "I feed him lunch because you are late. We talk. He wants to show me a little bit of the Sherman land. We talk some more. That is all!"

If he'd taken the time to think about it, Creed would've known as much. But the accusation tumbled from his tongue without his having the sense to keep from saying so.

"He is a good man, Creed," she said with more calm.

"He loves his home, his family. And he loves you. But you are too much like a mule to believe it."

She swung from him, then, with a flaring of her hems, and went inside, leaving him to fend for himself against a barrage of guilt from his own stupidity.

Chapter Seventeen

Gina knew it was only from Creed's need to make amends that he offered her a bath in the hot mineral springs.

Well, it worked.

Targeting her feminine side to soothe her annoyance with him had been a clever strategy. What woman would refuse such a luxury? And in the healthful waters, no less?

She could hardly wait to get there. A few miles, he'd said. Not far. A nice ride, with many things to see along the way.

He was right about that, too.

His knowledge of the plants and wildlife which roamed free on his father's land captivated her. The gray brush rabbits who fed on green clover; the small kit fox who watched them from his burrow; the condor gliding high in the California sky, graceful and majestic. The wildflowers and grasses that grew; the sheep and cattle grazing in the distance. The fields of wheat...

Proudly, he showed her all these things.

This place where he'd grown up was still a part of him. He didn't say so, but Gina knew it from the way his gaze soaked everything in, as if he were hungry to see it again.

Yet as they crested a hill and spotted a log structure snuggled in the belly of the valley, he drew up and frowned in puzzlement. He twisted in the saddle and swept his glance around him, a recheck of his bearings.

"What is it?" asked Gina.

"The hot spring should be down there. But I don't recall the shelter."

"It is not the bathhouse?"

He studied the place for a long moment. "He must've built it for her."

"Who?" she asked.

"My father. For my mother."

Gina returned her gaze there, too. She couldn't imagine having her own mineral spring bath, even one located by itself in the hills. "How fortunate she is."

"Was." He grew somber and resumed their ride. "She got sick. Living out here with the wind and dust made it hard for her to breathe some days. Her lungs weren't strong enough. So he'd bring her out here as often as he could." He squinted into the big blue sky. "She died a couple of years ago. At least, that's what they told me when I got back."

Gina's heart dipped in dismay. "Oh, Creed. I am sorry."

Their eyes met, and she read the pain of his regret that he hadn't been there with his mother when she would've needed him most. Being deprived of the opportunity to say goodbye would be a loss he'd feel all his life.

"If Mama dies, I cannot bear it." She refused to think of the possibility. By not thinking of it, she didn't go so crazy.

"You'll have her back," he said quietly. "It can't be much longer."

Gina clung to the memory of her *visiones*. The police, the nursing nuns at the infirmary, Graham…so many knew Louisa Briganti was missing. With their help, she would be found.

"Wherever she is, she'd want you to enjoy your bath, wouldn't she?" Creed's tone turned to a gentle tease.

Gina smiled. "I think the bath can make her a little envious, too."

They pulled up in front of the rectangular structure, and their conversation ended. Neatly made of logs, the place contained an open doorway at one end which invited entrance, yet the rest of the enclosure provided plenty of privacy. At the top, a skylight with a roof; open sides allowed illumination within. The odor of sulfur hovered in the air.

"Pa discovered this mineral spring when I just a kid." Creed made no move to dismount; his memories kept him in the saddle. "It's a runoff from the Santa Monica Mountains. The waters run below the ground, a couple thousand feet deep. They flow for miles, and along the way, they pick up the precious minerals in the earth. The waters absorb its heat, too. At some point, probably hundreds of years ago, cracks formed in the rocks beneath, and the water pushed up to form springs like this one."

The awe-inspiring force of nature paralleled that of the springs in Sicily. In her country's case, however, it'd been the volcanoes that formed many of them.

"The faster the water is pushed to the surface, the hotter it is," Creed added. "You'll like this one. It tends to run the perfect side of warm. At least it used to." He dismounted. "Ready to give it a try?"

"I cannot wait." She dismounted, too, taking her small valise with her.

"There's a clean towel in my left saddlebag. Help yourself."

He went inside to inspect the bathing chamber, and she

moved toward the palomino to take advantage of his offer of the linen.

"Will you use the waters, too?" she called to him.

His head poked out from around the doorway. "Is that an invitation?"

"To use them with me?" she asked, taken aback. She hadn't intended the question to be provocative, but it amused her that he took it as such.

"Just say the word, honey, and I'll dive right in."

She tried not to laugh. It would only encourage him. "I think again the price you want to charge me is too high." She flipped open one of the leather bags. "We will go separate."

He sighed dramatically, and she lost sight of him again. She rooted among his belongings, packed tight in their small confines, and finally found the towel. She pulled the article out, but something else came along, too.

A bundle that dropped to the ground. Small, wrapped in elegant, rose-colored paper. From the battered condition, he might have carried it with him from the far ends of the world, but wherever it came from, there was one thing for sure.

The package was meant for a woman.

The breeze tugged the crumpled wrapping loose and fluttered the filmy contents inside. Handkerchiefs, she realized. She scooped them up before they all went flying, and once they were safely in her grasp, she stared at them outright.

Delicate, lace-trimmed handkerchiefs, of the finest quality. A whole stack of them, from white to the softest pastels, some of them plain, some of them embroidered, and, oh, no...

He'd bought them for someone special.

Someone *female* special.

"Have to admit the Old Man did a nice job on the bath-house," Creed said, striding back outside. Seeing what she held, he halted. And frowned. "Hell, I forgot about those."

Well, he sure as blazes works fast, don't he?

Marcus's contempt dropped into her memory, and sus-picion stirred.

"Who are they for?" she asked. It was none of her business, but the question was out before she could think of it that way.

"Her name is Mary Catherine."

A beautiful name, and it conjured up instant images of the woman who bore it. A slow pique began to simmer, deep inside her.

His frown deepened. "At least, they were going to be."

"And she is…?" Gina held her breath, not wanting to know, but needing to and hating herself for it.

"Someone I planned to marry, that's all."

She gasped. "What?"

"It didn't happen," he said, watching her.

"You want to *marry* her?"

The pique spilled over, then. Hot and bitter. She shoved the bundle against his chest. Quick reflex kept him from dropping the whole bunch.

"Hey," he said, startled.

He's just havin' a little fun, that's all….

"But you kiss *me,* again and again," she snapped. "You hold me in your arms all night, like we are lovers. When there is another woman in your heart?"

His gaze dropped to the handkerchiefs, then back up at her. From his confusion, it was clear he hadn't made the connection she did.

"It wasn't like that." He shook his head for emphasis. "I swear it."

When had she been so furious? *"Bastardo!"*

Taken aback, he reached for her with his free hand. "Gina, wait a minute. Let me explain."

But she evaded him. Grabbing the valise and his towel, she all but ran inside the dim confines of the bathhouse. She stood on a buffalo skin and took quick, deep breaths to swallow down the hurt.

And the humiliating realization that she'd fallen in love with him.

Why had she let herself? Because he gave her strength and hope in her worries about Mama? Offered protection from the Sokolovs? Was excitement in her boring, mundane existence?

All those things, yes.

Yet he belonged to someone else. This Mary Catherine. Why did it have to be his love for her that made Gina realize her love for him?

What an *idiota* she'd been. Creed Sherman was born for more exciting things in his life than being with her in hers. And Mary Catherine was one of them.

Gina forced down the humiliation with a surge of resolve. If he followed her into the bathhouse, if he tried to sway her with more of his smooth words or bone-melting kisses to redeem himself, she would throw him out with her bare hands. She refused to be a toy to entertain him any longer, and she kept a close eye on him through the tiny slits between the logs.

"Gina, I want you to listen to me."

His shape moved, then transformed into a shadow in the doorway.

"Stay out!" she said.

The shadow froze. "The whole damn thing with Mary Catherine was a mistake."

"I do not want to hear it." Knowing of his intentions was enough. His details didn't matter.

"I'm not in love with her. I probably never was. And I'm not going to marry her."

Furiously, she blinked the sting of tears from her eyes. Once, she was foolish and gullible. Not again. "Now you say so, eh?"

"I can see why you thought what you did, and I'm willing to—"

And now he's drowning his sorrows in you….

"I am not listening." Carefully, she set the valise down, dropped the towel on top. "I am busy with my bath."

He swore. But the shadow still didn't move.

She waited.

Then she waited a little more.

It seemed he would stay outside, after all, and she dared to remove her hat. More than ever, she longed for the soothing waters, but now she needed them to help soak away the hurt, the humiliation, to convince herself she didn't need Creed Sherman like she thought she did.

And when she finished, when she dried herself and put on her last clean dress, she would leave him.

She took off her shoes and hosiery. The shadow in the doorway moved away, but her gaze found him again through the cracks between the logs, pacing back and forth. A caged lion, restless and impatient.

She worked the buttons at her throat down to her waist. Her Sunday dress and chemise drifted to her ankles, and warm, moist air touched her bare skin.

She stepped from the buffalo hide into the luscious heat, just deep enough to sit in. Faint tendrils of steam hovered over the swirling green spring, very different than the clear blue of those found off the coasts of Sicily.

But oh, this one was just as wonderful.

Smooth stones formed the bowl of the pool, and she sank against the side. A final glance revealed the doorway was still empty, all the permission she needed to lean her head back and close her eyes. Calming and tranquil, the water lapped gently at her breasts. Her muscles uncoiled; her body became attuned to the gently carbonating sensation flowing over her skin.

"You know, Gina," Creed called in, "I could ask you the same thing about Sebastian."

His demand intruded into her serenity. So now he thought he would turn the tables on her?

Sebastian had never bought her anything as extravagant as those beautiful handkerchiefs. There was no comparison between them, and Gina refused to discuss it.

"Go away," she called back.

He cursed. Boot soles tread closer. Her eyes opened, and there he was, right in front of her.

She yelped and crossed her arms over her breasts.

"Woman, this is ridiculous," he growled, pulling his shirt from his shoulders. "I'll be damned if I'll have a conversation with you through a wall. We've got a problem between us, and we're going to talk it out."

The shirt dropped onto her dress. He balanced on one leg to tug off a boot.

Her alarmed gaze shot upward.

"You cannot come in the waters with me!" she gasped.

The second boot landed next to the first. He unfastened his Levi's. "The hell I can't."

She darted a frantic glance to his towel and found it helplessly out of reach. She slid deeper into the spring, up to her neck. "Then I will get out. Turn away."

He stood on the rocks, a Roman god of perfection, as

oblivious to his nakedness as she was aware of it, and dear, sweet Madonna, she couldn't help but look at him. From the wide breadth of his shoulders down to his lean hips and well-hung masculinity.

"You're not going anywhere just yet, Gina."

His thigh bulged from the movement of stepping into the spring. The bulk of his body sloshed water against the rocks. He glided closer, and she drew her knees up. If she could slink any lower without drowning herself first, she would.

"Are you in love with him?" he demanded.

Her concentration scattered being with him like this, her legs only inches from his chest. Both of them naked. "Who?"

"Sebastian. He's crazy about you. Are you planning on making him your husband some day?"

"It is not your business."

"I'm making it mine."

"He would make a fine one," she said, goading him. "He is a good man, a hard worker. Very respected."

"But is he fine enough for *you?*" Creed insisted.

It'd serve him right if she told him she was in love with Sebastian. Then maybe he'd feel some of the same humiliation she did from the kisses they'd shared while he belonged to another.

But in truth, she couldn't.

"I will not marry until I have independence and the money I make from my dress shop." Many times, she had dreamed it. Vowed it. "I have love for Sebastian, yes. But it is not the right kind to marry him."

"Good." Creed nodded in approval. Some of the tension left him. "Very good."

"If I had, I would not have slept with you last night, Creed. I would not have betrayed him in such a way."

"And you think I betrayed Mary Catherine."

She arched a haughty brow. "You planned to marry her. You say this yourself."

"Yeah, well, my father married her instead."

Gina stilled. "What?"

Creed sighed heavily. "Her family's spread borders ours. Our mothers were best friends. Mary Catherine and I all but grew up together. Folks expected us to marry, so did we."

She remembered the work that meant so much to him. "But you leave to be a mercenary soldier first."

He nodded. "I wasn't in a rush to get back to her, either, and she got tired of waiting. Ma died about then. I guess the Old Man and Mary Catherine needed each other to get through the loneliness."

"And now they are happy?"

He grunted. "Happy enough to make a baby together."

"Oh." She pressed wet fingers to her lips in surprise.

Which melted into amusement.

"You think that's funny?" he growled.

She shook her head. It'd be almost impossible for him to marry Mary Catherine now, even if he wanted to. "No. The little one will be theirs to enjoy, but it is hard for you to think of what they did in their bed, eh?"

His head angled, as if he fought the image of it. "It's harder to think of him with another woman besides my mother. In bed or out."

"Did you expect him to mourn her forever?"

His expression hardened. "Mary Catherine is young. He watched her grow up. She was practically a daughter to him."

"That is only how you remember her," Gina admonished in a gentle voice. "You fight for America a long time. You do not see her grow into a woman. You do not know her desires and dreams. Or that she becomes lonely without you? Even before your mother dies?"

"If he would've married anyone else but her," Creed grated. "Maybe it'd be easier to accept."

"But he did not."

"No. But now, at his age, he's starting all over. With a baby on the way. *Her* baby."

"They are man and wife, Creed," she said firmly. "It is their privilege. You cannot deny them their right to be a new family with one another. Do you not want the same for yourself some day?"

He said nothing, but the deep almond in his eyes darkened.

"Be happy for them." Now that she understood the place Mary Catherine held in his life, or at least used to, much of Gina's hurt faded. She trailed her wet knuckles along his jaw in a tender caress, an easing of those things that pained him, deep inside. "I think they are sad you are not."

His lean fingers encircled her arm, and he pressed a kiss to the inside of her wrist. His eyes closed, the burden he struggled with.

"It will be fun to be a big brother again," she added. "Your father's baby is a gift he gives you. And Marcus, too."

For a long moment, Creed didn't move. When he did, he drew her closer and nuzzled his jaw against her temple.

"Seems I was in love with expectations," he murmured. "Not a woman. It was a long time ago, besides. And you're right. I'm a bastard. A selfish one."

The admission came low in her ear. She breathed in the scent of him, male and steamy and rousing. His warmth, his strength surrounded her, and how could Mary Catherine not have fallen in love with him when they were young and impressionable?

Little wonder she waited for him, year after year, until her hopes died. But even Gina knew Creed wasn't right for Mary Catherine, a woman who loved the Sherman ranch as much as the man who owned it. His father. So much that she accepted the bonds of marriage to live the rest of her life with him there.

Not Creed.

His destiny involved something no less honorable, but infinitely more dangerous and valiant. The ideals that he'd learned, that he instinctively embraced, ran strong within him.

His need to protect Gina, his ability to save her from Nikolai's revenge, was proof. Was it any wonder she'd fallen in love with him?

Her head lowered to rest against the warm skin of his shoulder, strong and broad, like the man. He was capable of love. Or of hate. He could harden his heart to kill or fill it with fierce loyalty. Enough loyalty to encompass an entire nation.

Or a single woman, like herself. Gina Briganti, a poor immigrant seamstress. A nobody.

Humbled beyond words, she squeezed her lashes to hold back the sting of tears.

He would always roam the world at his country's beckoning, always restless with the need to fight and defend.

And like Mary Catherine, Gina's fragile love could never be.

She couldn't wait for years in wasted hope. Her immediate fight lay in finding her mother. Creed's lay in something far different, that of finding the Sokolovs and ensuring his country's security.

She'd be a fool to expect anything more lasting than that.

Suddenly, being with him now, this moment, took on new meaning. An urgency which flickered and flared into a burning need to take a part of him with her, to hold in her heart and cherish when he was gone.

Slowly, she drew back. Time seemed to stand still, but in reality, it couldn't. She speared her hands into his hair and pulled him down to take her kiss. She would leave him. They would leave each other, and she had little to give him to remember her in return.

Except herself.

Chapter Eighteen

Creed tasted the fire in her.

The unexpected desperation.

She all but set him on fire, too. Her mouth opened wet and hungry under his, hot enough to stoke his own flames and get them going, but good.

He'd never been one to retreat from an opportunity, and they didn't come any sweeter than this. He wasn't a saint, nor did he claim to be, and what man could deny himself a beautiful, willing woman?

But something told him he needed enough control for the both of them, at least until he knew what was running through her mind, fueling her fire, and it took every shred of control he possessed to pull back.

"Gina, honey," he said, his voice husky. Ragged. He touched his forehead to hers, giving them both a little breathing room. "When a woman pushes a man too far, it makes it hard for him to stop. You've got me there, y'know that? Right on the brink."

Her arms curled to his neck. "Do you not feel what I feel? That soon everything will change for us?" She looked up at him, and the desperation was there, in the obsidian depths of her eyes. "We are together *now,* but only for a little while longer."

Creed knew about change all right. How fate could throw him in its path, force him into a whole new direction, whether he wanted to go there or not.

Like when he'd walked into the Old Man's house thinking he was going to marry Mary Catherine. He'd walked out, knowing he never would.

Gina knew change, too. The flick of a match kind of change. Loss. Uncertainty.

And yeah, they were here, together, in Ma's favorite hot mineral spring. Naked and alone.

His gaze dragged downward to Gina's breasts. Water glistened on the rounded globes, and her nipples hardened beneath his lusty stare.

His hand moved to cup one mound; his fingers flexed lazily over her supple flesh, and her breath hitched in response.

"No way to know what's going to happen in the time we have left," he said. "Is there?"

Her throat moved, and she shook her head. That uncertainty again. As if she was afraid of it.

He understood then, this need which drove her. The reason for her passion. To revel in the glory while they could.

"How could any man not want to make love to you?" he murmured.

He kissed her again, long and thorough, stirring the fires until they raged hot in him again. With a throaty growl, he lifted his head and changed their positions, twisting to sit against the back of the pool, bringing her with him. The warm waters gave her a buoyancy to smoothly straddle him. He clasped her waist, easily lifted her up and toward him, his mouth already open to take her nipple in.

She gripped his shoulders and hissed in a breath, revealing the newness of the sensation, the feel of a man suckling in pleasure at a female breast. His tongue laved across the rounded peak, over and around, again and again; he opened wider and used his teeth to nip and plunder.

She moaned something in Italian; her head fell forward, and her fingers speared through his hair, holding him to her while he seduced the other. A spiraling heat spread, deep in his groin. A wanting to consume her, send her hurtling to the peaks with him. Her hips swiveled as if searching, as if craving, and he groaned with a pretty hefty craving of his own.

"Touch me, Gina," he whispered.

He eased her lower into the water, and he took her lips in a greedy feast to take what she offered, his tongue swirling and thrusting, hers hot and wild, the passion in him escalating into roaring fire.

Her hands slid across the breadth of his chest, his skin as slick as hers. Her leisurely exploring continued downward past his belly. His muscles tautened in anticipation as she explored lower yet.

Her fingers found his blade and curled around him. He groaned and gloried in this power she held over him. She whispered his name, and he gripped her hips; she moved over him, finding her place. He entered her, slowly at first, then deeper, and deeper still, until the hot, slick feel of her stole his breath. Filled his body. Liberated his soul.

They found their rhythm. Sensation arced inside him while it built into a fevered pitch, thrust after mind-numbing thrust. Higher, higher, he climbed, until together, they exploded, triumphant, into a crescendo of ecstasy more dazzling than any he'd experienced before.

Ever.

She collapsed against him with a rocking of the waters, both of them deliciously spent. He heaved a satisfied breath into her hair and slid his arms around her back, holding her snug against him.

Creed couldn't move. For long minutes, Gina didn't, either.

"Next time, we'll use a bed," he said finally.

Her mouth curved against his shoulder. "Next time?"

"We'll use it longer, too. The whole night if we want."

She sighed. Dreamy and lethargic. "After how you make me feel now, I do not think I can."

He chuckled and relished the weight of her against him. A strange sense of contentment curled through his chest. The feeling he was right where he needed to be.

Man with woman.

Gina.

He didn't know what to make of it, this feeling she aroused in him. He'd not felt it from a woman before, not even Mary Catherine at the peak of his infatuation.

But Gina got him to thinking. And that got him to wanting. Long-term things, like the kind that came with a future. A succession of nights' worth of a future.

Had he fallen in love with her?

His eyes opened. Sunlight glinted through the doorway, and reality crashed in.

His mouth tightened. What was he doing? His thoughts came from the lust, that's all. The musings of a sexually satisfied man. The Sokolovs wouldn't get found while he was in here, loving her up. Nor would her mother, and that'd be most important of all in her mind.

He had no right thinking like he was. And he sure as hell

couldn't fancy himself being in love. Not when he had a war to fight not far beyond these bathhouse walls.

He needed all his willpower to get back to it.

"We have to get out of these waters, or we'll shrivel like prunes." He dropped a kiss on the top of her head. Gently, firmly, he lifted her and set her aside. "Besides, I have work to do."

The look she gave him revealed she didn't want to be reminded, and she leaned, pensive, against the rocks, giving in to the reluctance of leaving the warmth just yet. He rose and climbed out, and he could feel her gaze lingering over him.

He dried off his torso with the towel, started on his arms next. She still hadn't moved. "Come on, honey."

She stood, then, no longer shy with him. Water sluiced off her slender body, giving a sheen to her olive skin. His gaze sauntered over the dip of her waist and along the curve of her hips, touched on the dark curls at the juncture of her thighs. The slight wobble of her breasts stirred his blood all over again.

Feminine magnificence. Pure and simple.

How would he ever leave her?

She took his hand, and he helped her out of the spring. Easily, as if she'd done so a hundred times, she stepped into his embrace. Skin to skin. Delectable breasts pressed wetly to his chest.

"Stay with me a little longer, Creed," she whispered.

Her plea cut right through him. Had she read his thoughts? His dread of the inevitable?

"I can't," he said, hating it.

A moment passed, and she stepped back.

"I know." Her quiet voice stirred the air between them. "I will hurry."

She dressed in a plain black dress with a simple white collar, but somehow she made the thing look more elegant than it was. After refolding her navy Sunday dress and tucking the garment inside the valise, she buckled the clasps and stood.

"Ready?" she asked, the fine hairs at her temple wispy from the steam.

His mouth pursed. "Unfortunately."

She turned to leave. Creed swept a final glance around the bathhouse and noticed a small mound of dark fabric lying in the shadows. "Wait, Gina. You forgot something."

He bent to retrieve it. A scarf, he realized. Black and fringed.

She froze. The color drained from her cheeks. "Oh, no."

He paused at her reaction. "What's the matter? It's not yours?"

She took the scarf and examined it, front and back. "Yes." She managed to nod. "It is mine. I wear it to hide myself at the anarchist meeting. But I forget it when I tell Nikolai who I am."

The image of her at the old warehouse, rising from her chair, pulling the dark covering from her hair, hurtled back into his memory. "What do you mean, you forgot it?"

"I did not bring it with me today." Her breath quickened, the alarm growing inside her. "Someone else did."

The scarf must've fallen to the warehouse floor, left behind in the chaos that ensued. The room had emptied fast. No one took the time to pick up something so insignificant. Creed would've known if they had.

But two men stayed behind. One of them wounded. In need of warm, healing waters.

"Nikolai was here." Creed went cold from the certainty. "And he's hiding out around here, somewhere close."

* * *

Alex burst into the log shack, located on the Sherman ranch's North Camp, the hideout Nikolai had chosen for them. He slammed the door shut and tossed his knapsack onto the cot.

Nikolai glanced up from his work.

"Did you get the letter?" he asked without greeting.

"Yes." Alex reached into his shirt pocket and withdrew a folded piece of paper. "We have trouble."

A calm had settled over Nikolai since his time in the healing waters. A conviction he would succeed in his quest to bring about revolution in America, no matter who tried to stop him. Or when. Including Gina Briganti and the man she kept company with.

Alex, on the other hand, constantly worried. To him, the smallest concerns were big problems, whether he used the mineral waters or not.

"Why do you say so?" Nikolai asked.

"*I* do not say. The letter does." He extended the paper toward him. "Read it. The news is not good."

"My hands are busy. Tell me what it says."

He carefully measured black powder into a paper funnel. The time had come to prepare for the president's arrival. Building the bomb was the first step.

"Karlov sends word that an important general in the War Department has learned of our activities. He has ordered one of his men to investigate us on McKinley's behalf."

Nikolai glanced up sharply. "Here in Los Angeles?"

"Yes."

"Who is this general?"

Alex referred to the letter for the information. "It says his name is William Carson."

Nikolai committed the name to memory. He didn't

know of the officer, but then, why would he? Gleaning inside information on the military was Karlov's responsibility, not his.

"Do we have the name of the man Carson sent?" he asked.

"Yes." This time, Alex didn't need to look at the letter. "Creed Sherman."

Nikolai went still. Perhaps it was only a coincidence, the name being the same as the man who owned this ranch....

"He has returned home to his father. Here." Alex's arm swung outward, indicating the vast lands around them. "That is how Carson knew where to contact him."

From the questions Nikolai had asked before helping themselves to the isolated hot mineral springs, he'd learned that Gus Sherman had two sons, the youngest who lived with him on the ranch, the oldest who had left the country years ago. Nikolai hadn't thought to ask their names. At the time, it hadn't been important.

But now...

"You told me of just one son," Alex accused.

"Because the other did not live in America." Rarely did Alex challenge him. Nikolai disliked that he did so now.

"He left to be a soldier." Alex gave the paper a shake. "A *mercenary,* Nikolai."

His nostrils flared. A careless mistake on his part. He should've been more thorough. "That is what the letter says?"

"Yes. Karlov warns of his skill. He says the War Department hires Sherman to do their most dangerous work. They send him all over the world to collect intelligence for them and kill America's enemies, and his reputation—" Alex halted and rubbed his stomach with a moan. "We have to be careful, Nikolai. We cannot let him find us, or he will kill us, too."

"Do you think I do not know that now?" he demanded.

He declined to tell Alex of his sudden certainty it'd been Creed Sherman who infiltrated their meeting just last night, cleverly disguised with his beard.

Now, with this new information, it was clear Gina Briganti had aligned herself with him. A formidable weapon, it seemed, in her vengeance against them over the Premier fire.

A shrewd tactic, too. One Nikolai had not expected of her.

The pain in his thigh, eased from the healthful waters, stirred again.

"That is not all, Nikolai," Alex said grimly. "He was at our apartment, asking about us."

Unease lifted the hairs on his neck. The mercenary worked fast. "How do you know this? You were there?"

"Yes. For the last of our food and to find more cloth for bandages." He indicated his knapsack on the cot. "The landlord saw me. He told me."

Nikolai gritted his teeth. Not even his brother's thoughtfulness could alleviate his stupidity. The police could've been waiting for him. They could've followed him here, straight to the log shack.

Nikolai wouldn't have known until it was too late.

"Now, the mercenary knows where we live, and we cannot go back." Alex appeared pale, panicked at the prospect.

"Had you planned to?" Nikolai asked coldly. "After what we have done?"

"But what if he finds us out here next? On his father's land?"

"He will not."

It'd been sheer accident Nikolai had found the shack at all. From the desolate appearance of it, no one had been to the North Camp in weeks. Maybe more. To discover the place stocked with the basic necessities had been a baffling surprise.

Nikolai took the privilege of moving right in. Its seclusion, the opportunity the structure gave to continue his work, was a great advantage.

"We will not be here long," he said firmly. "Only until McKinley arrives."

Alex began to pace; his slender fingers stroked the pale moustache above his lip.

"You cannot be sure what will happen," he said. "Always you tell me we will be safe, but so much has gone wrong the past few days. What will be next?"

Nikolai studied him.

"Is your stomach bothering you again?" he asked.

Alex's mouth turned downward into a pout. "Yes."

"Rest, then. You will feel better after a nap. Did you take your medicine at the right time this morning?"

"Yes." Alex threw himself on the cot in a petulant huff.

"Good." He kept his voice soothing, the way his brother needed to hear it. "I will take you to the waters later. How about that?"

Alex heaved a sigh, long and suffering. He flung his arm over his face, the pout still strong on his lips. But he said nothing more.

Nikolai considered his mood. How he'd complained like an anxious old woman. He'd argued, too, defying the decisions Nikolai had made. Had even gone so far as to make a decision of his own, returning to their apartment without Nikolai knowing of it.

The risks...

Perhaps he was only showing signs of manhood by beginning to think for himself. Or perhaps he didn't believe he needed Nikolai as much as he once did.

But Nikolai squelched the thought. Of course Alex needed him. They needed each other.

Especially now, with President McKinley coming, and the allure of victory at hand. Victory they would share together.

Alex lay motionless on the cot, resting, and Nikolai returned his attention to his work. He tapped the black powder into a bottle and added oil of vitriol, the acid which would help the bomb explode. He mixed the elements, set the container carefully to one side, and prepared to make a second.

Suddenly, Alex sat bolt upright.

"Did you hear that, Nikolai?" he demanded in a hoarse tone.

The black powder hovered over the paper funnel. His senses leapt into place.

"I heard nothing," he said carefully.

But then, he'd been concentrating on the precise measurements of the mixture. He listened now. Hard.

Alex's gaze shot to the shack's lone window. "Something is out there."

Carefully, Nikolai set the jar of powder down, placed the funnel next to it. He thought of his .44 tucked in his knapsack, on the floor. He rose, in slow motion, to retrieve it.

Just then, the door crashed open, and the American, the mercenary named Creed Sherman, appeared in the doorway with a Smith and Wesson in each hand.

"Don't move," he snarled. "Or you're both dead."

Chapter Nineteen

Creed kept a hard eye on them, each standing still as stone. Alex looked scared enough to cry. Nikolai, furious enough to tear Creed apart.

"Now get your hands up. Make it slow and push 'em high," Creed commanded.

Alex's arms lifted to the rafters first. "Do not shoot us. Please."

Nikolai still hadn't moved. Creed watched him close. He knew firsthand the strength in those big burly arms.

"Do what I said, Nikolai!" he warned.

"I do not think you are capable of taking us both," the Russian taunted, but his hands inched into the air.

"You have no idea what I'm capable of," Creed said in a deadly voice.

But his muscles coiled at the assortment of chemicals on the table. The makings of a bomb. What *Nikolai* was capable of. Creed had to get him away from the explosives before he blew the three of them clear into the next county.

Gina flashed through his mind. She was tucked safe in the trees a fair distance back from the line shack. Regardless of what happened in the next few minutes, she was at least that.

Safe.

And she knew what to do if he didn't make it back.

He jerked the nose of his revolver at the youngest Sokolov. The easiest to subdue. "Take one step toward me, Alex. Any more than that, I'll kill you for sure."

Alex paled a little more. "What are you going to do?"

"Neither of you will get hurt if you follow my orders. Take that step. Now."

Alex darted a nervous look at Nikolai. An unspoken message seemed to pass between them.

"I will not let him hurt you," Nikolai said softly.

Acting reassured, the youth complied, but Creed sensed the tension hiking in his brother.

He could've used another pair of hands to get to the handcuffs hanging at his waist. He waited to make sure Nikolai didn't intend something rash before he sheathed his revolver, keeping the other aimed square at the broad Russian chest, letting Nikolai know Creed was as accurate shooting with his left hand as he was with his right.

"I'm going to put some cuffs on you, Alex," Creed said, unclipping the bracelets. His attention bounced between the brothers. "Turn around, real easy, so I can clamp them on your wrists behind you."

Again, Alex hesitated. Impatience spiked through Creed; he refused to tell him twice. He yanked one scrawny arm and did the turning for him, a rough move that almost cost the kid his balance. Creed snapped both manacles into place before Alex could think to fight him on it.

Alex yelped and tugged at the restraints. Nikolai jerked with barely constrained fury. And Creed cocked the Smith and Wesson.

He kept firm hold on the kid's elbow. Alex was Nikolai's weak point. Creed's ace up his sleeve to keep him cooperative.

"You're going to be next, Nikolai," he said. "Handcuffs, just like your brother."

The burly arms had lowered. Closer to the table. Closer to the bomb. Creed's heart pumped a little faster from it.

"No," Nikolai said.

Gut instinct told Creed he was ready to play dirty. Creed braced for it.

"Sit down, Alex. On the cot," he said.

"Ignore him, Alex," Nikolai said. "You are not a dog to be told what to do."

"You're wrong," Creed said. "I'm in charge. You'll both do what you're told."

He pushed Alex toward the cot, out of his way, to free up his concentration. Alex fell awkwardly against the mattress and rolled to the floor in a dramatic display of clumsiness. His head cracked against the wooden slats, and he cried out.

By then, Creed had both revolvers in his hands, cocked and aimed at both of them.

"Are you going to let him keep hurting me, Nikolai?" Alex yelled with a struggle to sit up. "Did you see him? He *hurt* me!"

The big Russian quivered. His cold gaze dragged to Creed and filled with contempt.

"The important American soldier is quick to harm the innocent with his tyranny, Alex," he said, his lip curled in a sneer. "Another of his country's hypocrisies. Tell me, Creed Sherman. Will your powerful General William Carson applaud you?"

Creed hid the burn of his own rage. There wasn't a finer man than General Carson in the military or one who loved

America more. And it was his devotion and respect for her president that put Creed right here in this shack, at war with two men who despised him.

But he refused to defend with words. The guns in his hands did it for him.

"I'm not surprised you know who I am, Nikolai," he countered, playing the game. A high-stakes gamble for his life. And McKinley's. "Your accomplice in the War Department has informed you well, it seems."

Shock flared in the ice-blue depths before Nikolai banked it with frigid disdain. "I do not know what you are talking about."

Creed shrugged. "When he's found, he'll hang for his treason."

Alex paled in horror. "Karlov—"

Nikolai whipped toward him. "Shut up, Alex!"

The gamble struck gold.

Alex whimpered and rocked back and forth. "He knows, Nikolai. He knows. Kill him. Kill him."

"He knows nothing!" Nikolai roared and with the speed Creed expected but couldn't stop soon enough, he snatched a filled bottle from the table and dangled it threateningly in the air. "Nothing, Alex. Do you hear me?"

Blood thundered in Creed's temples. "You drop that bomb, Nikolai, and we're all dead. Put it down."

"Get him out of here. Get him out!" Alex cried. He'd managed to get to his feet. "He's making me sick."

Creed bettered his aim with the revolvers, both men in his range of vision. One frantic, on the fringes of hysteria. The other, maniacal and cold. "Stay right there, Alex. Don't move a step closer."

Nikolai waved the bomb in the air, and cold fear knotted in Creed's gut.

"Kill him or let him go?" the big Russian taunted. "Which, Alex? You tell me. Think like a man. Which is the better solution?"

His brother seemed to recognize the menace he made. He took an anxious step forward. "What are you doing, Nikolai? What are you doing?"

Creed fired a shot into the floor, a reminder to stay put. Wood splintered. Alex screamed and leapt back.

"Next time, I won't miss," Creed snapped. He swiveled back to Nikolai. "Put the bomb back on the table. Do it now and do it careful."

"So you can arrest us and throw us in your squalid jails?" he demanded.

"Let him go," Alex cried again. "What will you do? Kill us with the vitriol, too?"

"He must surrender his weapons first." Nikolai circled the air over the table with the bottle. "Lay them here, soldier. Lay them right here."

"Never," Creed rumbled.

He would die first, a victim to the bomb. A less than favorable decision if Nikolai saw through his threat, but one where Creed would at least take the Sokolovs with him and spare the president his life. But to weaken, to give in to the fear and let the enemy win, was unthinkable.

It was then he heard the restless snuffles of the horses outside. They'd heard something, someone…

Creed forgot to breathe.

Nikolai lifted his gaze to the window.

Alex swung his to the open doorway.

Where Creed still stood, feet spread, legs braced, and his back to the free air, his front guarding the fanatics who threatened to blow him up with their damned bomb, and please, God, *please*, don't let it be her.

Or Markie.

Or the Old Man himself.

They'd be killed. They'd all be killed. And what a *hell* of a waste that would be because now everything had changed, and Creed wasn't ready to die yet.

Not by a long shot.

"A rider!" Alex croaked, staring at one somewhere behind Creed.

"Who is it?" Nikolai demanded.

Creed couldn't wait to find out. He had to leave. Fast. He had to save whoever was crazy enough to stumble in at one of the most remote places on his father's ranch at *the* most inopportune time of their lives.

His own being at the top of the list.

He bettered his grip on each Smith and Wesson. Dared to take a step back.

"A woman," Alex said, staring hard. His eyes widened. "Nikolai, it is Gina Briganti!"

Holy Lord.

He took another backward stride. Another. Only then did Nikolai notice, and a slow, feral grin spread across his harsh features. Chilling in their delight.

"Now the dangerous soldier runs, eh, Alex?" He moved toward the doorway, following him, the bottled-up bomb still in his hand. "He is not so brave when he knows she will die, too."

Creed's blood turned cold from resolve, and he fired into the opening, but too quick, Nikolai guessed his intent and dodged back inside before the bullet found its target. Creed fired again, for good measure, with the same rotten luck.

He gave up, then, and spun toward the horse, toward Gina, coming down the hill at a cautious lope.

"Go, Gina. Go!" he yelled.

She slowed. Frowned. Opened her mouth to shout. "What?"

"Go! Go! Go!"

He broke into a run toward her, his legs pathetically inept compared to the speed of a strong horse, his own left behind in the trees. Where Gina should be right now. But she wasn't. And if she didn't get the hell out of there, she'd be blown up right along with him.

In seconds.

He could feel it, and he ran even faster. Her alarmed gaze darted from him to the line shack. Her mouth dropped in horror, and Creed knew then. He knew…

A tremendous explosion sent him hurtling into the air.

And everything went black.

Gina prayed to the Madonna he wouldn't die, though deep down, she knew he wouldn't. Each shallow breath he took came when it should, but he had yet to open his eyes, and he lay so still in the grass.

The explosion, it was terrible.

She finished her prayer and crossed herself. It had taken all her strength and ingenuity to tie a rope around his leather holster and help the bay drag him up the hill to safety in the trees. After she untied him, made him as comfortable as she could, she prayed over him.

Now she must take him to his father's house. Gus Sherman would know what to do.

He must be told what happened. The Sokolovs might be hiding somewhere else on his vast ranch. After Nikolai threw his bomb, he had hurried to find a rock to break the links on Alex's handcuffs. Once Alex could use his arms again, they fled, taking the makings for their deadly bombs with them.

Gina knew getting Creed up on his horse wouldn't be

easy. He must regain his consciousness first, and from the way he stirred, she hoped it wouldn't be much longer.

Gently, she touched his forehead, bruised and swollen like the goose's egg. Tiny cuts nicked his face. Dust covered his clothes. His big strong body, which had made love to hers only a short while ago, had taken a frightening beating from the spray of earthen clods and rocks.

So easily, he could have been killed.

Again, she thanked the Madonna that he hadn't.

The tawny-gold lashes fluttered open, and his deep almond-colored eyes rolled as they tried to focus. They cleared and met hers.

"Gina," he said raggedly.

He tried to sit up. She nudged him back down again.

"Shh," she whispered. "Do not move yet."

"Are you…hurt?"

Her heart squeezed that his worry had been for her first, with none for himself. Was it any wonder she had fallen in love with him? "I did not feel the bomb like you did."

He grimaced and rolled to his side; one knee came up, his attempt to stand. "I have to…go after them."

"They are not here," she said firmly and pressed a hand on his shoulder to keep him down. "You cannot find them now."

His bleary gaze jumped to her. "How long ago?"

"Very long." She stretched the truth a little.

"Damn it." He lay back again. "I almost…had 'em."

"Yes." She didn't need to mention he'd almost been killed from his bravery at the same time.

"You were…crazy fool to come ridin' down that hill, woman."

She smoothed the hair from his forehead. "I hear the gun shoot. Two men are against you. When I see you in the doorway, I want to help, that is all."

The relief from knowing he wasn't shot or dead had left her knees wobbly. She would've done anything to help capture the Sokolovs, even in the smallest way.

She knew now he wouldn't have needed her, but he'd fallen so still, she began to worry he'd been injured worse than she thought. Her urgency to get to his father's house intensified.

A chill had settled into the air. The sun would soon sink from the sky, and the ride wouldn't be a fast one. She rose and left him, but only to walk their mounts right up to where he lay on the ground. Bending, she gave him a careful shake.

"We must leave, Creed. You must help me get you on your horse. Can you do that?"

He roused. Winced. Groaned. "Just…point me in the right direction."

"Come. Up, up."

With a fair amount of prodding and coaxing, she managed to get him into the saddle. He slouched in the seat with his eyes closed, and she feared he'd lose consciousness again and tumble right off. Worriedly, she took his reins, then climbed onto the bay and gripped hers.

He would think she was taking him back to the West Camp, the one he'd brought her to, closest to the city limits. But Marcus had told her how to find the main house. Just follow the fence line, he'd said, and she would get there.

That's what she did. Until night fell, and it seemed they rode forever. Eventually, it all came into view, though, and sprawled out before her. The Sherman homestead. A majestic place, with lights in every window on the ground level. Soon, with the late hour, they'd shine on the top one, too. Cattle grazed on distant pasture, their black shapes silhouetted in the moonlight. Various outbuildings were scattered along the horizon, their uses Gina could only speculate.

A testament to Gus Sherman's success.

But Creed's home, nonetheless.

It'd been devastating to leave hers in Sicily. She couldn't begin to think how it would feel to leave one like this in hurt and anger, to fight wars in lands which offered far less comfort or security. Or love. And how could his father not miss him during the years Creed had been gone?

Gina turned the horses into a tree-lined lane. Despite the troubles that kept him away, she was bringing Creed home again.

And she prayed it was the right thing to do.

Chapter Twenty

A muted confusion of noise dragged Creed upward from the fringes of oblivion. He fought the confusion, strained to identify it. Pieces. One by one.

He crawled higher. Noise came louder. Dogs barking, frenzied and persistent. Something slammed. A door. Footsteps running. A vague light shadowed the darkness in his mind.

He crawled faster. Shed the oblivion. He realized he was in the saddle, slouched over, barely hanging on. He slitted his eyes. A blurred shape of a woman sat beside him. A woman, Gina. Next to him on a horse.

He fought to comprehend it. The confusion.

"Gina! God Almighty, is that you? What happened?"

Lanterns appeared. Everywhere. The light hurt his eyes, and he closed them again. The voice talking to her, faintly familiar, asking questions. His brain churned to identify, to understand.

"Oh, Marcus. There is an explosion, and Creed, I bring him, because—"

"An explosion?"

"*Sì, sì.* A bomb, and—"

"God Almighty. Hey, Smoke. Get Pa out here. Y'hear me? Get him!"

"Who've you got there, Marcus? Is that Creed? What in blazes—"

"Do what I tell you, Smoke! Hube, give me a hand. Lonnie, you, too. Is he hurt, Gina?"

More light. More voices. More footsteps running in the dirt. Creed opened his eyes again. Wider. Clearer.

"There is no blood, but he does not want to stay awake."

Gina looked worried. Creed tried to talk. To tell her he wasn't anywhere close to dead. He just needed a little more time to bring himself out of the dark. But the words didn't come.

"The bomb throws him up into the air." Gina kept explaining, kept sounding worried. "And when he comes down again, he cannot stay awake very long."

Arms lifted. Hands grasped. Creed felt himself pulled from the saddle.

"Easy with him. Easy! Something might be broken."

Markie sounded worried, too. A door slammed. More light.

"What the *hell* is going on out here?" a voice boomed.

Crystal clear, recognition hit. The Old Man. Creed fought the hands. His father's disappointment. Failure that brought Creed back home.

"Whoa, easy. It's all right, big brother." Markie again, right beside him. His low voice soothing. Understanding.

Creed stopped fighting. Markie knew. Markie understood about Pa's disappointment.

"It's Creed, Gus. He's hurt," Hube said, voice flat.

"Creed? Sweet God. Bring him in the house. Mary Cat!"

Again, the Old Man's voice boomed. "Clear the table! They've got Creed out here."

The hands carried him up steps. He felt weightless, helpless, like a baby. Boot steps tromped across the porch floor. Into the main house.

They brought him to the kitchen. Creed squinted into the brightness; his brain registered smells. Brewed coffee, roasted beef, a strawberry pie, fresh-baked. Air, warm and fragrant.

"Lay him on the table," the Old Man ordered.

Mary Catherine whisked aside a plate, the last of their dinner dishes.

"Oh, please be careful with him," she said, the words sounding worried like the rest of them.

The hands eased him down, but Creed resisted and pushed them away. He struggled to sit up, swayed, caught himself before he rolled off the edge.

"Damned if you'll lay me here…like a slab in a morgue," he growled, the sound rusty and hoarse.

The men didn't move, as if stunned to hear him speak. They appeared cautious, uncertain of what he was capable of. What they should let him do, mostly.

Then, the Old Man pulled out a chair, thumped it next to the table.

"All right, son. Sit, if that's what you'd rather do," he said.

Son. Creed went still at the word. How long had it'd been since he'd heard his father say it?

Gus Sherman, acknowledging Creed as his son.

Creed's lip curled, and his bleary gaze slammed into the Old Man's. Eyes, the same shade of burnt brown as his own. Markie's, too. All three of them, bearing the same Sherman trait.

But Creed saw pain, too. Worry. Raw fear of what could have happened.

His rebellion died. More often of late, it seemed to. The anger with his father, the wounds Creed fought to keep from healing.

En masse, the men moved to help him into the chair, but he waved them off and managed it well enough on his own. His vision cleared in degrees. Somehow, being here, his strength eased back, too, where it belonged, in his muscles and bones. His head pounded like an Apache war drum, but he could think again, and that counted most.

They all stood around him. Staring. His father's men. Hube Clark, Smokey Gibson, Lonnie Rogers. Markie. All of them, years on the Sherman payroll. Loyal and honest and hardworking. As devoted to his father as he was to them.

And Creed had no grudge with the cowboys. Never had, and suddenly, the years fell away. All lousy six of them.

His father thrust a glass tumbler filled with whiskey at him, his hand, Creed noted, not quite steady.

"Drink up," he commanded. "Then tell us what happened."

Creed took the glass, lifted the rim to his lips, but he didn't drink. He caught sight of Gina, standing forgotten in the doorway.

He didn't need the whiskey to get his blood warming from the sight of her. She had some explaining to do, her reasons for bringing him home, to his father's house. But for now, it'd wait. She was as much a part of him as everyone else in this room. He refused to have her on the outside, looking in.

"Gina." He pulled out a chair, dragged it beside his. "Come here."

The men turned toward her. In unison, their hats came off, their respect for the female gender instant, genuine, especially one associated with a Sherman. They parted, and she walked toward him, a graceful mix of pride and woman. She sat, hands folded tight in her lap.

The straight line of her shoulders revealed she was nervous, overwhelmed at being the center of attention among strangers. The Old Man, likely, most of all.

Creed hadn't painted a friendly picture of him, and the regret stung. He handed her his glass. Liquid courage for the both of them.

But Mary Catherine made a sound of admonishment.

"No, not like that." She took a cup and saucer, pretty with pink painted flowers, from the cupboard. Ma's good china, he recalled. Mary Catherine filled the cup with coffee. "Gus, pour a little in here. It'll go down easier for her."

The Old Man trickled in some Old Taylor. She stirred with a spoon and handed the doctored-up brew to Gina.

Gina accepted with a hesitant smile. "Thank you."

"You're welcome. My name is Mary Catherine, but maybe you already know that."

She nodded once. Carefully. "I do."

"And your name is Gina?"

"Yes. Gina Briganti."

"Marcus told us he met you. I must admit, we've been most curious about you ever since." Mary Catherine pulled her white crocheted shawl from her shoulders. "You're not wearing a coat, and you must be chilled clear through. Here. Wear this."

"Oh." Gina didn't seem to know what to make of it, but she tugged the wrap closer about her. "Thank you."

Mary Catherine laid a gentle hand on her shoulder. "Both of you have been through a terrible ordeal. My husband—" she darted a quick glance at Creed "—Creed's father, must know everything." She moved away to stand at his side. "Please. Start from the beginning."

Her kindness toward Gina moved Creed. Left him shaken with the knowledge that while he was gone, she'd grown into Ma's role as matriarch of the Sherman family, wife to one of the most influential ranchers around.

And it humbled him that she did it well. With compassion and with ease, and damn it, had he been too hard on her and the Old Man? Had Creed's grief from losing Ma blinded him to the realization that life moved on, and why in hell should Pa be left alone the rest of his life while it did?

Creed's head pounded from confusion, and he threw back a healthy gulp of whiskey.

By the time his glass sat empty on the table, Gina had explained everything, from the moment the Sokolovs started the fire at the Premier Shirtwaist Company factory to their throwing the vitriol bomb at the line shack in the North Camp. Afterward, no one spoke. But tears shimmered in Mary Catherine's eyes.

"Oh, Gina. Your mother…how awful for you."

"She is alive. I feel it here." Gina pressed a fist over her heart. "I dream of her at night, and she tells me she waits. She knows I come for her. With Creed's help, it is not long before I see her again."

Pa nodded, grim. "Must be hard for you to be out here, so far from the city."

"Yes." Her dark eyes held his without wavering. "But I must have vengeance. It is important to me, too. I do not want to live in fear that Nikolai and Alex will kill again because I do nothing to help stop them."

"They'll be stopped." Pa's expression turned hard with the same fierce determination that drove him to defy innumerable odds in his life as a powerful rancher. The man he was. He turned to Creed. "You think they're hiding somewhere on Sherman land?"

With the whiskey's help, the fog in Creed's brain had all but lifted, the aches in his body numbed. He could think again. Feel the hate. Keep the hunger for revenge surging strong inside him.

"I'm convinced of it," he said. He recalled Nikolai's injury, his need of the healing waters. "Gina knows of their guilt, and they know she's with me. They want us both dead." His glance swept over Markie, the Sherman men. The Old Man and Mary Catherine. Creed never intended to involve them in his war, but now, he'd done just that. And it scared the hell out of him. "Once they get wind we're here, none of you will be safe."

"You think we haven't had enemies before?" Pa demanded.

"None like this," Creed shot back.

"They have the bombs," Gina added, miserable.

"That can kill a dozen men in the blink of an eye," Creed finished.

"Then we find them before they find you and the rest of us," Pa said, his tone hard. "It's that simple."

Simple? *Simple?*

It was all Creed could do to keep from yelling this fight couldn't be more difficult. The rise of anarchism was a secret enemy, as complex as the minds of the fanatics behind it. How could he possibly win? How could any soldier or army or even a military as powerful as the one right here in the United States?

"And the president is coming." Markie shook his head. "Hell of a thing."

"Complicates things, for sure." Smoke nodded, grim like the rest of them.

"We'll handle it," Pa said.

Creed stared at him. He'd always known the Old Man was a stubborn cuss, but this stiff-necked tenacity in the face of fear and adversity was, hell...

Something inside Creed broke.

Admirable.

His frustration crumpled. Might be the Old Man was an example to follow, after all. Creed had plenty of fear built up inside him. He'd just have to let go of some to formulate a strategy.

He'd done it before. Survived on strategy. A mercenary's plan to fight and win.

But, then, except for Jeb, he'd had only to think of himself the past six years. Save his own life or die trying.

Never his family's. And that painted the picture a different color.

"The details of McKinley's journey are confidential," he said. "His itinerary isn't final. But he'll be here. Soon."

"Tell us what we can do," Lonnie said.

"Just name it," said Hube.

"Anything," Markie and Smoke added in unison.

Their loyalty hit him deep. He'd forgotten what it was like to be surrounded by the devotion of his father's men.

"Short of sending for the entire United States Army so they can comb every inch of Sherman land to find the Sokolovs?" Creed's head hurt, just thinking of it. "We wait."

"That's right." Pa nodded. "Let them come to us." A ghost of a grin showed up on his lips. "Simple."

Hell.

Creed angled his head away. He didn't want to feel the effects of his father's wry humor, and he sure didn't want to give any back. Not now, when times were serious. Too many years of pride and resentment kept him from it.

Mary Catherine took Gina's empty coffee cup and set it on the sideboard, saving him.

"I trust you menfolk will have plenty to talk about

without us," she said. "Gina's exhausted. I'll take her upstairs to Marcus's room. She needs some sleep."

"Oh, but I cannot take his room," Gina protested, darting a helpless glance at Creed.

"It's no trouble, truly," Mary Catherine said. "He stays in the bunkhouse with the rest of the outfit."

Her explanation was another reminder to Creed his kid brother had grown up to become one of his father's men. In time, the ranch would be his, and he'd move back into the main house to rule over it all.

Patriarch of the Sherman regime.

In Creed's place.

And that threw him into a damned confused feeling again.

Gina remained hesitant despite Mary Catherine's assurances. Had it been so long since anyone offered her any kind of hospitality?

"Go on," Creed said quietly. "The room's yours for the night."

She nodded, stood, and he rose with her, the courtesy Pa taught and always expected, what a man gave a woman in polite society. Funny how it came back, now, in his kitchen.

Her hand lifted, a farewell and acknowledgement of the others. "Good night, everyone."

Creed nearly took a step forward to give her a kiss, but stopped himself before he could. He had no claim to the intimacy, the possessiveness of such a gesture. Something a husband would give his wife every night for the rest of their lives.

He watched the women climb the stairs, talking softly amongst themselves. They were about the same age. They could be friends if circumstances were different....

Family, even.

And where did *that* thought come from?

Smoke sighed, long and lusty. Years ago, he was hired to work in the bunkhouse kitchen, and his tendency to burn anything he tried to cook earned him the nickname of Smokey. Wasn't long after that he was booted out to cowboy on the range, and he'd grown into one of Pa's best.

"She's as fine as cream gravy, Creed," he said.

"Yep." Lonnie sighed, too. "Them eyes, all black and shiny."

"Like patent leather." Hube stared at the now-empty staircase.

"She's sweet as sugar, too." Markie rubbed his jaw. "Reckon she's got us all sufferin' from a case of Cupid's cramps, don't she?"

Creed scowled. When had they gotten so damn poetic?

"What kind of claim you got on her?" Smoke asked.

Smoke always fancied himself a ladies' man. Far as Creed knew, he was the only one who did. "Who's asking?"

He hitched up his britches. "I am."

"You touch her, you die."

The whole bunch guffawed at their success in getting his hackles up, and Markie smacked him on the arm.

"Aw, pull in your horns, Creed," he drawled. "Smoke's just stirrin' your oats, that's all."

Yeah? And he did a damn fine job of it. But Creed kept the complaint to himself.

"That's enough, boys," the Old Man said. "Save your play for later. We've got some decisions to make."

Instantly, they turned serious again.

"What would you like us to do, Creed?" he asked. "Your call."

Creed, too, had to shift his thoughts, from Gina to war, the hell of it being Pa asking his opinion for once.

"We'll need to send a man to each of the line camps in

case the Sokolovs go there to hide," he said. "And we need to circle guards around the main house, a couple of acres beyond." He hesitated. The whole outfit had to know the risks. "In case they hurl a bomb."

For a moment, no one spoke as the implications of what he'd said sank in.

"Consider it done," Pa said finally.

Creed thought of the time. "I need to ride back out to the West Camp. Gina and I left some things behind."

The rest of his weapons, for one. Her coat and sketches, for another.

"I'll go," Markie said. "I've ridden that trail so often I can do it blindfolded."

"I don't expect it of you," Creed said. His brother would have to ride most of the night. "I'm willing."

"Let him do it," Pa said. "You got a good crack on the head tonight. Rest up so you'll be sharp in the morning. Who knows what we'll have to deal with?"

The rest of the men took his words as an order. They put their hats back on and headed toward the door. Creed followed them out.

The crisp night air filled his lungs, made him glad he was in better shape now than when he rode in. He strode toward Gina's bay, his legs still a shade wobbly, but getting him where he needed to go.

He untied her valise, then stepped to the palomino for his saddlebags; he flung them over his shoulder. Markie approached from the direction of the barn, and Creed noted how quick he'd been to mount up and ready himself to ride out.

"Markie!" he called out. His brother trotted toward him, and Creed unsheathed his Remington .44, one of the finest the company made of its caliber. The rifle had saved his life more times than he cared to think about. "Here."

He sent the weapon sailing. Markie caught it one-handed.

"Hope you don't have to use it," Creed said.

Markie glanced down at the rifle, then back up. In the lantern light, his appreciation showed. "Thanks."

"Be careful."

"Sure thing, big brother." His horse pranced, ready to run. "Hey, Creed?"

"Yeah?"

"Call me Marcus, will you? I'm not twelve anymore."

Once again, the sting from time lost rolled through him. But oddly, not as deep. Creed liked what he saw. The man his brother had become. A corner of his mouth lifted. "I will from now on."

"See you in the morning." He rode off with a wave, leaving Creed to stand alone in the lane, watching him until the night swallowed him whole.

Pa had gone off to the bunkhouse to gather up the rest of the outfit and inform them of the situation. Creed's arrival had put them all in danger, and if he could take his battle to different soil, spare them the scare and the trouble from what lay ahead, he would.

But it was too late for that. They were as involved as could be, and, troubled, Creed headed back into the house.

Chapter Twenty-One

He found Mary Catherine in the kitchen, washing dishes, an apron tied to her round belly. His stride slowed. She would still remember the ugliness of his homecoming, and he figured he had some amends to make.

She glanced at him over her shoulder and smiled. "She's a lovely woman, Creed."

Gina. More woman than any he'd ever known, her being lovely not even half of it. Did Mary Catherine understand how Gina had changed his life? The sheer unexpectedness of it? Or that he was on the brink of falling in love with her, if he hadn't already?

"She is," he said instead. "Thanks for making her feel welcome, by the way."

"Anyone out here would've done the same." She turned and reached for a towel.

"Mary Catherine," he began.

"Creed," she said at the same time.

She held up a hand, rosy and damp from the dishwater. "I'll go first, if that's all right."

His gaze spilled over her pale hair, shining in the

kitchen's light, the creaminess of her skin, the freckles on her pert nose. Funny how his preferences had swung toward thick and sable hair, skin with an olive hue, and a nose with a charming little hook.

"We were never right for each other, you know," she said quietly.

Dreams from the past settled over him, like a misty rain. "At first, Mary Catherine, we were. You know we were."

"Maybe not even then." She shook her head in regret. "Oh, we were young, Creed. Our worlds were narrow. We never looked beyond what was directly in front of us. We didn't know how. And we didn't know that we should."

"Until I left."

"Then we had no choice, did we? In my case, I didn't have to look far."

"No." The Old Man had always been there. Losing Ma helped him find Mary Catherine. And she'd always been there, too. Both of them in each other's world.

"I don't think you had to, either," she said. "Look far, I mean."

He frowned and resisted what she might imply.

"No farther than the city." She smiled.

"It's not like you're thinking." He was leaving. He had no room for Gina in his world. And she sure as hell didn't need someone like him in hers. "It's not."

She shrugged. But her eyes stayed on him.

He shifted to the other foot and gave up. Why bother to explain? Nothing would change if he did. He felt the weight of his saddlebags on his shoulder and recalled what was inside. He opened one of the flaps, pulled out the crushed, rose-colored package and thrust the thing at her.

"Here. These are for you. I bought them at Collette's when I, well——"

He halted. At the time, he'd thought the handkerchiefs were an appropriate gift for his homecoming and impending engagement. But now...

"Oh, Creed." She stared down at the package in her hands. "Collette's? For me? You must've paid a fortune."

"I didn't."

Not really, and even if he had, seeing the pleasure in her expression now would've been worth it.

"They're beautiful."

Carefully, as if she feared the contents would get up and fly away, she laid the gift on the table, parted the paper wide and gasped in delight at the miniature squares of cloth, each clearly a treasure.

But of all of them, her fingers lingered over one in particular, in pristine white, delicately edged in lace.

"I'll make a christening bonnet with this," she breathed. "It will fit her little head just right." He must've looked confused; her smile grew. "The baby's, Creed."

Something swelled inside him. "'Her'?"

"I'm hoping." Her eyes twinkled. "Would you like a sister?"

Emotion pushed up into his throat. When he left, he'd miss the baby's birth, like he'd missed Ma dying, because life went on, his family living it every day without him. The happy times and the sad.

She regarded him again. "All of this is hard for you, isn't it? The changes since you've been gone, I mean."

"I'm sorry." He blew out an agonized breath. "I don't want it to be."

"I wish it wasn't. Maybe this will help." Gently, she took his hand and pressed his palm to the side of her belly. Tiny kicks patted against his palm. "Your father's baby is real,

Creed. I hope you'll be able to love her as much as we already do."

The anguish broke. Creed bundled Mary Catherine into his arms and held her tight. He'd been an ass to resent the innocent growing in her womb. And he'd been unfair to disdain the happiness she found with the Old Man, too.

"She'll be lucky to have you as her mother," he said, voice husky. "And Pa, he never would've married you if he didn't love you enough."

"Nor I him." Eyes shimmering, Mary Catherine drew back and kissed his cheek. "We'll not speak of it again. Go on upstairs now. Your old room is waiting for you."

His mood lighter, he released her and headed toward the stairs. "Yeah? Does it still look the same?"

"*Exactly* the same."

He climbed the first step.

"Creed?"

He halted, one hand on the rail.

"He never gave up hope you'd come back, you know."

That helped his mood, too. "Good night, Mary Cat."

He climbed the stairs; at the top, down the hall to the right, was his old bedroom, the door open and inviting. Instead, he turned left, toward Marcus's room, where Gina would be.

The door was closed, and he didn't bother to knock before going in. A breeze drifted through the open window; curtain hems flitted and swayed. Moonlight shone in through the glass, illuminating her shape under the covers.

He latched the door, turned the lock. Her dark head swiveled on the pillow, and he could feel her watch him, the awareness between them building. This need in him, too, that wouldn't go away, even in his father's house.

Setting her valise on the floor, he dropped his saddlebags on top, and pulled his shirt free from his Levi's.

"I hoped you would come," she whispered.

She threw the covers back for him. In moments, the mattress took his weight, and he gathered her into his arms. Desire swept through him, hot and sweet. He succumbed to the power of her kisses, the allure of her body, and fulfilled the promise he'd made in the bathhouse.

By making love to her in a bed. All night long.

The *visione* came again. But this time, different.

Mama sat in a soft haze of light with her slender body propped against fluffy pillows and immaculate white blankets over her lap. Shining and thick, her hair flowed over her shoulders, a contrast against the brilliance of her gown. A smile filled her face, her happiness as vibrant as the light illuminating her.

Gina called to her, and Mama laughed, her black eyes twinkling. Her arms lifted. Reaching...waiting.

"Mia bella figlia. *My beautiful daughter. Come, come to me...."*

Gina began to run, her arms reaching, too. Elation filled her heart, the need to embrace her mother consuming. Finally, finally. It had been so long, so frightening....

She ran and ran, yet it was as if her legs were filled with sand, and she could not reach her. Mama sat, smiling, elusive but patient, waiting and waiting....

Gina awoke with a start.

Her pulse pounded. The certainty her mother was safe and alive had never been this strong. This real.

The vision faded, and comprehension of the new morning took its place. Sunshine streamed through the window, freshened by a crisp, clean breeze.

Creed was gone. Startled by it, she sat up. His saddle-bags were gone, too. But her valise sat on the floor, where he'd left it last night. On a chair, her coat, neatly draped, along with her sheaf of sketches.

Marcus would have returned from their line shack at the West Camp. Creed was with him, then, and an urgency to tell Creed of her new *visione* sent her hastening from the bed to find him.

After she dressed and tidied up the room, she rushed down the stairs and into the kitchen. A pot of coffee sat hot on the stove, a skillet heaped with fried potatoes on an adjacent burner. On the sideboard, a basket of eggs and a platter of sliced bread. A stack of plates and cups and forks, too.

Breakfast made, but not served.

Mary Catherine was nowhere to be found, and alarm flickered through Gina. She kept moving, into the front room and out the door. Her footsteps quickened across the porch and down the steps.

A shiny black runabout sat in the lane, and she recognized it as Graham Dooling's. Why was he here? *Where* was he? Why hadn't the Sherman family welcomed him into their home?

Where was Creed? Where was *everyone?*

Her gaze searched beyond the yard and found nothing; she lifted her dress hem and ran toward the barn, and there she spied a group of cowboys standing with the Shermans and Graham under the wide-reaching shade of a stately cottonwood tree growing nearby. All of them in a circle, their expressions somber beneath their Stetsons, and her alarm intensified. Gina tried hard not to be afraid and hurried toward them.

Several of the men she knew, those of the Sherman outfit she'd met last night. Several others, young and old, she hadn't seen before. Creed and Graham were hunkered next to the cowboy named Lonnie, lying on the ground with his Stetson beside him, his forehead wrapped in a blood-smeared bandanna.

He lay so still, she gasped from the fear he was dead. Heads lifted toward her, and the circle widened, letting her in.

Creed's grim gaze raised to hers. A rough beard shadowed his cheeks. He wore his Stetson low, like the holster strapped to his hips. The hard glint in his eyes revealed none of the loving he'd given her last night. He was a different man now. Cold and full of hate.

"The Sokolovs bombed the East Camp," he said. "Lonnie was there, taking a turn at watch, and got caught in it. Hube found him this morning and brought him in."

"Oh, no." Horrified, Gina made the Sign of the Cross.

The cowboy peeped up at her through barely opened lids. "Now, don't you go…prayin' over me, Miss Briganti. I ain't dead yet, far as I know."

She knelt beside him on a wave of relief. "How bad are you hurt?"

"Bad enough, I reckon."

"You're going to pull through," Creed said. "Pa's called for a doctor. He'll tell you the same thing."

"It gets worse, Miss Briganti. Read this." Graham tossed a newspaper into her lap. "The announcement was made yesterday."

She glanced at the headline emblazoned across the top of the *Los Angeles Daily Times,* enthusiastically proclaiming President McKinley's impending arrival that very night to the thousands of people who would read it.

The secret, no longer secret.

"The article reveals the time his train will arrive," Graham said. "Preparations are being made as we speak to give him a proper California welcome."

"The Sokolovs will know exactly where he'll be. And when," Creed said, mouth tight.

"Yes," she said, feeling his worry, too.

"To complicate matters, the president has requested a visit to a hot mineral spring as soon as possible for his wife," Graham continued. "This ranch has one of the nicest private bathhouses around. I rode out to request permission of the Sherman family and make arrangements. Needless to say, the attack on Lonnie has raised the risks against McKinley dramatically."

"But the brothers will know where to find him," she said in alarm, the memory of finding her scarf, the knowledge that Nikolai had used the waters, too, still vivid in her mind.

"If the president of the United States wants his wife to use the bathhouse, we'll damn well find a way so she can," Gus said.

"We just have to capture them before she does, that's all," Creed said.

Gina stared at him. "Why do you make it sound so easy?"

"It won't be. And it sure won't get any easier the more we waste time talking about it."

The tension shimmered from him. His urgency to vanquish the enemy before it was too late. Cold fear clutched her by the throat. He could be hurt or killed, and how could she possibly stop him from going?

Creed gave the injured cowboy's shoulder a squeeze. "Take it easy until we get back."

"Sure thing, Creed. Whip their hides for me, will you?"

"Count on it. Stan and Charlie will help Pa get you into the house." He rose, swept the men with a grim glance. "Handle him with care, boys. The rest of you, get ready to ride out."

Gus didn't move. "I'm coming with you, Creed. Don't for a damned minute think I'm not."

Creed shot him a stern look. "It's too dangerous. You've got Mary Cat to think of. The baby."

"There's a war happening on Sherman land," he rumbled. "You're defending the president of the United States, but I've got things just as important to fight for."

For a long moment, Creed didn't move, as if he weighed the risks against the need. The loss, too, if the fight turned wrong. Finally, he gave his father a curt nod. "Be ready in five minutes."

The circle broke quickly. Creed lingered, making sure his orders were followed. Only afterward did he glance down at her.

"I'll be back as soon as I can," he said.

His lack of emotion chilled her. For the first time, she saw him for who he truly was—a soldier, prepared to kill. A mercenary consumed with the desire to destroy.

He cared little about her concern for him. Or that he'd be leaving her behind. Obviously, he'd forgotten the closeness they shared only hours ago, too. The love they'd made, again and again.

The hurt roared through her. His interest in her had only been physical, entertainment to enjoy until the time came to confront the enemy. Would he remember her when the thrill from the battle was over?

"You do not have to do this," she said, hovering on the brink of pleading with him.

His eyes narrowed. "The hell I don't."

"Wire General Carson if you must. He has more men—the Army can find Nikolai and Alex faster. It is their job to—"

"It's my job as well. You *know* it is."

She crossed her arms to keep from reaching for him. "I do not want you to go. Does the attack on Lonnie mean nothing? You must save the lives of your father and his men." She swallowed, hating herself for being as scared as she sounded. "And you must save your own."

"Of anyone, Gina, I thought you'd understand." His cold gaze switched to Graham. "You riding with us?"

"I am, sir. Most certainly."

"I'll have a horse saddled for you."

He turned, then, and headed for the barn. Graham hastened to keep up with him.

Suddenly, he pivoted back toward Gina, his expression stricken.

"Forgive me, Miss Briganti. I neglected to tell you— another reason I rode out here—in all the excitement over the cowboy, Lonnie—" His throat bobbed. "I forgot to mention your mother has been found."

Her fingers flew to her mouth.

Creed swung toward him.

"What?" they said in unison.

His apologetic gaze jumped between them. "I'm sorry. Oh, God, I'm so sorry. It completely escaped my mind. I received the news only minutes before I drove out here."

Gina's bosom heaved. "Where is she? Is she all right? Where has she *been?*"

"She's been in the care of Good Samaritan Hospital. The Los Angeles Infirmary was simply too full after the Premier fire, and when she was found, she wasn't conscious, and thus she was unable to—"

"Unconscious?" Her breath quickened.

"Please be assured, Miss Briganti, she's doing as well as can be expected considering her injuries—"

"Injuries?" Gina's voice raised an octave.

"She's quite coherent, as I understand it, and has been asking for you, so please try not to worry too much until—"

"Try not to *worry?*" Gina had heard enough. "I must go to her." She spun toward the main house, for her coat and hat in Marcus's room.

But an iron grip clamped on her arm, holding her fast.

"No," Creed said.

Aghast, she stared up at him. "What?"

A muscle ticked in his cheek. "Not yet, Gina. It isn't safe for you to leave."

"You would deny me my *mother?*" The quaver in her tone revealed her shock, her absolute fury, that he would dare to do such a thing after all the pain, the tears, the heartache—oh, how *dare* he?

"The Sokolovs are on Sherman land," he grated. "I'd swear on Ma's best bible that Nikolai is watching us now, from somewhere close. I can feel him, the bastard, breathing down our necks, and damn it, Gina, you're not going anywhere until I have him dead or behind bars, I don't care which."

"Mr. Sherman is quite right," Graham added, looking so sympathetic Gina wanted to choke him. "Even if he were to engage a detail of armed men to escort you into the city, you'd be defenseless against a bomb thrown at you along the way." He seemed to draw courage from his own logic. "For someone of Mr. Sherman's expertise, it shouldn't take long at all to track the brothers down. You'll see."

Her mind raced. She forced down the fury.

"When will you be back?" she asked, sounding calmer.

"Tonight." Creed hesitated. "Maybe tomorrow."

Did he really think she would wait so long?

"Fine," she said.

He regarded her warily. "You'll stay with Mary Cat. In the house. Nikolai can't get to you there. She could use a hand taking care of Lonnie, besides." His grip eased on her arm, but only slightly. "Agreed?"

Gina nodded. Once. "Agreed."

"All right. I'll see you soon."

He stepped closer, his intent to kiss her goodbye.

She stepped back, so he couldn't.

The muscle in his cheek moved again. "Go on in, Gina. I'm staying right here until you do."

"Fine."

She turned. With a controlled, even stride, she walked away. Toward the house. Into the yard. Onto the porch. Feeling him watch her, her hand reached for the doorknob....

She dared a look over her shoulder. In his haste to begin the fight, Creed turned away and walked with Graham toward the barn, his trust in her obedience complete.

And foolish.

She hurriedly crouched into a corner of the porch, out of sight. Inside the house, she could hear Mary Catherine fussing over Lonnie. Outside, the sound of men's voices near the barn melded into the thunder of horses' hooves.

Gina waited until the drone faded away. She didn't dare enter the house to retrieve her coat and hat. Nor did she dare hurry to the barn to saddle her bay.

But she dared to steal Graham's runabout.

With the reins grasped tight in her hands, she drove fast toward the city and prayed to the Madonna to forgive her for the sin.

Chapter Twenty-Two

Nikolai watched them ride away through the field glasses. An army of Sherman men, led by the tall American. Creed. All of them armed and smelling the blood of the hunt.

His blood.

He watched until only their dust remained. He slid the lenses slowly along the perimeter of the yard, past the barn and toward the big house, until he found her again, the beautiful Gina Briganti, on the porch. He kept his sights on her, his interest building as she climbed into the black rig parked in front. She drove down the lane at great speed. In the opposite direction of Creed Sherman and his men.

Nikolai lowered the glasses in surprise.

Toward the city?

His mouth curved from his good fortune. He thrust the binoculars at Alex, sitting next to him on his horse. "We will go after her."

Alex peered through the lenses. "The Briganti woman?"

Impatience flitted through Nikolai at the stupidity of his brother's question. He felt it more often of late, this impatience. "Who else would I speak of? Yes. Gina."

He fought down his annoyance with a quick swig of vodka. Worried about the fever that had ravaged Nikolai last night, Alex had brought a bottle back with him from Los Angeles early this morning, along with another wire from Karlov and the latest edition of the *Los Angeles Daily Times*.

At last, the information Nikolai needed to set his revolution in motion had arrived, yet so little time remained to prepare for McKinley's arrival.

For that, he needed Gina Briganti.

"Forget about her, Nikolai. It is the American you should be concerned about," Alex said, dragging the lenses over the horizon.

Nikolai grunted and shoved the vodka back into his knapsack.

"He has guards posted everywhere to protect his family," Alex said.

"I saw them."

"He is angry you bombed the line camp and injured one of his father's men. You should not have played games with him. Now he wants revenge."

Nikolai steeled himself against the complaining and took up the reins. The vodka's heat slid into his veins, numbed the pain in his thigh and diluted the fear.

"Be strong, Alex. I will not let him hurt you." But it wasn't the mercenary who filled his thoughts. Instead, another gave him focus, drove him with a sweet urgency. His gaze touched on the lane, now empty of the black rig. "We must hurry, or we will lose Gina Briganti inside the city."

Creed squatted next to the banked campfire and leveled his hand over the embers. A faint heat shimmered against his palm.

"They were here," he said, grim. "A couple of hours ago."

"How can you be sure?" Marcus asked, seated on his horse behind Creed. "Might be anyone drifting through these parts."

"The East Camp isn't far from here." He squinted, gauging the distance, figuring in a ride from the bathhouse, too. "Nikolai's wounded in the leg. It'd be hard for him to stay in the saddle long."

"This might be just the evidence you need, son." Pa strode closer and handed him an empty bottle. "Found it in the weeds over there."

Creed read the label. "Manganese dioxide."

"Mixed with sulfuric acid, it becomes explosive," Graham said.

Marcus slid a whistle through his teeth. "There you go, big brother."

"I wonder how many bombs he's made by now." Graham looked worried enough for all of them.

Creed tapped the mouth of the container against his palm; only a few remaining granules of black powder came out, and he tossed the bottle aside in disgust. "Enough to use up his supplies."

Pa's glance met his. "Hard part's knowing which way they went from here."

Creed read a different kind of worry in that glance. The close proximity to the main house. The possibility the brothers could slip undetected between the men keeping watch around the place.

And damn, the damage a single bomb could do…

"A rider's coming, Creed."

Smoke's warning cut through his thoughts. He stood. His gaze clawed rangeland before snagging on a figure emerging from a shroud of dust. The frenzied tattoo of the horse's hooves made it plain whoever rode him was in one hell of a hurry.

Leather creaked as Smoke all but stood in the stirrups to identify him. "Oh-oh. It's Hube."

Creed's mind ran wild with reasons why the cowboy would search them out when he'd been given orders to guard the road leading to the main house.

And every reason ended with bad news.

Hube pulled up with a spray of grass and dirt and with an expression as frantic as his ride had been.

"It's Miss Briganti," he choked out. "She's up and gone."

Creed's heart dropped to his toes. "What do you mean, she's gone?"

"Didn't know it was her at first. She was in the runabout, driving like her tail was on fire. Hell, Creed, I thought it was *Graham* until I remembered he'd stayed behind to ride with you."

"And you didn't go after her?" he thundered, pivoting toward the palomino.

"I started to, but then I saw a couple of riders watching her from on top of a ridge. I couldn't get a good look at 'em, but I had a pretty fair guess who they might be, and I figured you'd want to know about it." He sucked in a breath. "I'm sorry, Creed. I didn't know what else to do but come lookin' for you."

Creed stabbed a boot into the stirrup and swung up into the saddle. Pa, he noted, was already in his.

"You did the right thing, Hube." He clutched the reins. The adrenaline kicked through him, hot and thick. "You told us what we needed to know."

He spurred the palomino into a hard run and fought the sick feeling that he'd never get to her in time.

Gina rounded the bend in the road with the fervent hope she wouldn't get lost somewhere on the vast Sherman rangeland. She had to believe she was going the right way, that this road would take her straight to the outskirts of Los Angeles.

Her entire being ached with the need to reach her mother's bedside. Her pulse drummed a desperate beat with every second, every agonizing minute, keeping her away.

She slapped the reins again. Faster, faster. Mama would be afraid. She would be confused and worried about why her daughter wasn't with her, and oh, Gina couldn't get the horse to run fast enough.

The wind blew at her face, her hair. Her gaze clung beyond the road, onto the horizon, and then, they appeared. The faint shape of buildings. Tiny, indistinct, but they were there, and giddy, dizzying relief soared through her, filling her thoughts, her mind, with the glorious anticipation of soon seeing her mother again.

An anticipation so intense she barely comprehended the sight of two men in front of her, on the road, blocking her path.

Too late, she reacted, bracing her feet against the floorboard and pulling on the reins with all her strength. The horse reared; his shrill whinny streaked through her ears. The rig lurched and swayed; she screamed from the sensation of tilting to one side, of being turned upside down. From the awful realization she would be hurt or killed, and oh, sweet Madonna, no, no, no…

And then, nothing.

Except for the air filling her lungs, helping her breathe. And the awareness that she lay full out on the ground with the rough prickle of range grass against her back.

Her eyes opened, strained to focus, and blinked against the brilliant blue of the sky. She waited for pain, but the fire didn't come. She expected noise, but heard only silence. She moved muscles, arms and legs and feet, and managed it.

A shape formed above her. A giant of a man, blocking the sky. The weapon in his hand formed, too, and the bottle of vodka he pressed to his lips. He nudged her ribs with the toe of his boot.

"Stand up, beautiful Gina," he purred.

Shaken and furious, she sat bolt upright. "Damn you, Nikolai!"

"You will come with me," he said and capped his bottle.

"I will not."

She scrambled to her feet. Her gaze clawed over Graham's rig, lying on its side, its rigging twisted and tangled. Dismay rolled through her, her only means of escape destroyed.

"We must talk," Nikolai said.

Her glance jumped back to him. "No."

"I have much to teach you."

She took a step away, out of the grass and toward the road, a feeble attempt to distance herself from him and his fanatical ideas. "You will not convince me of anything you say."

The ominous-looking revolver waved a broad arc in the air. "President McKinley is coming today. Did you know that?"

She kept his weapon in her range of vision. "Many people know."

"We must be ready for him."

A rosy flush stained his cheeks, and sweat glistened on his forehead. The fever that ravaged him.

"I must go into the city, Nikolai." Her fury died into desperation, but there was no help for it. "My mother needs me. She waits for me to come."

The ice-blue eyes, glazed and wild, bored into her. "You are lying!"

The vehemence of his accusation startled her. "It is the truth!"

"You say so, but you will go to the police and tell them all that I have done."

Her breath quickened. She would, of course. She had to, for the justice he deserved. But only after she reunited with her mother first.

Nikolai didn't seem to notice her lack of denial. He took a step toward her, then another.

"We must prepare for our act of demolition, beautiful Gina, so that a better society can be built for the people."

"You talk crazy," she said, going a little crazy herself.

"Man must be free to create his own happiness!"

"Then let me *go*."

From behind her on his horse, Alex snorted. "Do you really think he will? After what you did to him?"

Her gaze dropped to Nikolai's thigh and the blood seeping through bandages. She swallowed and dared a different way to convince him.

"I hurt you, Nikolai," she said. "You need a doctor. Strong medicine. Come with me. The hospital will help you."

He faltered, his hand finding his injury. "I must go to the healing waters again."

She shook her head carefully. "Not even the waters can help you. You are too sick."

"There is no time for the waters," Alex said. "And we cannot keep sitting here having useless conversation." He leaned forward, looking pale and distressed. "The mercenary will come after her, Nikolai. He will find us and kill us."

"Quit whining!" Nikolai snapped.

"He will." Gina seized upon Alex's worry. "He is a skilled soldier. You cannot win over him."

A sniveling sound slipped from Alex's throat. "Kill her, Nikolai. She is only a burden to us!"

The burly Russian's fevered glance jumped over each of them. He swiped his forehead with the cuff of his sleeve.

"Get on my horse, Emma," he said, as if his brother had never spoken. "The president is coming. Together, we will ride to meet him."

A shiver wrapped around her spine from his confusion, his intent. "I will not help you hurt him. I swear I will not."

The revolver jabbed toward the waiting mount. *"Get on my horse!"*

Alex appeared distraught. "Do it, will you? Just do it!"

She had no choice. Nikolai wouldn't hurt her if she didn't resist, and she wouldn't be able to thwart an assassination attempt if she was dead.

Because, for now, there was no one else. No guarantees, only dwindling hope, that Creed and his father's men would find her in time to help her save President McKinley's life.

Talons of fear gripped Creed at the sight of Graham's runabout lying on its side in the road.

He pulled up sharply, and the others reined in beside him. He twisted back and forth in the saddle, a sweeping search for some sign of Gina, hoping against hope she'd been thrown clear in the accident and not left crushed and broken from it.

Marcus searched, too. "Maybe she went looking for help."

Smoke veered right and walked his horse off the road. He pointed to the ground. "She landed here. By the trampled look of it, the grass cushioned her fall."

The carriage lay on its right side. The theory fit, and Creed took some comfort from it.

"No blood that I can see," Smoke added.

Pa rubbed his jaw in consternation. "Then we have to believe she walked away, free and able."

Creed nudged the palomino forward, skirting the downed carriage. "Able, maybe, but not free. She would've been hell-bent on getting to her mother." He studied the tracks in the dirt, smeared footprints with two sets of iron hooves, as plain as rain. "And she sure as hell didn't walk. The brothers took her."

He ambled the palomino beyond the hoof prints, but the search yielded nothing more. Since there were no more tracks in the dirt, it could only mean the brothers had turned off the road.

His glance lifted to the left. The horses had trod over the range grass on this side, breaking the stems and leaving an obvious trail to where they were headed.

He scanned the horizon, on the right. If the Sokolovs intended to lose themselves in the bowels of the city, it would've made for a faster ride to stay on the road. Had they left it to avoid being pursued?

Or did they have a different destination?

His scrutiny swung back to the left again. Not much lay beyond the Los Angeles boundaries except for the Santa Fe and Southern Pacific Railroad lines.

And the warning bells began to clang.

"Graham, what time is it?" He urged the palomino onto the trail of trampled grass, and the others followed.

The Secret Service agent pulled his watch from his vest pocket. "Just after noon, sir. Twelve thirty-two."

"What time did the newspaper say the President's train was due?"

"Nine o'clock tonight. Why?"

"It's coming sooner than that."

The men exchanged puzzled glances.

"You know something we don't?" Marcus asked.

"As a matter of fact, I do." He thought of the coded

message he'd sent to Washington and was confident his orders would be followed, that Jeb and General Carson would see that they were. He thought, too, of the little-used siding he hadn't seen for more than six years, the auxiliary track off the main line that was far enough away from the train depot that no one would see McKinley ride in. "Forget what the papers say. The president is coming in on an express train that'll pull into the Diamond Bar Station in a little over an hour's time. A carriage will be waiting to rush him and his wife to a private hotel for the duration of their stay."

Graham whistled, long, low and surprised. "I'm impressed, Mr. Sherman."

"Don't be. He's not out of danger yet." Apprehension churned through him in waves. The brothers had fled in the very direction the train would be coming from. "And neither is Gina."

"But having him arrive this far in advance of the publicly announced time and at a different station besides will have the anarchists waiting for a train that's not going to come," Graham exclaimed. "By nine tonight, the McKinleys will be safely hidden away."

"That's the plan," Creed said, grim.

"Smart thinking, son," Pa said. Pride flowed rough and genuine from his voice, but Creed couldn't allow himself to take pleasure from it.

"A tunnel leads up to the line, doesn't it?" he asked.

His father nodded. "Several miles back from the Diamond Bar. The tunnel opens up right next to the trestle bridge."

They drew closer to the foothills of the Santa Monica Mountains, blanketed with the oak woodlands which grew thick amongst the sage scrub.

He held up a hand, and the men halted. He studied the

gaping mouth of the tunnel, hewn out of a low hill and capped with a roof of scrub and grass. The bridge butted up against the hill and carried the tracks over a narrow canyon, where they connected on the other side with the main lines leading into Los Angeles.

He stared hard at the tunnel roof and caught movement. Three indistinct figures, but there wasn't a doubt of who they were.

Once they realized it was President McKinley's train heading toward that tunnel, Nikolai would seize the chance to kill him. There wouldn't be a better place to try than right there, on top, while the train was running through. No one would see a bomb drop, and even if they did, there'd be no way to stop the train before the bomb exploded.

Creed had to stop the brothers. He had to get Gina out of their clutches.

A slow, feral smile formed on his mouth.

And he knew just how he was going to do it.

Chapter Twenty-Three

"Does nothing scare you, Creed?"

The Old Man looked plenty serious as he crouched in the stand of ponderosa pines and handed over the Remington. Creed put his arm through the leather sling and slid the weapon high over his shoulder.

"Not when I have a job to do," he said.

"A battle to fight, you mean. Another war to win."

Creed shot him a hard look. Pa's cynicism put a bite in his tone. Reminded Creed of the long stream of arguments they'd had before he left for West Point.

"Call it what you want. Won't change things." He tossed his Stetson aside to retrieve later.

"Don't reckon it would."

With the way he pressed his lips together, Creed couldn't help but think his father was determined not to say the words right there on his tongue.

Creed had no time to wonder what they were, anyway. The rest of the Sherman outfit was in position and waiting. All that was left was for Creed to make the first move.

"I'm heading up," he said. "You know what to do."

The Old Man nodded. But he reached out and grasped Creed's shoulder with one callused hand.

"Be careful, son," he said roughly.

Creed went soft. The closest thing he'd gotten to an embrace from the Old Man in how long? "This is what I do, remember?"

"Yeah. That's what scares me."

Creed's mouth curved. Adrenaline curled through him, and he turned his mind toward what lay ahead.

Getting Gina away from Nikolai first and foremost.

It'd been hard being apart from her, harder not being able to see her, but his gut instincts told him Nikolai wasn't going to hurt her just yet. He wouldn't have brought her all the way out here and onto the top of a tunnel to wait for McKinley without having a perverted reason for having her there.

Whatever that perverted reason might be tied his stomach into knots. He left the shelter of the pines and sprinted toward the rim of the canyon, out of sight from the Sokolovs on the tunnel.

He could hear voices. Nikolai's, mostly, on one of his anarchist ramblings, and Creed regretted Gina's being forced to endure it. He squatted beside some brush and sought out Smoke and Marcus, both of them perched like crows on the wooden beams bracing the bridge.

Each gave him a silent nod to indicate their readiness. Graham would be farther up the side of the tunnel, closer to Gina. Hube, too, his job to cover the Old Man. And all of them would cover Creed.

He took a breath and leapt to the nearest truss. He monkey-climbed upward, his movements stealthy in the shadow of the rails. He pulled himself through the ties, then crept up the side of the hill to the transom. A few careful steps took him to the center of the ledge; he pulled his rifle from his back, acutely aware that one wrong move, one wild shot, would send him hurtling backward to the bottom of the canyon.

He straightened, high enough to peer over the tunnel's top. He took in the trio's positions with one swift glance: Gina sitting, looking miserable with her knees folded to her chest. Nikolai standing in front of her, one leg bearing his weight, preaching like a professor to his student. Alex, never still, pale and anxious and looking ready to throw up any minute.

But it was the knapsack lying open at Nikolai's feet that turned Creed's blood cold. The vitriol bombs waiting to explode.

Creed had the advantage. The Sokolovs wouldn't expect him to appear like this, from below the tunnel, like a devil from the fires of hell.

Slowly, he straightened, lifted the butt of the rifle to his shoulder...

"We must assert our independence!" Nikolai railed, his back to Creed. He flaunted a bottle of vodka, but his .44 hung loose at his side, as if he'd forgotten he still carried it. "We must rebel for the benefit of the masses."

Gina lowered her dark head and covered her ears with her hands. "Stop, Nikolai! I will not listen to you anymore!"

He flung aside the vodka. "You must listen so you will believe!" He lunged toward her with an awkward limp, grabbed her wrist and jerked her to her feet. "I have a way to end the hypocrisy, Emma. See?" He swung back toward the knapsack. "I know the ways for revolution."

Creed had heard enough. He cocked the rifle, and the sound cracked through the air like a whip.

"Get back from that knapsack, Nikolai," he snarled. "Drop your gun at the same time."

Nikolai jolted in surprise, as if struck by a lightning bolt. Gina and Alex cried out in shock.

Creed stepped from the transom onto the tunnel roof. They stood frozen. He kept his aim true.

"I'm not going to tell you again," he said slowly, succinctly.

Nikolai's lips curled back in a sneer. "Do you hear what the American says, Emma? He thinks he can fight all three of us."

"He knows I will not fight him." Gina's bosom heaved. "Do as he says or he will kill you."

Nikolai let loose with a drunken, maniacal laugh. "Karlov, do you hear what he says?"

Alex appeared near tears. "I hear him."

The man was delusional in thinking Gina was Emma Goldman, that Alex was their informant in Washington. Creed dared to take a step closer. He willed Gina silent strength to trust him, to know he'd get her out of this mess if it was the last thing he ever did. And he had to use every skill he possessed to make sure that it wasn't.

"You're surrounded, Nikolai," he said. "I'll bet you didn't know that, did you?"

To punctuate the announcement, Marcus popped up over the tunnel roof and cocked his rifle. Smoke did the same, standing beside him on the transom. From the side, Hube and the Old Man and then Graham appeared, each with their weapons pointed.

Gina tugged against the Russian's grip. "Give up now while you still can. Please!"

Sweat poured from Nikolai's forehead, his face flushed. His breathing rasped harsh, labored, in the tense silence. He appeared to waver, weighing his dedication to his cause against the merits of his life.

Creed's finger moved over the trigger. It wouldn't be easy for Gina to see him kill Nikolai in cold blood. He held back, waited until the time came when he couldn't wait anymore…

"Do something, Nikolai!" Alex pleaded.

Gina darted a quick glance to Creed, and he read the message she implored in her dark eyes. That it was his turn to trust her. She faced Nikolai again. "The American does not believe as we do, comrade." Her arm lifted, and she placed her hand over his. "Go with him for a little while." Her voice had turned soft, soothing. "He will see that you get the medicine you need to be strong again. Then, when the time is right, you will be free to join me in our dream for revolution."

The Russian's gaze dropped to her hand, then lifted to meet hers. The ice in his eyes melted with indecision and pain.

"Emma, Emma," he whispered.

She gave him a tentative smile of encouragement. "Trust me, Nikolai. Karlov and I will continue your work while you are gone. Will you trust me in that?"

"She is lying, Nikolai," Alex yelled. "She is *lying!*"

"Shut up!" Creed snapped.

Nikolai's head swiveled toward his brother. "Why must you always complain, Karlov? Do you not know by now you must be strong like her?"

Alex choked on the tears streaming down his face. "Nikolai. Oh, Nikolai!"

"Silence!" he thundered.

The kid whimpered but obediently fell silent.

"Drop your gun," Gina said, and the Russian turned back to her. "Over there, by the American."

He glanced down at the .44. Frowned. Then, amazingly, he tossed it toward Creed.

She sagged a little in relief and patted his hand in

approval. "You are a man of honor, Nikolai. Our comrades will soon know of the sacrifices you make for the sake of our revolution."

"My revolution." He released a worried sigh.

"Now, let go of her." Creed kept her strategy going by keeping his voice smooth, calm. "Step back when you do."

Again, the man hesitated.

"It is all right," she cooed. "We will be reunited again soon."

He released her, as trusting as a child. "I will write you, Emma. Every day."

She nodded. "Yes, yes. Our work must continue."

Nikolai swayed from the effects of the vodka and fever and limped backward. She wet her lips and slowly, slowly, bent down to the knapsack at her feet.

"Your ways for revolution will not be forgotten, Nikolai. I will act. In your place."

Gingerly, she grasped the bundle and straightened. One quick move, one careless knocking of the explosives inside could blow them all into pieces. Creed's pulse pounded at her nerve when his own was at the breaking point.

Chuff, chuff, chuff...chuff, chuff, chuff...

The distant sound seeped into his awareness, and he dragged his sights from Gina to the short train clattering down the tracks on the other side of the hill, rounding the bend and heading toward the tunnel.

A top-secret junket, sleek and dignified, and arriving right on time, with the most important man in the United States of America.

"McKinley's train, Nikolai!" Alex screamed. "The paper lies! He's here! He's here!"

Gina cried out, and with more speed, more courage, more *patriotism* than any woman Creed had ever known, she pivoted and hurled the knapsack away from all of them. The bundle sailed through the sky in a perfect arc downward toward the opposite side of the hill, out of sight—

Ka-boom!

Ka-boom!

Ka-boom!

One after the other, the vitriol bombs exploded, rocking the earth from its force. Clods of dirt and range grass flung upward. A cloud of dust mushroomed through the air.

Nikolai roared in pure, diabolic fury and lunged for her in retaliation.

Five Sherman rifles fired instantly. His big body jerked. Blood bloomed from his back and chest, and he dropped like a rock. Dead.

Gina screamed. Terrified she'd been shot, Creed spun toward her. She'd been close. Too damned close, and if one of his father's men missed their mark, if one stray bullet slammed into her, oh, holy Lord—

But she was alive, standing there, beautiful and horrified and blessedly alive. Graham bolted toward her, grabbed her, and ran with her, taking her away, sparing her the ugliness of war, the ugliness of what Creed, of what all of them, had done....

Chuff, chuff, chuff...chuff, chuff, chuff...

The junket chugged closer to the tunnel. Closer, closer, and in the blink of an eye, the engine disappeared inside the gaping mouth. The roof shimmered from its roar.

Alex shrieked. He bolted for the Russian Army .44, plucked it from the grass, and kept running. And before Creed could stop him, before he could react to the train's engine barreling out the other side, Alex leapt over the transom and onto the flat top of the car rumbling through beneath him.

Creed swore. Viciously. He flung aside the rifle and leapt off the tunnel's roof after him.

Wind tore at his clothes and body. He crouched, his feet braced against the motion of the ride. Ahead of him, on the car hitched to Creed's, Alex wobbled with legs spread and arms flailing but his hand keeping a firm grip on the revolver.

The kid was crazy enough to go looking for the president inside the railcars to shoot him down cold in his brother's place. Creed sprinted after him.

Chuff, chuff, chuff…chuff, chuff, chuff…

The train barreled closer to the Diamond Bar Station. Creed jumped onto the next car.

"Alex, no," he yelled.

The kid whirled. His pale face twisted in contempt. The wind whipped at his thin hair, giving him a wild, demonic look. He swung the nose of the .44 toward Creed, leveled it with both hands.

But Creed kept going and tackled him to the wooden roof. His hand banded the bony wrist; one swift yank eliminated the .44's threat, and he tossed the revolver overboard, out of sight.

"You're in a hell of a lot of trouble, kid, so you might as well give up right now," Creed grated into his face.

Alex spat out a string of words, Russian blasphemies, most likely, and punctuated them all with a stream of spittle against Creed's cheek. Creed let loose with a few choice curses of his own.

"You really think you'll get to McKinley?" he demanded. "Even if you make it past me, this train is crawling with Secret Service agents that'll shoot you dead on sight. Now stand up."

He roughly jerked the kid to his feet. He lifted an arm

and swiped at the saliva with his shirtsleeve. Beneath his boot soles, the train rocked and rumbled.

Chiff, chiff, hiss-ss...chiff, chiff, hiss-ss.

The train slowed in its approach toward the station. Half-crazed and desperate, Alex watched him with his teeth bared, like a trapped mongrel, ready to attack.

"You've done a serious thing, attempting to assassinate the president. You're a prisoner of the United States government now. When we get off this train, you're going to tell the authorities what you know," Creed commanded.

"I will tell them nothing!"

"You'll tell them how you got your information from the War Department. They'll want to know who Karlov is, what he's done, and why," Creed shouted above the clackety-clack of the iron wheels over the rails. "Cooperate while you have the chance. You're young enough to still have a life once you get out of prison."

"I will not go into your filthy American jails!" Alex yelled.

"Yeah? Well, maybe they'll hang you instead."

The blood drained from the kid's face, and he gagged. Creed braced for him to get sick right there, on top of the train.

"Your revolution isn't going to happen, Alex," he said, ruthless in driving his point home, even if it was a waste of his breath to try. "And especially not without Nikolai."

Alex's face crumpled on a strangled sob. "Nikolai, Nikolai."

"He's dead, Alex. He's not here to take care of you, and he's not going to tell you what to do anymore."

The kid looked so distraught that pity stirred inside Creed, in spite of everything. The young Russian's life up to now hadn't been an easy one. From here on out, it wouldn't get any better.

The Diamond Bar Station appeared ahead. With it, the

inevitability of Alex's arrest and time in the jails he despised so much.

As if the same realization struck him, the kid wailed in anguish. The keening sound all but curdled Creed's blood.

Then, without warning, without giving Creed a chance to stop him, Alex hurled himself over the edge of the railcar.

Chapter Twenty-Four

Two Days Later

The sweet-faced student nurse bustled in with a bouquet of flowers almost bigger than she was. She set the arrangement on Mama's bedside table and stepped back to admire the effect.

"What is this?" Mama exclaimed. "The flowers are for me?"

The sparkle in the girl's eyes showed her delight. "Well, of course they are, Signora Briganti. Your name is on the card. Gina's, too. The flowers are for both of you!"

"Who are they from?" Gina was as astounded as her mother. The elegant roses, exotic lilies and vibrant chrysanthemums—who would be so extravagant?

"No one seems to know, and the card doesn't say." The young nurse hurried toward the door with a giggle. "But does it matter?"

She was gone before Gina could declare someone had made a mistake. Gina studied the miniature card tucked in amongst the greenery and found only their names listed, just as the girl said. Bemused, she dipped her nose into the delicate petals and inhaled their fragrance.

"Something strange is happening, Gina," her mother said, leaning back against the pillows with a sigh. "Too many surprises for us, eh?"

"Yes, Mama. One after the other."

Yesterday had been the first, when the nurses announced that her mother would no longer be cared for on the main floor of Good Samaritan Hospital, in the dormlike quarters where the beds were lined up in rows. Instead, they moved her upstairs, where the rooms were private. Even more amazing, she had been given the finest room of all, a suite reserved for the most important of hospital patients. All their meals were feasts prepared at their whim. Whatever they asked for, they received.

Not that they asked for much. Mama had been suspicious of the staff's generosity. Gina, too, confused and burdened from guilt. Who would think a pair of Italian immigrant women were worthy of such luxuries? And were they expected to pay for them in the end?

The doctors and nurses waved aside her insistent questions. They strictly, gently, told her again and again not to worry over the costs, that arrangements had been made by a secret benefactor who ordered their every need be met.

No one claimed to know the benefactor's name, but oh, everyone was curious. Many times, Gina heard the whispers, the speculations, of who he might be. And yesterday, when the *Los Angeles Daily Times* announced in their headlines how the Premier Shirtwaist Company factory seamstress named Gina Briganti helped to save President McKinley's life by destroying the bombs made by the anarchists who intended to assassinate him, well…

Gina was embarrassed to be the subject of so much

gossip. She'd simply done what anyone else would've done in the same situation.

All that mattered was Mama. To be with her again.

Gina's gaze lingered over her, and her heart swelled with a resurgence of love. Of gratitude and relief. How beautiful she looked against the crisp, white bed linens! Her thick wavy hair, the strands of gray only beginning to peek through, flowed about her shoulders and curled against her cotton hospital nightgown. The worry was gone from her face, and she appeared rested, relaxed. But happy, most of all.

Just like in Gina's *visione*.

Graham had whisked Gina away from the Santa Monica foothills after the bombs exploded and brought her straight to Good Samaritan Hospital. At first, she'd been devastated by her mother's bruises and injuries, the bandages around her hands which hid the burns and scars already beginning to form on her skin. In her frantic distress to follow Gina down to the first floor after finding her purse with their pay envelopes safe inside, Mama had hastily covered her hands with layers of shirtwaist fabric and used the wire ropes to slide down the elevator shaft. But the fabric burned through, the cable broke, and she fell. It was a blessing she lost consciousness until the brave firemen found her and rushed her to the hospital.

Many times, Gina thanked the Madonna for saving her mother from the terrible fires. But never again would her scarred fingers be nimble with a needle and thread. Nor would she sit at a Singer sewing machine and maneuver the delicate fabrics of the shirtwaists. And she could never be employed in a factory again.

Gina's teeth worried her lower lip. She'd have to work

harder than ever to support them both. The dismal prospect of going back to her dreary life of factory work and living in the dingy tenements depressed her. But what choice did she have?

With a heavy sigh, she stepped to the window. Brilliant sun sprayed the lawn and warmed the profusion of flowers in the manicured gardens. A stream of elegant carriages cruised up the road leading to the hospital. Good Samaritan was located in the heart of Los Angeles. Here, everyone and everything thrived.

Like it did at the Sherman ranch. She was only there a short while, but she'd always remember the openness and natural beauty of the land, the kindnesses of the Sherman family, the devoted cowboys who worked for them...

And Creed. Creed, most of all.

Had she ever met anyone more exciting?

Would she ever miss anyone more?

She'd not heard from him, or seen him, since Graham spirited her away to the city. But then, on the night they infiltrated the anarchist's meeting, Creed had told her he intended to leave America. The Sokolov brothers had only delayed his plans. Now, he'd won his fight. There was nothing to keep him in America any longer.

Not even her. Gina Briganti. The woman who'd paid the price in full for the services of his protection. She'd given him everything he wanted, hadn't she? The pleasures of her body because of the love she had for him.

And he hadn't even given her a chance to tell him goodbye. Would the hurt ever go away that he'd been so quick to forget her, leave her?

"Do you think of him again, Gina?" Mama asked softly.

She turned from the window. Her mother's ordeal had

been horrific. Gina refused to let her melancholy mood dampen her mother's healing.

"Who?" Her mouth softened with her teasing. "Sebastian?"

Mama snorted. "I wish you would be this lovesick over that one."

Gina moved to the bed and sat on the edge of the mattress. "You would like him to be my husband, yes, but you see how he flirts with the nurses when he comes to see us. We are friends, Mama. Nothing more."

"He knows you are in love with Creed Sherman. He tells me he sees it in your eyes. In your heart."

Gina fought a sudden sting of tears, and her mother's tongue clucked in sympathy. She brought Gina's head against her shoulder; her bandaged hands caressed her hair.

"What an *idiota* I am, Mama."

"Maybe you do not think an Italian immigrant woman is important enough for him?"

Gina drew in a weepy breath, let it out again. Many times, she had feared that very thing.

Her mother kissed the top of her head. "You tell me he is a man of honor in this country. If he truly loves you, nothing else will matter to him."

Before Gina could take the advice into her soul and allow herself to hope, footsteps mingled with the low murmur of voices in the hall. The sounds drew closer to their suite, and she sat up in puzzlement. By the time she regained her composure and rose from the bed, Graham appeared in the doorway, dressed in his usual dark suit and shiny shoes.

He grinned broadly. "Would you mind if we came in, Miss Briganti?"

Gina had no idea who "we" might be, but she nodded politely. "Of course not."

He stepped aside, and another man strode in, powerful and dignified and without announcement. Silver glittered at his temples, and a cleft creased his chin, and recognition left her positively speechless.

President William McKinley took her hand and dropped a light kiss to her knuckles. "I'm pleased to make your acquaintance, Miss Briganti."

She managed to find her voice. "Thank you, sir."

"And you must be Louisa, her mother."

Her black eyes widened at meeting one so prestigious. Mama clutched the bedsheet to her bosom. "*Sì, sì.* It is an honor to meet you. Oh, an honor."

Another Secret Service agent entered the room. He stood silent and respectful beside a woman in a wheelchair.

"My wife, ladies," the president said. "Ida Saxton McKinley."

Though her face was thin, and her once-auburn hair now short and gray, her features were lively and kind. She held a small bouquet of flowers, a discreet refusal to shake hands in light of her frail health, and she acknowledged their introductions with a gracious smile.

"America is indebted to you for what you did to save my husband's life, Miss Briganti," she said.

Gina thought of Creed, the risks he'd taken again and again. Graham, too, and the rest of the Secret Service, their devotion to protect their leader.

"I do only a small part, truly," she said.

"I will be forever grateful." McKinley smiled and swept an arm outward. "I trust your accommodations here are acceptable?"

Gina's glance touched on the lovely arrangement of

flowers, the spaciousness of their immaculate surroundings. "Oh, yes. More than we can dream of."

"Good, very good." He beamed. "You are guests of the American government. It's important to me your stay here be as comfortable as possible. A small token of my appreciation, you understand."

Gina exchanged a stunned glance with her mother. Their mysterious benefactor was President McKinley himself?

"The anarchism troubling our country is not to be tolerated," his wife added.

"Nor the despicable conditions in which many of this country's laborers must work." He grew somber. "The horrible ordeal you and the rest of the Premier Shirtwaist Company factory employees endured has not gone unnoticed. Those responsible will pay the price in the courts for their negligence and blatant disregard for the very people who make them profitable. I assure you Washington will work hard to make sure this tragedy won't happen again."

His avowal touched Gina. If anyone could bring about change, he could.

"Thank you," she and Mama murmured together.

"One more thing, Miss Briganti." He clasped his hands behind his back, his smile returning. "Would you honor the First Lady and me with the pleasure of your company at a private dinner tomorrow night?"

Gina's hand flew to her breast in surprise. "What?"

His wife's soft blue eyes sparkled. "I understand you have a talent for dress design. I'd be most pleased if you'd help me with my upcoming winter wardrobe. We'll make time after dessert to discuss your selections."

Her mind spun with panic, with pure elation. Never had she dreamed...how could she have ever thought...what if her sketches weren't good enough…oh, heavenly Madonna. One of her gowns, worn by the *wife of the president of the United States?*

"It's been a pleasure." In a polite signal that it was time for him to leave, McKinley patted Mama's bandaged hand. "My best wishes for your continued recovery, Signora Briganti."

"Thank you, sir." Her mother's face glowed with pride, with complete happiness.

"Likewise, Miss Briganti." He bent gallantly at the waist. "Until tomorrow night?"

"Yes," she said softly. "I will be there."

The Secret Service agent turned the First Lady's wheelchair around and rolled her toward the door. Her husband followed, but he paused in the hall.

"Mr. Dooling. See that she has everything she needs, won't you?"

"Yes, sir. Certainly."

The president winked and left.

Gina stood stunned at the exchange, her mind captive with all she must do, all she didn't have, her precious sketches left behind at the Sherman ranch, most of all.

She peered up at Graham in utter dismay. "I have nothing to wear!"

He chuckled. "I know the perfect dress shop. Be ready in an hour, and I'll take you there."

Gina stood in front of Collette's Fine Ladies Wear. She'd never been inside, but many times she'd window-shopped with Mama, and together they had admired the breathtaking gowns artfully displayed on mannequins. Now, she would soon have one of Collette's gowns for her very own.

Gina still couldn't believe it. And oh, she felt guilty, too, but Graham insisted she must accept McKinley's gift in the manner in which he intended it, another sign of his gratitude for what she'd done. To refuse him would be an insult.

Well, Gina couldn't very well insult America's president, could she? Because of her own stubborn pride?

"Any time you're ready, Miss Briganti, we'll go in," Graham said.

She sensed he tried not to laugh at her dawdling. Perhaps it'd serve her right if he did. She was acting as naive as she felt.

She sighed. "As soon as you open the door for me, we will go in."

He did laugh, then. "My sister is looking forward to meeting you. You'll like her, I think."

They entered. A tiny bell tinkled in announcement, and even the chime sounded as exclusive as the rest of the shop. Her gaze soaked in the array of colorful gowns, feathered hats and glass cases containing a wide assortment of accessories, all more beautiful up close than they had been from outside.

A tall, broad-shouldered man stood with his back to the door while he stared intently at something through the window. He appeared to wait for his wife and young daughter while they admired several parasols near him. By the look of his fine-cut frock coat in deep chocolate brown, he could afford to shop in the establishment, but his masculinity seemed out of place amongst all the feminine contrivances.

Yet it was the woman standing at the counter who hooked Gina's attention. Collette Dooling was strikingly gorgeous, shamelessly pampered and completely engrossed in the sketches spread out before her.

Gina's sketches.

The entire sheaf, right here in this shop.

Collette's glance lifted. She appeared stunned by what she'd been studying.

"These are exquisite," she breathed.

Gina pressed her fingers to her lips. It didn't matter how Collette got them or that she took the time to look or that she hadn't bothered with the formality of introductions since they knew who the other was, anyway—

She *liked* them!

"Do you think so?" she asked.

"Your talent excites me, Gina!" Her perfectly tinted lips formed an awed *O* as she picked up one design after another. "These are as good as any in Paris or London, and yet you don't imitate a particular style. You've taken what's fashionable and adapted it for the American woman. You've designed her as special and unique. She'll feel heavenly in your gowns, Gina. And she'll pay any price to be that way."

Gina tried not to be swept away by Collette's enthusiasm. Surely she had a tendency to exaggerate. The gowns couldn't be *that* striking.

Could they?

"This one—I must have it." Collette held up the tea gown design, the one Gina envisioned created in old-rose peau de soie and brocaded with delicate flowers, the one she'd been working on at the West Camp. "It's inspired by *la maison Rouff,* isn't it?"

"Yes." Gina marveled that she recognized the style. "But it is not finished yet, and—"

"And it's extravagant and glorious already. I *want* it in my shop."

"Oh." Her mind swam from the possibility. "You do?"

Collette set the design down and leaned forward, her heavy-lashed eyes wide with excitement. "Come work with me, Gina! We'll go to New York and buy bolts and bolts of luxurious fabric and every kind of trim imaginable. I'll give you room in the back and you can sew the dresses yourself. Or I'll hire you a staff. You'll have your own exclusive clientele in no time, and then you'll have your very own shop and be rich and reputable, and oh, say yes, Gina!"

Gina didn't know what to think, much less whether to agree. Could her dream be coming true? Was it possible?

"She'll never let you go back to a factory, you know," Graham said, smiling. "Might as well say yes and save yourself the trouble later."

Happiness swept through her, and she smiled, then, too. "I am honored to work in your shop. Thank you for asking me."

Collette laughed gaily and hurried toward her on a cloud of perfume. She flung her arms around Gina. "It is I who should be thanking *you!*" Suddenly, she drew back. "We'll have to discuss the details later. You're having dinner with the president tomorrow, aren't you? You need something exquisite to wear. Let me look at you." Her approving appraisal took Gina in from head to toe. "With a body like yours, you can wear anything. Come with me."

She led Gina toward an elegantly appointed corner of the shop. Along the way, she scooped up corsets, petticoats and hosiery. Upon reaching a small dressing area, she laid them all out on a brocade settee.

"We'll get you started with lingerie. I already have several gowns in mind for you. You'll look stunning in them. I'll be right back."

Swishing the heavy velvet drape closed and cloaking Gina in privacy, she left. Gina stood before the full-length mirror and considered her Sunday best dress, the navy-flowered one once her favorite, but now looking hopelessly simple and drab amongst Collette's elegance.

Gina was afraid she'd wake up and find herself living in another of her *visiones.* Yet after she removed her dress, the cool air against her skin felt real. She stepped into one of the ruffled petticoats and tied the narrow ribbon at her waist, and well, the crisp fabric felt real, too. And oh, the corset, black sateen and edged in lace, the way it fit and plumped her breasts was more feminine and alluring than anything she could have dreamed.

Her struggles to fasten the corset were real, too. This one hooked at the side, from under her arm down to her waist, and how could she manage it all but one-handed?

The velvet drape swished open again, and a rueful laugh escaped her. Her glance lifted to ask Collette for help—

But she found Creed instead, wearing the deep brown wool frock coat and creased trousers.

She took a startled step back. He'd never left America, after all. And he'd been in the shop when she arrived, not somebody's husband, and no longer a war-hardened mercenary. Instead, a man who exuded polish and sophistication and power.

"Don't be shy, honey," he drawled, his whiskey eyes drifting in a lazy perusal over the sagging corset she clutched against her. "I've seen you naked, remember?"

Her breath caught. Did he think she could forget?

"You should not be in here," she insisted. "What will Collette think?"

"She'll think this is where I belong." He appeared amused. "I'm not the first man who claimed the right to help his woman dress. Or undress, as the case might be."

Her chin lifted. "We both know I am not what you say. Your woman."

"No?" He stepped closer, filling the miniature room with his presence, rocking her world with his blatant masculinity. "What are you then?"

Her brow arched. "Someone to entertain you until it is time for you to leave again?"

He stilled. "I'm not going anywhere without you, Gina. I'm staying in America. For good."

She rolled her eyes. She knew better, the deep need he had to protect his country. "What makes you think such a thing?"

"You do."

"I make you not think like a soldier anymore?"

"Something like that." With one lean finger, he traced the curve of her bare shoulder. "I've fallen in love with you. Been hard to think about anything else once I realized it."

Sadness settled heavy in her chest. To believe him, to hope for a life together…how could she, when it would be impossible?

"Comes a time when a man's priorities shift and change." His head lowered, and he pressed his mouth where his finger had been, his lips warm against her skin. "I've missed having a family. Going back to the ranch helped me see that." He trailed kisses to her neck, and she savored the sensation. "I want a wife, kids. I want them with you, Gina."

"We cannot." She vanquished a stirring of hope. "We are too different."

"How?"

"Many years, you travel the world. Soon, America, the War Department, will need you again. It cannot be helped." She hated the words she had to say. "Already, I have left one home. The one I have in Sicily. I find a new life with Mama here in Los Angeles. And now, Collette gives me my dream…I cannot leave here if you must fight for your country again, Creed."

"I know."

"It is not fair to expect you not to be a soldier anymore because of me."

"There are lots of ways to be a soldier, Gina. Fighting overseas is just one of them."

She eyed him doubtfully. "I cannot ask you to change who you are."

He turned pensive, trailing his fingertip along the curve of her breast, then into the valley between, his palm brushing against the lace trimming of the corset along the way. She shivered, and his arms took her against him, warming her.

"You may as well know President McKinley invited me to his private dinner tomorrow night, too. He's asked that I take a position with the Army based here in California. He'd like me to work with the War Department to fight anarchism and revolution in this part of the country."

She gasped at the honor. "That is wonderful!"

"I've spent some time with the Old Man the past couple of days, too. Guess fighting the Sokolovs helped him see the importance of what I've been doing the past six years."

"He is proud of you, too."

"So he says."

But she heard the warmth in his low voice, the pleasure that filled him in knowing such a thing. She thought of his bravery in climbing the trestle bridge, the shrewd strategy he'd devised to surprise Nikolai, his reckless determination to keep Alex from reaching McKinley. How could Gus Sherman not be proud of what his son had accomplished?

"He has missed you," she said. "He is happy when you are with him on his ranch."

Creed frowned. "I'm not a cowboy. Took him a good long while to understand that."

"And now he does."

He nodded. "He's got Marc to lean on. The Old Man's learned to appreciate that, too."

She toyed with the button of his shirt. Thinking of the Sherman legacy which had formed Creed into the man he was, she couldn't help feeling small and ineffectual.

"He likes you, Gina," he murmured, as if he could read her mind. "Mary Catherine, too. You fit in, like you were born to be with us."

She recalled their kindnesses, their quick need to make her feel welcome. "You have a fine family, Creed. The ranch, it is so beautiful."

"Glad you think so, because you'll be staying there a spell."

She blinked up at him. "I am?"

"You think I'd let you go back to those damn tenements? We've already moved your things out."

She stared in disbelief. "What? Who?"

"Smoke and Hube, Marcus and me. We went in and cleared the place out." He frowned. "Didn't take us long. You don't have much."

Gina wasn't sure if she should be thrilled or annoyed with his high-handedness. Had he even thought to consult her?

He kissed her nose. "Your mother can recuperate in the main house once she's released from Good Samaritan. She's healing well, I hear."

She needed a moment to comprehend it all. "Graham tells you so?"

He nodded. "He's been keeping me updated on everything you've been doing the past couple of days. I'm looking forward to meeting her, by the way."

Then Creed hadn't forgotten her, as she'd feared. She cocked her head. "You bring my sketches to Collette, too?"

"They're damned good, Gina. I hoped she'd give you

the opportunity you deserved." He hesitated, looking more vulnerable than a mercenary should ever be. "You're an independent businesswoman now. Might be you won't have room in your life for a man right now, but I'm asking that you'll find some for me." His head lowered, and he kissed her with incredible tenderness. "I love you, Gina. I want to marry you. Will you be my wife, for always?"

The remnants of her misgivings vanished—poof!—and elation soared through her. Having Creed for her husband would complete her perfect life in America. The Great Land of Opportunity. She abandoned her unfastened corset and flung her arms around his neck. "Yes, yes, yes!"

The velvet drape swished open. Collette, her arms full of exquisitely expensive gowns, stopped short.

"Oh, my." But she didn't look surprised. Or offended. She smiled. "I brought dresses."

Creed's glance lifted. He winked at her in the mirror. "You got any for a wedding?"

Her gaze took in Gina, half-clad in his arms. She winked back. "As a matter of fact, I do."

"We're in need of one."

Her eyes twinkled. "It seems so." She stepped past the drape again, but held back. "She'll make a beautiful bride, Mr. Sherman. Don't you think?"

But Gina kept him too busy with her kisses for him to answer.

* * * * *

*Experience entertaining women's fiction for every
woman who has wondered "what's next?" in her life.
Turn the page for a sneak preview of a new book from*
Harlequin NEXT,
WHY IS MURDER ON THE MENU, ANYWAY?
by Stevi Mittman

On sale December 2006, wherever books are sold.

Besides, I am so not looking for sports

Ambience is everything. Imagine eating a foie gras
at a luncheonette counter or a side of coleslaw at Le
Cirque. It's not a matter of food but one of atmo-
sphere. Remember that when planning your dining
room design.

—Tips from *Teddi.com*

"Now that's the kind of man you should be looking for,"
my mother, the self-appointed keeper of my shelf-life
stamp, says. She points with her fork at a man in the corner
of the Steak-Out Restaurant, a dive I've just been hired to
redecorate. Making this restaurant look four-star will be
hard, but not half as hard as getting through lunch without
strangling the woman across the table from me. "*He* would
make a good husband."

"Oh, you can tell that from across the room?" I ask,
wondering how it is she can forget that when we had
trouble getting rid of my last husband, she shot him.
"Besides being ten minutes away from death if he actually
eats all that steak, he's twenty years too old for me and—
shallow woman that I am—twenty pounds too heavy.
Besides, I am *so* not looking for another husband here. I'm

looking to design a new image for this place, looking for some sense of ambience, some feeling, something I can build a proposal on for them."

My mother studies the man in the corner, tilting her head, the better to gauge his age, I suppose. I think she's grimacing, but with all the BOTOX and Restylane injected into that face, it's hard to tell. She takes another bite of her steak, chews slowly so that I don't miss the fact that the steak is a poor cut and tougher than it should be. "You're concentrating on the wrong kind of proposal," she says finally. "Just look at this place, Teddi. It's a dive. There are hardly any other diners. What does *that* tell you about the food?"

"That they cater to a dinner crowd and it's lunchtime," I tell her.

I don't know what I was thinking bringing her here with me. I suppose I thought it would be better than eating alone. There really are days when my common sense goes on vacation. Clearly, this is one of them. I mean, really, did I not resolve less than three weeks ago that I would not let my mother get to me anymore?

What good are New Year's resolutions, anyway?

Mario approaches the man's table and my mother studies him while they converse. Eventually Mario leaves the table with a huff, after which the diner glances up and meets my mother's gaze. I think she's smiling at him. That or she's got indigestion. They size each other up.

I concentrate on making sketches in my notebook and try to ignore the fact that my mother is flirting. At nearly seventy, she's developed an unhealthy interest in members of the opposite sex to whom she isn't married.

According to my father, who has broken the TMI rule and given me Too Much Information, she has no interest in sex with him. Better, I suppose, to be clued in on what they aren't doing in the bedroom than have to hear what they might be doing.

"He's not so old," my mother says, noticing that I have barely touched the Chinese chicken salad she warned me not to get. "He's got about as many years on you as you have on your little cop friend."

She does this to make me crazy. I know it, but it works all the same. "Drew Scoones is not my little 'friend.' He's a detective with whom I—"

"Screwed around," my mother says. I must look shocked, because my mother laughs at me and asks if I think she doesn't know the "lingo."

What I thought she didn't know was that Drew and I actually tangled in the sheets. And, since it's possible she's just fishing, I sidestep the issue and tell her that Drew is just a couple of years younger than me and that I don't need reminding. I dig into my salad with renewed vigor, determined to show my mother that Chinese chicken salad in a steak place was not the stupid choice it's proving to be.

After a few more minutes of my picking at the wilted leaves on my plate, the man my mother has me nearly engaged to pays his bill and heads past us toward the back of the restaurant. I watch my mother take in his shoes, his suit and the diamond pinkie ring that seems to be cutting off the circulation in his little finger.

"Such nice hands," she says after the man is out of sight. "Manicured." She and I both stare at my hands. I have two popped acrylics that are being held on at weird angles by bandages. My cuticles are ragged and there's marker decorating my right hand from measuring carelessly when I did a drawing for a customer.

Twenty minutes later she's disappointed that he managed to leave the restaurant without our noticing. He will join the list of the ones I let get away. I will hear about him twenty years from now when—according to my mother— my children will be grown and I will still be single, living pathetically alone with several dogs and cats.

After my ex, that sounds good to me.

The waitress tells us that our meal has been taken care of by the management and, after thanking Mario, the owner, complimenting him on the wonderful meal and assuring him that once I have redecorated his place people will be flocking here in droves (I actually use those words and ignore my mother when she rolls her eyes), my mother and I head for the restroom.

My father—unfortunately not with us today—has the patience of a saint. He got it over the years of living with my mother. She, perhaps as a result, figures he has the patience for both of them, and feels justified having none. For her, no rules apply, and a little thing like a picture of a man on the door to a public restroom is certainly no barrier to using the john. In all fairness, it does seem silly to stand and wait for the ladies' room if no one is using the men's room.

Still, it's the idea that rules don't apply to her, signs don't apply to her, conventions don't apply to her. She knocks on the door to the men's room. When no one answers she gestures to me to go in ahead. I tell her that I can certainly wait for the ladies' room to be free and she shrugs and goes in herself.

Not a minute later there is a bloodcurdling scream from behind the men's room door.

"Mom!" I yell. "Are you all right?"

Mario comes running over, the waitress on his heels. Two customers head our way while my mother contin- ues to scream.

I try the door, but it is locked. I yell for her to open it and she fumbles with the knob. When she finally manages to unlock and open it, she is white behind her two streaks of blush, but she is on her feet and appears shaken but not stirred.

"What happened?" I ask her. So do Mario and the waitress and the few customers who have migrated to the back of the place.

She points toward the bathroom and I go in, thinking it serves her right for using the men's room. But I see nothing amiss.

She gestures toward the stall, and, like any self-respecting and suspicious woman, I poke the door open with one finger, expecting the worst.

What I find is worse than the worst.

The husband my mother picked out for me is sitting on the toilet. His pants are puddled around his ankles, his hands are hanging at his sides. Pinned to his chest is some sort of Health Department certificate.

Oh, and there is a large, round, bloodless bullet hole between his eyes.

Four Nassau County police officers are securing the area, waiting for the detectives and crime scene personnel to show up. They are trying, though not very hard, to comfort my mother, who in another era would be considered to be suffering from the vapors. Less tactful in the twenty-first century, I'd say she was losing it. That is, if I didn't know her better, know she was milking it for everything it was worth.

My mother loves attention. As it begins to flag, she swoons and claims to feel faint. Despite four No Smoking signs, my mother insists it's all right for her to light up because, after all, she's in shock. Not to mention that signs, as we know, don't apply to her.

When asked not to smoke, she collapses mournfully in a chair and lets her head loll to the side, all without mussing her hair.

Eventually, the detectives show up to find the four patrolmen all circled around her, debating whether to administer CPR, smelling salts or simply call the paramedics. I, however, know just what will snap her to attention.

"Detective Scoones," I say loudly. My mother parts the sea of cops.

"We have to stop meeting like this," he says lightly to me, but I can feel him checking me over with his eyes, making sure I'm all right while pretending not to care.

"What have you got in those pants?" my mother asks him, coming to her feet and staring at his crotch accusingly. "*Baydar?* Everywhere we Bayers are, you turn up. You don't expect me to buy that this is a coincidence, I hope."

Drew tells my mother that it's nice to see her, too, and asks if it's his fault that her daughter seems to attract disasters.

Charming to be made to feel like the bearer of a plague. He asks how I am.

"Just peachy," I tell him. "I seem to be making a habit of finding dead bodies, my mother is driving me crazy and the catering hall I booked two freakin' years ago for Dana's bat mitzvah has just been shut down by the Board of Health!"

"Glad to see your luck's finally changing," he says, giving me a quick squeeze around the shoulders before turning his attention to the patrolmen, asking what they've got, whether they've taken any statements, moved anything, all the sort of stuff you see on TV, without any of the drama. That is, if you don't count my mother's threats to faint every few minutes when she senses no one's paying attention to her.

Mario tells his waitstaff to bring everyone espresso,

which I decline because I'm wired enough. Drew pulls him aside and a minute later I'm handed a cup of coffee that smells divinely of Kahlúa.

The man knows me well. Too well.

His partner, whom I've met once or twice, says he'll interview the kitchen staff. Drew asks Mario if he minds if he takes statements from the patrons first and gets to him and the waitstaff afterward.

"No, no," Mario tells him. "Do the patrons first." Drew raises his eyebrow at me like he wants to know if I get the double entendre. I try to look bored.

"What is it with you and murder victims?" he asks me when we sit down at a table in the corner.

I search them out so that I can see you again, I almost say, but I'm afraid it will sound desperate instead of sarcastic.

My mother, lighting up and daring him with a look to tell her not to, reminds him that *she* was the one to find the body.

Drew asks what happened *this time*. My mother tells him how the man in the john was "taken" with me, couldn't take his eyes off me and blatantly flirted with both of us. To his credit, Drew doesn't laugh, but his smirk is undeniable to the trained eye. And I've had my eye trained on him for nearly a year now.

"While he was noticing you," he asks me, "did *you* notice anything about him? Was he waiting for anyone? Watching for anything?"

I tell him that he didn't appear to be waiting or watching. That he made no phone calls, was fairly intent on eating and did, indeed, flirt with my mother. This last bit Drew takes with a grain of salt, which was the way it was intended.

"And he had a short conversation with Mario," I tell him.

"I think he might have been unhappy with the food, though he didn't send it back."

Drew asks what makes me think he was dissatisfied, and I tell him that the discussion seemed acrimonious and that Mario looked distressed when he left the table. Drew makes a note and says he'll look into it and asks about anyone else in the restaurant. Did I see anyone who didn't seem to belong, anyone who was watching the victim, anyone looking suspicious?

"Besides my mother?" I ask him, and Mom huffs and blows her cigarette smoke in my direction.

I tell him that there were several deliveries, the kitchen staff going in and out the back door to grab a smoke. He stops me and asks what I was doing checking out the back door of the restaurant.

Proudly—because, while he was off forgetting me, dropping by only once in a while to say hi to Jesse, my son, or drop something by for one of my daughters that he thought they might like, I was getting on with my life—I tell him that I'm decorating the place.

He looks genuinely impressed. "Commercial customers? That's great," he says. Okay, that's what he *ought* to say. What he actually says is "Whatever pays the bills."

"Howard Rosen, the famous restaurant critic, got her the job," my mother says. "You met him—the good-looking, distinguished gentleman with the *real* job, something to be proud of. I guess you've never read his reviews in *Newsday*."

Drew, without missing a beat, tells her that Howard's reviews are on the top of his list, as soon as he learns how to read.

"I only meant—" my mother starts, but both of us assure her that we know just what she meant.

"So," Drew says. "Deliveries?"

I tell him that Mario would know better than I, but that I saw vegetables come in, maybe fish and linens.

"This is the second restaurant job Howard's got her," my mother tells Drew.

"At least she's getting *something* out of the relationship," he says.

"If he were here," my mother says, ignoring the insinuation, "he'd be comforting her instead of interrogating her. He'd be making sure we're both all right after such an ordeal."

"I'm sure he would," Drew agrees, then looks me in the eyes as if he's measuring my tolerance for shock. Quietly he adds, "But then maybe he doesn't know just what strong stuff your daughter's made of."

It's the closest thing to a tender moment I can expect from Drew Scoones. My mother breaks the spell. "She gets that from me," she says.

Both Drew and I take a minute, probably to pray that's all I inherited from her.

"I'm just trying to save you some time and effort," my mother tells him. "My money's on Howard."

Drew withers her with a look and mutters something that sounds suspiciously like "fool's gold." Then he excuses himself to go back to work.

I catch his sleeve and ask if it's all right for us to leave. He says sure, he knows where we live. I say goodbye to Mario. I assure him that I will have some sketches for him in a few days, all the while hoping that this murder doesn't cancel his redecorating plans. I need the money desperately, the alternative being borrowing from my parents and being strangled by the strings.

My mother is strangely quiet all the way to her house. She doesn't tell me what a loser Drew Scoones is—despite his good looks—and how I was obviously drooling over him. She doesn't ask me where Howard is taking me tonight or warn me not to tell my father about what happened because he will worry about us both and no doubt insist we see our respective psychiatrists.

She fidgets nervously, opening and closing her purse over and over again.

"You okay?" I ask her. After all, she's just found a dead man on the toilet, and tough as she is that's got to be upsetting.

When she doesn't answer me I pull over to the side of the road.

"Mom?" She refuses to meet my eyes. "You want me to take you to see Dr. Cohen?"

She looks out the window as if she's just realized we're on Broadway in Woodmere. "Aren't we near Marvin's Jewelers?" she asks, pulling something out of her purse.

"What have you got, Mother?" I ask, prying open her fingers to find the murdered man's ring.

"It was on the sink," she says in answer to my dropped jaw. "I was going to get his name and address and have you return it to him so that he could ask you out. I thought it was a sign that the two of you were meant to be together."

"He's dead, Mom. You understand that, right?" I ask. You never can tell when my mother is fine and when she's in la-la land.

"Well, I didn't know that," she shouts at me. "Not at the time."

I ask why she didn't give it to Drew, realize that she wouldn't give Drew the time in a clock shop and add, "...or one of the other policemen?"

"For heaven's sake," she tells me. "The man is dead, Teddi, and I took his ring. How would that look?"

Before I can tell her it looks just the way it is, she pulls out a cigarette and threatens to light it.

"I mean, really," she says, shaking her head like it's my brains that are loose. "What does he need with it now?"